MURDER BY MEMORY

By

William M. Jones

This book is a work of fiction. Places, events, and situations in this story are purely fictional. Any resemblance to actual persons, living or dead, is coincidental.

© 2002 by William M. Jones. All rights reserved.

No part of this book may be reproduced, restored in a retrieval system, or transmitted by means, electronic, mechanical, photocopying, recording, or otherwise, without written consent from the author.

ISBN: 1-40330-015-1

This book is printed on acid free paper.

1st Books - rev. 3/8/02

Dedication

This book is dedicated to my daughter, Lori, who has been my biggest supporter in promoting my other novels.

CHAPTER ONE

1999

Herbert Chalmers yawned as he slowly lifted his slightly overweight body from his soiled recliner. Wearing an old, torn in one knee, pair of sweat pants, a faded paint splattered collegiate sweat shirt which barely covered the pot belly of his recently acquired extra four inches of stomach girth, and sporting a week's growth of a whitish coarse beard, Chalmers crushed his cigarette in the over full ashtray on the lamp table and sauntered towards the kitchen to fetch yet another beer. Stopping part way, he belched almost to the point of vomiting. Delaying his venture to the kitchen, he instead plopped his miserable body into the nearest chair and involuntarily started to cry. Slowly recovering some semblance of reality, he remained in the chair with his hands covering his bloodshot eyes and reflected on what a miserable wretch he'd become. Wasn't supposed to be like this. Early in his career he'd been one of the most respected detectives on the police force and his golden retirement years should've been filled with happy times expended on hobbies plus finally traveling to all those interesting locations he'd dreamed of finally getting to see after all the hard years of toiling in the same job year after long year. But reality and dreams seem to have a way of taking different paths. Herb was retired now because when offered the early retirement option at age fifty-five, he reluctantly agreed to call it quits. Where he'd once been a hard charging, highly motivated detective sergeant, he'd slowly become extremely cynical and displayed classic burnout symptoms. Over the years he'd also progressively become more and more negative in his thinking and seemed to only see the worst in others. He also became less and less focused in performing his detective duties and also had almost zero compassion for those he dealt with in the line of duty or with his co-workers. Simply stated, what had once shown signs of becoming a brilliant career had over time deteriorated to the point where his presence and future on the police force were seriously questioned. When approached by his superiors with the early retirement option, they made it crystal clear how for the best of all concerned he should accept it and get on with other things in his life. It was simply time for him to move on. Take the gold "thank you" watch and find something else to do to pass the time away. He knew it, and they knew it, so on his fifty-fifth birthday a few months earlier there had been a mutual parting of the ways. Oh, yes, there'd been the usual retirement party with the usual "feel good" speeches from those who long ago had been his buddies, but he knew everyone was just going through the motions and were really glad to finally be getting rid of him. But now what was he going to do and where could he go? His life had continuously spiraled downhill. Where he should be enjoying these retirement years with a loving wife, he didn't have one and besides, he was basically broke. His once loving wife had seen to this. Waiting until his mid thirties before getting married, in retrospect, he figured he'd already been to set in his ways to make the marriage work. The first few years had been okay, but when his wife couldn't get pregnant she became increasingly more unsatisfied and unfulfilled and they consequently slowly drifted apart. She had a meager day job at a bookstore which she thoroughly loved and he made sure he worked the first watch which began at 11 p.m. This work arrangement kept their personal contact to a minimum but also created an immense emotional void in each of them. His wife compensated by conducting colossal shopping sprees which overtaxed their credit limit on the multiple credit cards she was able to obtain. With his mental and physical health deteriorating from the debt stress she'd caused him, coupled with their

Murder by Memory

total loss of emotional support, he finally filed for divorce. He wrongly deduced it would be a simple proceeding and much to his chagrin it quickly turned ugly when knowledge of his one brief affair was brought out in court. In the end, even though the divorce was granted, he was left with basically nothing while his former wife bore none of the responsibility or accountability. He was left not only with the responsibility of paying off her enormous credit card debts, but she got their row house and the judge also awarded her a sizable monthly alimony allowance. Had been five years now since the divorce and by moving into his current spartan apartment and consolidating the debts he'd been able to slowly reduce his debt burden, but he still had a ways to go. And now with his reduced early retirement benefit, well, he couldn't afford to go anywhere else even if he wanted to because it took almost every penny he had to pay the rent, alimony and debt payment. Didn't seem to be much light at the end of the tunnel. His existence seemed beyond hope and wallowing in his self pity didn't afford any time to try to figure out some way to dig out of this seemingly bottomless pit he'd fallen into. Instead, what few extra dollars he did have, lately he'd blown on cigarettes, beer and highly carbohydrated foods - thus his newly acquired pot belly and his nearly incessant inebriated state. He knew he'd become a pitifully depressed creature, but without anything to look forward to in the future, he simply continued in his spiraling decline and had lost all desire to do anything about it. Thoughts of suicide routinely entered his thought process, but so far he'd just grabbed another beer and wallowed deeper in his self pity. As he slowly took his hands from his face, raised his head and slowly stood back up, his door bell suddenly rang. Taking a few rings for it to register in his brain, he eventually comprehended what it was and grabbed for the door knob which was only a few feet away. Not even asking who was there, he slowly opened the door.

"You look like hell, Herb!" Detective Lieutenant Benjamin Mitchell greeted Chalmers with.

"Nice to see you again too, Benny. How long's it been? Three months? What do you want?"

"You. Can we come in?" Mitchell requested.

Herb thought about it for a few seconds and eventually replied, "Don't see why not. Who's she?" Herb then asked while glancing at Ben's female companion. He'd never seen her before and thought he at least recognized all the detectives on the force. But not her, if in fact she was a detective. Whoever she was, he found her quite attractive. In his beer-numbed mental capacity he figured her to be mid forties but wasn't sure of her nationality. She was of medium height with a beautiful, smooth complexion and dark hair and big brown eyes. Possibly some Jamaican blood, but definitely African American with a hint of oriental. Maybe Filipino or Chinese. He couldn't tell, but one thing was for certain - this was the first woman he'd looked at in years who aroused any erotic feelings in him.

"Detective Sergeant Lizabeth Barcay." Mitchell introduced.

"Elizabeth." Herb responded while extending a hand but quickly retracting it to cover his mouth from a sudden burp.

"Lizabeth." She emphatically pronounced. "There's no E."

"Okay, Lizabeth it is then," Herb understood as the two detectives entered his filthy apartment. He could sense their disgust for his current living conditions when they refused to have a seat and preferred to remain standing with Lizabeth as close to the door as possible.

"What do you really want, Benny?" Herb questioned.

"Like I said, old buddy, we need you."

"What do you mean by you need me, old buddy?" Herb returned sarcastically. "What could you possibly need from a disreputable retired drunk like me?"

"Don't be so hard on yourself, Herb."

"Cut the crap, Benny. Look around for yourself. It ain't exactly the Ritz you know," Herb fired back while observing Lizabeth's obvious discomfort. "Who sent you here? You certainly didn't come on your own for a chatty social call. Either of you want a beer?" he then asked.

"No thanks," Benny calmly answered while Lizabeth simply shook her head indicating no.

"Well, I do," Herb proclaimed. "Was on my way to the frig when you showed up. Once again, Benny, who sent you?"

"The Chief."

"The Chief!" Herb repeated in total astonishment. "Thought he couldn't stand the sight of me. Word I got was how he threw a good riddance party the day I retired. We weren't exactly bosom buddies if you remember."

"The Slaughter House Murderer is back." Benny formally declared.

"What did you just say?" Herb questioned with a disbelieving look.

"You heard me correctly the first time, Herb."

"You sure?"

"Looks like it."

"How long's it been? Twenty-three, twenty-four years?"

"Something like that."

Comprehending the conversation and quickly sobering up, Herb abandoned heading for the beer and took a seat in the nearest chair. "When?"

"Last night," Benny answered.

"Damn, after all these years. Unbelievable." Then looking directly into Benny's eyes, Herb asked, "Who'd he kill?"

"Alvin Reinhold. Ring a bell?"

"Alvin? You sure?"

"No question about it."

"Son of a bitch!" Herb exclaimed. "And all these years he was my number one suspect. Just couldn't ever prove it and then when the killings suddenly stopped we couldn't make any arrests so the case kind of just faded away over the years. Damn! Alvin Reinhold. Still can't believe it."

"Chief wants your help on this one." Benny next calmly stated. "He knows you never really let go of the case and probably know more about it than anyone else."

"Yeah, but the guy I thought was the killer is now dead."

"And the real Slaughter House Murderer still lurks out there," Benny finished Herb's statement. "Doesn't matter. The Chief, and me also, Herb, know if this guy's going to finally get caught, well, you're the best detective to do it."

"But I'm retired. Or have you forgotten? And just look at me." Herb declared.

"Doesn't matter, Herb. If you want back in, you're in. Plain and simple. You could use the extra money, couldn't you?"

"What do you think, Benny?" Herb snickered.

"Still paying off Irene's debts?"

"Well, I wouldn't be living like this if I weren't. That bitch!"

"Sorry I brought up the subject."

"Yeah, me to. Now, if I come back, is the Chief unretiring me?"

"No, you'll still draw your retirement and then be paid additional as a special detective consultant just to work this case. Herb, this case is bound to get big time press. It's really important to finally put an end to it and the Chief knows it."

"The Chief, or the politicians?" Herb wondered.

"Well, I'm sure the Chief's getting a lot of pressure from the mayor's office already on this." Benny offered knowing the truth was the mayor threatened to fire the Chief if he didn't catch this killer soon because of the negative press it was going to draw starting with the morning's front page headliner. It was Benny, then, who approached the Chief

Murder by Memory

with the idea of bringing Herb back to work the case because even though they had drifted apart over the years, they'd been partners for years back in the early days and he knew what Herb was capable of doing when he put his mind to it. Plus, Herb hadn't ever really let go of this case. Where most new detectives hadn't even heard of the Slaughter House Murderer since the case was so old, Herb had thought about it constantly as the one big murder case which he just couldn't ever solve. It had haunted him more and more as the years passed on and had a major impact on his mental well being. Benny knew it'd also been a factor in Herb's marriage. Irene had gotten fed up with his obsession with the case - it seemed to consume him and sucked the spirit right out of him. But now with the killer back, Benny was the first to realize how Herb was the best detective to save the Chief's ass on this one, and maybe his own, if the killer wasn't caught soon. After quite a heated discussion, the Chief also realized the truth and reluctantly authorized Herb's return.

Liking the idea of being needed again, Herb felt a twinge of hope from his depressed state for the first time in years. "When do you want me?"

"Tomorrow morning okay?" Benny asked.

"I'll be there. We'll get the SOB this time! You going to be my partner again like the old days, Benny?"

"Not exactly, Herb. You'll be under my command, but Lizabeth is your new partner."

"Lizabeth!" Herb replied.

"Got a problem with her?" Benny questioned.

"No, none at all," Herb answered as the thought of working with this mysteriously attractive woman warmed his being, "but don't you think you ought to ask her if she's willing to work with me after what she's seen here tonight."

"No problem, Detective Chalmers," Lizabeth responded with a smile which melted his heart. "Lieutenant Mitchell thoroughly briefed me on your situation and I have faith you'll come around. Catching this murderer depends on it, you know."

"You hear what she just said, Benny?" Herb excitedly stated. "The lady has faith in me. Nobody's had that in years. Where did you find her?"

"After you retired, the department started a detective exchange program. Lizabeth is with us for six months from Syracuse."

"Long way from home," Herb proclaimed, "but we'll make it worth your time. You help me catch this creep and I'll guarantee you'll be the most famous detective in the country. Probably get your pretty face plastered on the front page of every major newspaper in the country."

"First things first," Lizabeth responded with a slight smile. "Let's just concentrate on catching this killer before he strikes again. See you at the precinct in the morning?"

"Eight o'clock sharp, Detective Barcay," Herb promised as he shook Benny's hand and opened the door for the two detectives to depart. Watching them walk towards their patrol car, he viewed a brightly shining full moon and a sudden chill quickly spread through his body. The Slaughter House Murderer only struck with a new moon, not a full moon. Who really killed Alvin Reinhold last night? He and Lizabeth would just have to find out, but it definitely wasn't the original Slaughter House Murderer!

Returning inside his rat trap apartment, Herb took a good look around and reflected again on the disaster his life had become, but this time he possessed the strength and will power to do something about it. He was needed and he'd prove to everyone he still had what it takes. May not get him out of debt, but certainly could restore his dignity and pride and those, he concluded, were worth more than anything else in life. Getting royally pissed at himself for sinking so low, he vowed right then and there to get rid of all the self pity and take charge of his life. He started by straightening up his apartment and taking out the countless

Murder by Memory

bags of beer canned trash which consumed his kitchen. Then he proceeded to the bathroom where he first shaved twice to assure a close shave and then took the first hot shower he'd taken in probably over a week. Standing under the pulsating shower head, he thought back twenty-four years to when this case had first started. Was called the Slaughter House Murderer because the weapon used had been a blank .22 caliber pistol used in slaughter houses to kill cattle. Since the blank cartridge forced a metal rod out the barrel into the back of each victim's head, he always felt the killer had to know each of his unsuspecting victims because there wasn't any other explanation of how he could get that close to them. Until last night's killing of Alvin Reinhold, there had been three murders, or should he say assassinations, in this case. Herb had been the only detective to propose the theory of how the killer only struck when there was a new moon. But then the murders suddenly stopped and the case was never solved. And now, Alvin Reinhold was dead from a slaughter house pistol shooting, but his obvious copycat killer apparently didn't know about the new moon connection because Herb hadn't allowed that detail released to the press; it was only written on his official detective work sheet and it had long ago been filed in the archives. Determined to make a good impression in the morning, after finishing his shower, he next pressed his best suit and shined his shoes for probably the first time in years. Too excited to sleep, he laid awake in bed for the remainder of the night and ran all aspects of the case, past and present, over and over in his mind. In the morning he ate, for the first time in weeks, a nutritious breakfast of scrambled eggs, bacon, toast and juice and then headed for the old precinct with a renewed purpose to his life. He wasn't sure what aspect of the day excited him the most - being needed on the job or the prospect of being close to Lizabeth Barcay. Whatever it was, he realized the dynamic dichotomy of the situation - how the death of Alvin

William M. Jones

Reinhold had resurrected the life of Detective Herbert Chalmers.

CHAPTER TWO

1975

Alvin Reinhold slowly dragged his bruised and bloody body up the outer garage stairs to his private room above his parent's spacious garage. Gasping for a breath upon reaching the top step, he slowly turned the knob, opened the door, and painfully limped inside. Holding his ribs with his right hand while wiping the trickling blood from his throbbing nose with his left, he slowly crawled onto his old, worn couch. Now feeling somewhat safe inside his private room, he closed his eyes and tried to forget the pain while his bleeding nose slowly clotted. Gagging a few times on the drying blood, he eventually got up and slowly made his way to the small bathroom and spit out a wad of bloody clotting mucous in order to clear his throat. He'd never felt so miserable in his life. He didn't deserve this beating tonight. Why was he always being harassed? Probably just because he was Alvin Reinhold. He was a high school senior and was preparing to graduate in just a few months. He'd already been accepted to a local college and was excited about his future plans. Where many of his classmates were clueless about their futures, he seemed on the right path to making something out of his life. His motto over the last ten years had become "sticks and stones can break your bones, but names can never hurt you," but tonight he'd simply had enough and look at him now - his body aching from multiple punches to his stomach and ribs plus probably a broken nose. He'd always been of a slight build and had worn thick glasses from early childhood. He was also a good student and loved music, reading, and writing poetry instead of sports, but due to his diminutive stature, family name and personal mannerisms, he'd for years been the object of verbal harassing from a local bully.

William M. Jones

He'd been taunted with everything from "four eyes" to "Alvin the chipmunk" for no other reason than he was an easy target to be picked on by the bully who felt a need to do so to somehow feel superior. His only sanctuary now was inside his garage room. He had a normal bedroom inside the adjoining house, but since turning eighteen late last year his parents had allowed him to move into the garage space. They realized he'd become somewhat of a loner, but as long as he continued to get good grades in school, stay out of normal teenage troubles, and was happy in his room, they were okay with it. They had no idea of the verbal torture he'd endured since grade school. He'd never told them and up until tonight that's all it had only been - just a verbal bashing. In his room he could shut out the cruel world, dream of a better future and play his music. His other redeeming consolation was his lovely girlfriend, Rita Powers. She lived only a few blocks away with her mother and one year older brother. Alvin had known Rita since first grade and over the years had become inseparable soul mates. There wasn't anything they couldn't discuss and he assumed they'd marry in the near future. With his pain subsiding slightly, he began thinking more and more about her when unannounced there was a slight knock at his door. Fearful the local bully and his gang were outside, he quietly, but slowly, locked the inside door chain lock which he'd forgotten earlier due to his pain and desire to simply escape inside. He then asked who was there.

"It's me, Rita," came the reply. "Where you been? You forget about our date?"

Now remembering he'd been on his way to meet her at the local music store when he'd been accosted, without saying a word he opened the door.

She started to say something, but quickly froze when she beheld the dried blood smeared on his face. "Oh my god, Alvin," she gasped while reaching for him.

Taking a painful step backwards, he reluctantly stated, "Don't touch me. Please. It hurts too much. Think I may have a broken rib."

"And your face, Alvin. What about your poor face?" she cried.

"I don't know. Feels like my nose may be broken."

Slowly grabbing his right forearm, Rita led Alvin back inside, re-locked the door and helped him back onto the couch. "Who?" she next needed to know.

"Bruno and his gang," he replied.

"Damn them," she pronounced as tears began flowing down both of her cheeks. "Why?"

"Because I'd finally had enough from them. Couldn't take it any longer! Guess I kind of snapped tonight," he admitted.

"What did you do to deserve this, Alvin?"

Rubbing his hair back with his left hand, he then again told her, "I'd had enough. Couldn't take their abuse any longer. Enough's enough and without hesitation I decided to do something about it."

"Did you try to fight them?"

"Guess I did."

"No," Rita cried out again.

"I remember swinging at Bruno," he said while remembering. Then massaging a sore right hand he affirmed, "Yeah, guess I did hit him."

"What happened next?"

"What do you think?" Alvin tried to laugh. "Three of his buds held me while Bruno beat the living crap out of me!"

"You shouldn't have provoked them, Alvin. They're just a bunch of bullies."

"I know, Rita," he agreed, "but I'd had enough. All these years of verbal abuse. Just couldn't take it any longer. It's got to end."

"Well, I'm afraid it's just beginning now, Alvin," Rita proclaimed. "Think we ought to go to the police?"

"Heavens no! No way! What would they do anyway? Probably nothing!" Alvin stated as he felt a feeling of hopelessness. "It's just my word against theirs and then they'd get really pissed off and take it out harder on me. No telling what they'd do then."

"Then let's take care of them ourselves!" Rita boldly declared.

"What are you talking about, Rita?" Alvin fearfully questioned.

Holding both of his hands and looking directly into his wondering eyes, she coldly asserted, "We get rid of them so they can't ever hurt you again!"

"Get rid of them? How?"

"Like you said, Alvin. Telling the police won't do any good. Probably just make matters worse. We can't allow that. Time we took matters into our own hands. Alvin, now listen carefully. We've got to have them killed!"

"Are you serious?" Alvin stated as he stood up and began to tremble uncontrollably.

"Yes, it's the only way!"

"I can't kill anybody!" Alvin screamed at her.

"Keep your voice down, Alvin. Of course you can't. Neither can I, but I know someone who can."

"You're crazy, Rita. No one's going to kill Bruno and his gang for us!"

"Yes he will."

"He?"

"Raymond will do it," she calmly promised.

"Ray?" He wouldn't kill anyone either. He's never been in any serious trouble in his life. He won't do this!"

"Yes he will!" Rita emphatically replied. "If he thinks someone's out to hurt me and my life's seriously in danger, then he'll do it."

"But it's not," Alvin interjected.

"But Raymond doesn't know that, does he?"

Murder by Memory

"You seriously believe he'd kill someone to protect you?"

"No doubt about it! When daddy died, Raymond pledged to always take care of me. If he honestly feels I'm in trouble, he'll do whatever is needed to keep me safe."

"So you're saying we lie to Ray and tell him Bruno beat me up and also threatened to hurt you if we told anyone about it?"

"Yep."

"Unbelievable."

"I know, but it will work. Think about it. Nobody would ever suspect Raymond. He knows Bruno, but there's no history between them so there's no way he'd ever be suspected. And then why would anyone suspect us? Did anyone else see them beat you up?"

"No. Not that I know of. They got me in that dark stretch in the park where the lights have been out for months. Can't the city ever fix anything? I didn't see anyone else around. Guess Bruno and his guys followed me into the park. They hadn't actually harassed me in a few months. Oh, you know, they always gave me looks whenever I saw them and in ways those were worse because I always wondered what and when they'd do something next. Kind of like a silent torture. So I guess they decided it was time tonight to have some more fun with me."

"Okay. So then there's no reason anyone would suspect us. To be sure, we make certain we're seen other places when the murders occur. It's the perfect murder and Bruno won't ever harass you again! Alvin, you shouldn't have to live in fear for the rest of your life. It's just not right. Sometimes you've just gotta take matters into your own hands. Bullies like Bruno need to be dealt with and if the police won't, then we will!"

With his ribs still aching and his nose throbbing, Alvin carefully weighed Rita's argument and slowly came around to her way of thinking. "Can't hurt to at least talk to Ray about it," he finally acknowledged.

"I'll do it," Rita stated. "Don't need you with me. Better if I do it by myself."

"Okay." Alvin gladly agreed since he probably didn't have the stomach to actually discuss the subject with Raymond. "But there's one more thing."

"What?" Rita asked.

"I want Bruno's three buddies taken out first."

"Great idea, Alvin. That way Bruno will have to sweat it out for awhile and see what it's like to be mentally toyed with."

"Exactly! Isn't revenge sweet?"

CHAPTER THREE

With his mother working the night shift and his sister, Rita, probably out somewhere with Alvin, Raymond Powers and his steady girlfriend, Carla, had the house to themselves. Nursing a stiff neck, headache and slight fever, Raymond felt somewhat drained as he and Carla laid together on his bed in his planetarium lit bedroom. Being obsessed with astronomy, Raymond had a miniature planetarium which projected the stars on the walls and ceiling of his room. Feeling slightly sick, he didn't feel like messing around much with Carla tonight, so the two had been silently laying embraced for around an hour now while occasionally making out in between Raymond studying the various star constellations projected around his room. His nagging physical ailments weren't seriously debilitating, but since he'd had them now for over a month, earlier today he'd finally gone to see a doctor about them. The first diagnosis had been mononucleosis; probably from making out too much with Carla he thought, but the blood test for it had come back negative. The doctor then diagnosed him as being slightly anemic and prescribed rest and iron pills. Raymond had forgotten to mention feeling nauseous or the numbness he'd felt a few times in his right arm. He wasn't used to feeling zapped of his energy like this, so hoped the prescribed rest and medication would clear everything up quickly, but while laying here on the bed tonight he'd also suddenly developed a nagging stiff neck; hopefully just from twisting his neck from the position it was resting against Carla.

Raymond was a year older than his sister, Rita. He'd graduated from high school last year. Not being a serious student, he'd graduated in the lower third of his class. He was one of those countless teenagers who was basically faceless as he progressed through the school years - never in trouble, but again never getting any special recognition for excelling in anything such as sports or academics. Matter of fact, he'd shied away from organized sports for fear of getting hurt and hadn't participated in very many extracurricular activities so he didn't have many close friends - just lots of acquaintances. Many knew him, but just not very well and he didn't hang out with any particular group. Luckily for him, he'd met Carla in the one club he did enjoy - the science club - and they'd hit it off immediately and had been together since that first meeting back in tenth grade. He also enjoyed working out by himself so ran three to four times a week and lifted weights in his basement. Being six feet with an athletic build was probably the reason he wasn't ever picked on like his sister's wimpish boyfriend, Alvin. Life could certainly be cruel to a lot of people just because of physical appearances. This fact greatly disturbed him when he saw others, like Alvin, being harassed for no particular reason by the bullies of the world.

Raymond's goal in life now was to someday become an astronomer, but first he needed to raise his GPA in order to get accepted by any major university's astronomy program. He was currently enrolled full time at the local community college with the hopes of meeting the required enrollment criteria. Many times now he berated himself for not studying harder back in high school, especially in the core courses required for college entrance such as English and math. He could easily excel in any subject he put his mind to, but unfortunately that only occurred in his science classes with him barely receiving a passing grade in most others. Oh, well, he figured the school of hard knocks would make him better in the long run because he'd better appreciate an eventual astronomy degree more after everything he was having to go through just to get into a program. He also thanked his lucky stars that Carla shared a similar interest in the universe because with his obsession

Murder by Memory

he figured any other girlfriend would have long ago left him.

Another variable which shaped his personality had been the death of his father some ten years earlier. He'd basically been at the wrong place at the wrong time and had been killed by a bully in a fit of road rage. Driving along in his own little world, his dad had inadvertently cut off a hot head on a busy road. When his dad mouthed that he was sorry, the other motorist gave him the finger, mouthed back an obscenity and then broadsided his car. After stopping, the pursuing argument rapidly turned deadly when the belligerent motorist shoved his dad against the side of his car and then shot him point-blank with one pistol shot to the forehead. From that instance on, Raymond was forced to become the man of the house and take care of his mom and Rita. He vowed he wouldn't ever knowingly allow anyone to mess with any member of his family. Knowing how Rita felt about Alvin Reinhold and having witnessed some of the verbal harassment he'd periodically received at school, he'd discussed the matter with her, but had been asked to stay out of it. He had reluctantly consented to her wishes when she stated they feared the harassment would just get worse if he tried to do anything to help. Rita and Alvin figured things would eventually get better as the bullies grew up and matured and recently it appeared as if they'd been correct as Rita hadn't mentioned anything in months.

Embracing Carla closer to him, Raymond gave her another long, passionate kiss. Then looking at the constellation projections on his ceiling, he hoped he'd feel better soon so he'd have the energy to get outside on the next clear night to stargaze. His favorite time was during a new moon and over time new moons caused a cultist affect on him. He could spend hours out on dark, clear, new moon nights almost to the point of being hypnotic. He enjoyed being out on other nights also, but clear new moon evenings were the only which truly invigorated him. He felt invincible on those nights and felt as if he were one with the universe. Other times he realized how small and insignificant an individual was when compared to the grandiose expanse of space, but new moons caused a transformation within him. Why? He really didn't know. Just did and the anticipation level rose with each approaching new moon. New moons were the closest thing to a religious experience he knew. Where others witnessed Christ or raised their hands while singing hallelujah, he felt redemption during a new moon. He'd never mentioned this fact to anyone, not even Carla or Rita. It was his personal, secret salvation.

Rita suddenly burst unannounced into Raymond's room and flicked on the light switch. Temporarily blinded from the sudden light, Raymond promptly sat up causing his head to violently throb for an instant. Regaining his sight, he recognized his sister and yelled, "What are you doing, Rita? Can't you knock first?" Then clearly seeing her, he saw she was clearly distressed as she was crying and her clothes were disheveled. "Rita, what's wrong?" he then asked with compassion while walking over to hug her. Due to her distressed mental state, he then turned to Carla and stated "I think you'd better leave us alone."

"Sure," Carla agreed as she got up, buttoned her blouse, kissed Raymond lovingly on the cheek, and left the room. "Call you in the morning, Ray," she announced while closing the door.

"Okay," he replied and then led Rita to the chair next to his bed and sat her down.

Putting on the best acting job she'd ever performed, Rita sobbed and forced a steady stream of tears to flow from her eyes. "Raymond," was all she initially said.

Not having any idea what was wrong with his sister, he again asked, "What's wrong?"

"Bruno," she next said.

"Bruno? Did he do something to you?"

Murder by Memory

Making exaggerated sobbing sounds, she answered, "Yes, and he really hurt Alvin!"

"Son of a bitch!" he blurted.

"Raymond."

"What?"

"I think Alvin and I need your help now."

"Thought you wanted me to stay out of things."

"Can't any longer. Things have just gone too far."

"What happened, Rita? You've got to tell me."

"I know," she said while feigning greater distressment. She then provided him with her grossly fabricated story. "You know that dark spot in the park where the lights have been out for months?"

"Yeah, I know where you're talking about. What happened?"

"Alvin and I had just left the library at school," she lied, "and I guess Bruno and his buddies decided to follow us. We didn't see them at school and didn't know they were following us. We were a little scared when we came to the dark stretch, but decided to walk through it since we didn't think anyone else was out there. Well, about half way through we suddenly heard running footsteps. Being startled, we both froze and grabbed each other. Within seconds we were tackled and thrown to the ground. It was Bruno and his three regular buddies," she stated while asking for a Kleenex to blow her nose and wipe the crocodile tears from her eyes.

"What happened next?" Raymond asked with vengeance boiling inside him.

"They immediately put duct tape over our mouths to keep us quiet. Then while they called Alvin various demeaning names and pushed him around, Bruno and another placed my back against a small tree and tied my hands behind my back. Then they brought Alvin close enough so he could watch what they were doing to me."

William M. Jones

"Did they rape you?" Raymond interrupted and demanded to know.

"No," Rita assured. "Bruno did unbutton my blouse, though, and then lifted my bra to expose my breast."

Raymond was having a hard time composing himself enough to hear the rest of his sister's story. This was his baby sister who had been sexually abused and he wouldn't stand for it. Nobody would do this to her and get away with it. Visualizing the mental picture she was describing was making him crazy.

Rita continued. "Bruno then fondled my breast and forced Alvin to watch. Raymond, believe me, there wasn't anything either of us could do. We were completely helpless."

"I know," Raymond agreed.

"But when Bruno started to lift my skirt."

"That son of a bitch!" Raymond protested.

"Alvin got a leg free and kicked one of them in the groin."

"Good for him!"

"But that really made them mad and that's when Bruno started hitting Alvin. Raymond, I think he's got some broken ribs and a broken nose. When they saw he was really hurt, I think they got scared and realized things had gone too far because then they suddenly quit and ran away as quickly as they'd originally come at us. Before leaving, though, Bruno said he'd hurt us both a lot worse if we told anyone and I think he really meant it."

"Did anyone else see them?"

"No, and that's another reason we didn't call the police because it would just be our word against Bruno's with no witnesses and we were afraid the police wouldn't be able to do anything and then Bruno would just get angrier and come after us again. We need your help, Raymond. Will you help us?" Rita finally requested as she really laid on her made up sobbing.

Murder by Memory

Filled with rage, he quickly answered, "Of course!"

"Thank you, Raymond, thank you," she stated over and over while hugging him. "Can you kill them?" she next bluntly asked.

"What?" Raymond suddenly replied. But with the rage he was carrying coupled with the promise he'd made after his dad's senseless death at the hands of another bully, it only took him a matter of seconds to agree to his sister's desperate request which in his normal frame of mind he'd never have even considered. "I will, Rita!" he avowed. "Probably need your help, though."

"You've got it. Whatever you need. Alvin and I just want them gone so we can live in peace. We're so tired of living with fear and the constant harassment."

"You want to stay here tonight with me? You can have the bed. I can put a sleeping bag on the floor."

"I'd like that," she agreed.

After he thought she'd fallen asleep, Raymond left the room and headed for the attic. He remembered his dad had long ago worked at a slaughter house and his memento from those days was his slaughter pistol. He'd been required by the company to purchase it himself, and instead of selling it when he quit, he'd stashed it in an old trunk which for years had been up in the attic. Raymond hadn't seen it in over ten years, but figured it was still up there. As he left the bedroom, Rita, who was faking being asleep, smiled.

CHAPTER FOUR

When Rita woke up, it was already late morning and she found herself alone in Raymond's room. Where he'd gone, she didn't have a clue. Laying in bed another fifteen minutes before finally getting up, she proceeded to her own bedroom to get cleaned up. On the way, she checked in on her mother who had been at work when she came in last night. She found her already up and ironing in her utility room. Her mom informed her Raymond had told her how she'd fallen asleep in his room late last night after coming in from Alvin's and then having one of their brother/sister chats. After getting cleaned up and eating a quick breakfast, Rita decided to walk over and check on Alvin. Opening the front door, she was greeted with a blast of cold air and the sight of a light dusting of snow. Weather had been quite pleasant last night, she remembered. Apparently an early spring cold front had rapidly passed during the night. Walking to Alvin's, she was careful to watch her step as the late morning sun was making slush out of the night's light snow cover. Turning the last corner to his house, she was startled to observe him and his faithful dog, Mutt, just walking into the driveway from the other direction. Yelling his name and waving, she got their attention so they stopped in the driveway and waited for her.

"What are you doing out?" she quizzed with a concerned expression.

"Feel a lot better, Rita."

"And your face looks better now too," she added.

"Don't think anything was actually broken last night, just badly bruised."

"Good," she replied grabbing for his hands and tenderly kissing him on the cheek.

"Ought to be fine by the time my folks come back in a few days so they won't suspect anything. Still hurts to take a deep breath, though, so am still moving pretty slow."

"Where you and Mutt been?" she again inquired.

"Oh, you know, we just wondered up into the woods back behind the house a little ways. Always helps to just go back there and think things through. Wrote a new poem this morning. Want to read it?"

"Of course I do," Rita acknowledged. "You know how much I like your poems."

Reaching inside his pocket, he pulled out his scribbled work and handed it to her. Having read much of his other drafts, she was used to his handwriting so had no trouble deciphering his chicken scratching as she faithfully stood beside him in the driveway and absorbed the words of his latest composition. She knew this was part of the special bond they had for each other; they could talk about anything and through his writings she'd gained a special inner insight into his true feelings and sensitive personality. A sincere tear now dripped from both eyes as she slowly read the poem.

WOODS VENTURE

Today I took an astonishing step, from my house warmth did I go,
To the woods, through mud and slush, the half patch work of snow.
My only friend on this odd day, a half-breed dog, age eight,
Who ventures wildly through the woods, for my whistle he gallantly waits.

Here I sit on a fallen tree; rotten, dead, and brown,
I hear only the natural woods' and animal's queer sounds.

William M. Jones

All else is still. Heaven surely must be similar to all this,
    For all is so peaceful, people should not miss.
    The wind does so gently blow from the chilly blue sky,
    This is my type of world, until the day I die.
    From my tree I can see, the whole rustic woods below,
    And at my feet, the half frozen snow tingles about my toes.
    The majority of the sound I hear, comes from my speechless friend,
    But now I hear a voice at far, over the hill it sends.
    The birds in the barren trees, an occasional call let out,
    And in the distance bombs are bursting, keeping the outer world out.

    Everything is so peaceful, just sitting and thinking here,
    My dog just returned for a quick glance, to the woods he disappears.
    I wish I could stay forever, not leave this still solitude,
    But I must depart for now, the warmth of home is calling, taking away my mood.

Rita wiped the tears from her eyes when she finished the poem. "It's beautiful, Alvin," she admitted. "I think it's your best one," she then honestly stated while squeezing his hand and giving him another kiss. "I love you, Alvin. You're such a sensitive and caring person. Why can't others see you for that and why must the bullies of this world, like Bruno, be so cruel to decent people like you? I just don't understand it! Don't know what I'd ever do without you."

    "I feel the same about you," Alvin professed.

    "I know, I really do," Rita replied. "Let's get out of this cold and go inside," she then said while tugging gingerly on his hand and guiding him toward the stairs leading to his garage room. "Come on, Mutt, you can come up too," she called to his tail wagging companion.

Murder by Memory

Once safely inside his room, Alvin broke the mood by asking, "What happened with Raymond?"

"Like I promised, when he heard what happened last night he agreed without hesitation."

"What exactly did you tell him?" Alvin asked but not sure he really wanted to hear the answer.

Rita then told him exactly the fabricated story she'd fed to trusting Raymond.

"Rita!" Alvin proclaimed while taking a step back from her. "How could you?"

"Alvin, it'll be okay. Remember, I told you Raymond needed to believe my life was in danger. You still want to get rid of Bruno and his thugs, don't you?"

"Yes, Rita, of course I do. It's just, well, that's quite a story you came up with. You sure Raymond believed it?"

"Absolutely."

"You seen him this morning?"

"No, he was gone by the time I got up," she answered as there came a knock at the door with Raymond's voice calling Alvin's name. "Guess we'll know for sure in a second," Rita then stated as she walked over and opened the door to let her brother in.

"Rita."

"Hey, brother, come on in."

"You okay, Alvin?" he next asked. "Scary night last night?"

"Sure was, but I feel better today and thank goodness Rita wasn't harmed."

"Maybe not physically, but definitely emotionally," Raymond declared. "No one will ever do what they did to you and my sister last night and get away with it as long as I have something to do with it!"

"Then you'll help us?" Alvin sheepishly inquired.

"Sure will. Got it all figured out," he promised. Raymond then laid out his plan for handling the situation. Rita and Alvin simply sat quietly and nodded with agreement as he filled in the details. When everything was finally said and mutually agreed upon, Raymond left by stating, "I think it's best if we're not seen together for the next few months." As he left, he noticed how much the bright sunshine was bothering his eyes.

CHAPTER FIVE

Detective Herbert Chalmers was exhausted when he finally returned to his office at the 14th District Police Station. He'd been out alone most of the night investigating the normal myriad of routine crimes which occurred nightly within his district. Nothing major tonight, just small incidents through the course of his shift which, without the assistance of his partner and mentor, Detective Sergeant Benjamin Mitchell, made for a rather long and fatiguing tour of duty. Benny had been reassigned to the police academy for a week to teach his periodic quarterly class on criminal investigations. Being an expert in the field, one week each quarter he pulled the additional duty. Good thing for Herb, he'd been a quick study and figured he'd learned well from Benny during the short three weeks he'd been a detective or else the endless required reports from each investigation would have overwhelmed him. And the last thing he wanted to be when Benny returned was behind with his administrative responsibilities. Being the new detective in the district, he needed to prove to everyone that he could hold his own and get the job done without constant supervision. Reputation was everything and he knew it. Being initially surprised when he wasn't temporarily assigned another partner for the week Benny was away, he quickly realized he was actually being tested and how well he performed this week could have a profound affect on his future as a detective. Bone tired when he finally collapsed at his desk, Herb was determined to complete all of his reports before heading home. Didn't matter if he worked past his shift time, he would get everything done and correctly. He'd put a smile on Benny's face when he returned in a few days. Taking a quick break, Herb headed for the detective lounge and grabbed two jelly filled donuts and a hot cup of coffee. Taking a deep breath and looking around, even though he was dead tired, Herb reflected on the fact of how he was happier right now than he'd ever been. Thirty-two years old now and finally he'd found his niche in life. This was exactly where he wanted to be and he could easily see himself remaining a detective for the remainder of his police career. But the road to this point in his life had been excruciating long and arduous. Graduating from high school back in '62, he didn't have any set goals or career choices in mind. Trying to discover himself and thus find something he enjoyed doing, he first attended a local community college for the next two years. Hoping to find himself there, he took all the required general courses and then spread his electives around to as many different areas as his schedule allowed. After spending two years in this revolving academia void, he still considered himself a lost sole absent of any future direction. Still living at home, he next entered the working world by taking an unfulfilling construction job. It provided him with some extra spending money for the first time in his life, but didn't provide him with a personal sense of worth. And then what little extra money he did have, he always seemed to squander it by going out for beers with the others from the construction gang. Six months into his construction job, his life suddenly took a drastic change. Was now 1965 and the Vietnam War was starting to escalate. He could still vividly remember his dad bringing his draft notice to him while at work. He recalled how his heart sank when he read the words from his draft board that he was to report at 0800 the very next Monday morning for induction into the Army. He remembered being stunned as he walked away from the construction job with his dad. His life now had a direction and he knew where he most likely was headed - to Vietnam - and he was really scared for the first time in his life. He remembered the looks on his fellow construction workers as he left the job site that day. Most knew it was only a matter of time before their notice arrived. Reporting to the Army as ordered, he was

Murder by Memory

immediately given a complete physical along with a battery of intelligence and psychological tests. By the end of the day, he, along with about fifty others, was officially sworn in to the Army. After the swearing in, Herb and three others were pulled aside and taken into the head recruiter's office. Being a little older than the average draftee and possessing some college, Herb was asked if he'd be interested in the warrant officer helicopter program. The decision seemed like a no brainer for him. Whereas the other draftees would go immediately to basic training where the majority would most likely become infantry privates and be trying to stay alive in the deadly rice paddies of South Vietnam within four or five months, he'd remain in the states for maybe up to two years for warrant officer and flight training. Plus, he knew enough about the military to understand how he'd be treated a heck of a lot better as a warrant officer than as a drafted private. He also fully understood how probably at least half of the young men sworn in with him this morning would most likely be dead before the year was over. And then if he was really lucky, the war would end before it would be time for him to go. But that wasn't the case. When he finally completed his flight training in '67 and earned his wings along with his warrant officer bars, Vietnam was bigger than ever and, as feared, his first assignment was as a Huey pilot flying smack dab in the middle of the war in South Vietnam. Scared out of his wits when he first arrived in country, he soon discovered he rather enjoyed the flying. The countryside was absolutely beautiful from the air and he'd been fortunate not to receive much hostile fire during his missions. He mainly flew medevac sorties with the occasional recon team insert/extraction flights. When his year tour was over, he thanked his lucky stars that he'd survived. Matter of fact, he was one of the few helicopter pilots he knew who hadn't at least been shot down once or twice. Returning to the states in '68, he quickly became disillusioned with how things were "back in the real world".

William M. Jones

He was stunned with the treatment he and his fellow servicemen received from the general population. You'd have thought they were all rapists, murderers and baby eaters. How far from the truth that was. They were all just average American youth drafted during their prime by their country and sent to a far away country to perform their assigned duty for God and country. And that's all he'd done; serve his country, do the job asked of him and survive. Wasn't his fault the war had become so political and unpopular. He couldn't understand how the protesters could be so angry with him and his comrades in arms for simply doing their sworn patriotic duty. Disillusioned with the hatred he returned home to, Herb shocked even himself by volunteering to go back to Vietnam. He remembered counting the days until his first tour was over and praying harder and harder with each flight that he'd survive and make it home in one piece to see his parents and friends again. Now he counted the seconds until leaving the states and getting back to Vietnam. What a dichotomy; he'd initially gone to flight school in hopes of the war ending and thus missing it, and now he couldn't wait to get back into it. His mother was devastated with his decision. She pleaded with him to reconsider, but he refused. His mind was made up. The sight of her crying when he left to return to Vietnam would permanently remain ingrained in his mind forever. He hated causing her so much pain after all she'd done for him over all the years, but he simply had to go. With the war drastically escalating during this second tour in '69, he found himself flying more and more missions and his luck finally expired about three fourths of the way through his year tour. He'd been flying a recon extraction mission from close to the Cambodian border when his helicopter was suddenly hit by hostile small arms ground fire. Fighting for control of his chopper, he autorotated into a nearby rice paddy. His copilot and two recon soldiers riding in the rear of the aircraft were killed, but the other

Murder by Memory

four from the recon team survived and helped pull him out of the wreckage since he'd been rendered unconscious during the crash landing. After pulling him out, the surviving recon soldiers quickly set up a hasty defense around the downed helicopter and radioed for cobra gunship support and a medevac chopper. Using their M-16s in the semi-automatic burst mode in order to conserve ammo, they held off an approaching enemy platoon until their help arrived. After the gunships eventually dispersed the enemy, Herb and the recon soldiers were rapidly extracted by a medevac Huey. Still unconscious when they arrived back at base, Herb had been swiftly transferred to a field hospital where he remained for the next week. During the impact of his crash landing, he'd taken a severe jolt to the head. Even though he'd been wearing his flight helmet, he'd still been knocked unconscious. When he finally awakened, his mind remained somewhat fuzzy and he had quite a throbbing headache. Small price to pay, he figured, since he could've ended up dead like the three others. Not wounded seriously enough to be returned to the states, but his concussion serious enough to keep him from flying duty for quite awhile, Herb volunteered to serve his recovery period attached to the base military police unit. He'd gotten to know one of the military police warrant officers quite well during the last few months during their almost nightly card games and the two had talked at length about law enforcement. Before getting to know this individual, Herb hadn't ever even thought about going into law enforcement, but now it seemed quite appealing. Returning to the states in a few months, Herb was given the opportunity to attend Officer Candidate School and thus make a career out of the Army, but he quickly declined and was subsequently honorably discharged. Returning home, he was immediately accepted into the police academy. Graduating in '72 at the top of his class, he next found himself assigned as a patrolman attached to the 10th District. During the next two

William M. Jones

years he performed his duties as a beat officer walking the 1023 beat. Continuously working the night shift, he used his veteran's benefits to attend college during the daytime and in June of '74 received his baccalaureate degree in criminology. With degree in hand and superior evaluations as a uniformed patrolman, Herb returned to the police academy for follow-on detective schooling where he learned additional subjects such as polygraph and interrogation techniques along with investigative and fingerprinting techniques. And now, here he was, a brand new detective assigned to the 14th. Smiling to himself before taking another sip of coffee, he couldn't be happier with his position in life. His thought process returned to the present when the watch commander came in and informed him of a homicide which had just been reported in the park down by the 22nd beat. Swallowing his last bite of doughnut, Herb promptly proceeded to the murder site.

Arriving there, he first walked up to the uniformed police officer responsible for securing the crime scene. When that officer recognized him, he said, "Hey Herb, when'd you get assigned here?"

Recognizing the officer from his original police academy class from '72, he replied, "Hey, Jim, good to see you again too. How's it going?"

"Oh, pretty good. You know. How long you been a detective?"

"Just a few weeks."

"Didn't you go down to the 10th after the academy?"

"Yep, but came up here after getting my detective shield since the 10th had their detective quota."

"Surprised I haven't seen you around the precinct."

"Well, you know, old Benny Mitchell keeps me pretty busy."

"You got Mitchell for a partner?"

"Sure did. Is that good?" Herb wondered.

Murder by Memory

"The best. He'll break you in right. Where is he anyway?"

"Teaching at the academy this week."

"And they're letting you operate alone?"

"Looks that way," Herb answered.

"Man, you must be doing all right for old Benny to turn you loose so soon," the patrolman exclaimed.

"Well, guess I haven't been here long enough yet to really step on my pork," Herb laughed.

"But if you do, old Benny will definitely let you know about it."

"I'm sure he will. He really seems like a by the book, no nonsense type of guy."

"You've got that right, Herb."

Getting back to the matter at hand, Herb terminated the chit chat and inquired, "What've we got here so far?"

"Not much," the uniformed police officer responded, "just the dead guy over there and those two joggers," he stated while pointing to the two female joggers talking with his partner.

Before talking to the witnesses, Herb first walked over and viewed the victim. Was a relatively clean cut looking white teenager with a single gunshot wound to the base of the back of his head. Looked like the round probably entered around C-1 or C-2 before going through the spinal cord and then lodging in the lower brain. He deduced the victim had died instantly from the shot which most likely had been fired from a close range. Then moving over to the two female joggers, he first showed them his badge and introduced himself before asking for details.

"We were simply out for our early morning jog through the park," the prettier of the two joggers started.

"You jog here regularly?" Herb then asked while writing down their names and addresses from identification they presented.

"Yes, sir. Come here almost daily. Usually around six as we like to run before getting ready for work."

"No time during the rest of the day to work out," the other jogger added.

"I hear you there," Herb responded. He then confessed, "You're definitely more dedicated than me. I can't seem to fit it much into my schedule lately and know I really should." Focusing back on the prettier of the two girls, he then asked, "So, what did you see?"

"Well," the jogger started, "we've got this mile loop we run here in the park since it's close to our apartment building. First time by this spot this morning we noticed this guy sitting by the tree over there. Seemed quite odd for so early in the morning and especially since it's so cool out here. We commented to each other about him as we continued to run."

"Okay, so what happened then?" Herb asked.

"Next time around the guy was laying on the ground."

"So you stopped and checked him out?" Herb finished her statement for her.

"Yes, sir. We called to him, but when he didn't respond we walked over and that's when we saw the blood and suspected he was dead. I stayed here while Jane ran home and called the police."

"You see anyone else in the park?"

"No. I think we were the only joggers out so far this morning. Most others tend to come out a little later. We usually see a few during our cool down walk back to the apartment building."

"Either of you ever see the victim before?" Herb then asked.

"No, don't think so. Never pay much attention to the teenagers. They all kind of blend together and pretty much look the same after awhile."

"Okay. Well, thanks for the information and you're free to go," Herb added while handing each one of his detective

Murder by Memory

cards and informing them to call him if they happened to remember anything else. He then performed a cursory search of the crime site before radioing in for a crime scene investigating unit to conduct a thorough search of the area. Hopefully they'd turn up some sort of clue so he'd have something solid for the Homicide Squad from the County Prosecutor's Office. Since the body couldn't be removed until the area was thoroughly checked out, Herb stayed for awhile and finally left once the CSI unit arrived. Returning initially back to his precinct office, he wrote his preliminary report, passed what information he had to the next shift's detective team and headed home. He was exhausted. He'd worked all night plus this morning so had been on the job for about fourteen straight hours. He desperately needed to get some sleep before his next shift started. In his short tenure as a detective, that's the one difference he'd learned in being one from his days as a regular uniformed officer. Uniformed patrolmen rarely worked longer than their eight hour shift and so far in his three short weeks as a detective rarely had he only worked his required shift. Seemed like something, and was usually the paperwork, seemed to always keep him an hour or two past the shift's end. But he didn't care. He really enjoyed this; it was his life now. He was glad, though, that he was still single. No way he could work these hours and keep a family happy, but in a few years he figured he'd be able to handle it after he got some seniority and hopefully moved up to detective sergeant like Benny. For the time being, he'd work like a dog to learn his business, remain single, and hopefully love every minute of it.

Watching TV to unwind when he first got home, Herb eventually fell asleep on his couch with his clothes and TV still on. He was awakened mid afternoon when his phone kept ringing. Finally comprehending what the ringing noise was, he slowly got up and answered the call. It was the precinct's day shift watch commander notifying him that this morning's shooting victim was now at the city morgue and the medical examiner had requested to see him as soon as possible since he was the lead detective on the case. Hearing the words lead detective made him feel quite proud. Quickly shaving and washing his face, Herb immediately headed for the morgue to talk with the medical examiner.

Arriving at the morgue, for some unknown reason, Herb flashed back to Vietnam and all the body bags he'd medevaced over the course of his two tours. Back then, the regularity of the dead soldiers didn't phase him after awhile and they eventually seemed like handling any other type of cargo. Back then he couldn't allow himself to think of the body bags as actually containing human bodies. Numbing ones soul to such atrocities was a common defense mechanism for mental survival during Vietnam as well as all other wars throughout time. But going to view this homicide victim was different. He'd seen the young teenage victim at the scene plus shortly he assumed a name would also be attached to the corpse, not just a metallic dog tag attached to the remains like during the war. This was quickly turning personal for him and he was feeling the affects. He figured it was a normal human response since it was the first shooting victim he'd dealt with since becoming a detective. He figured that the more homicide cases he worked over the years he'd eventually become personally numb to them also like the countless dead soldiers back in Nam. But that was in the future, right now he personally felt the loss of this particular young teenager. He decided he'd have to discuss these feelings with Benny when he came back next week. Oh well, right now he had a job to do and it involved viewing the body, talking with the medical examiner, and most likely also talking with the victim's parents sometime in the near future.

Checking in at the front desk, Herb was informed the medical examiner was finishing his autopsy and wanted to talk with him at the body. Herb thought this to be quite odd,

Murder by Memory

but kept his thoughts to himself while being guided to the appropriate room. After greeting the elderly doctor, Herb next inquired, "What caliber pistol killed him?"

"Good question," returned the doctor.

"What do you mean?" Herb asked. "Didn't you get the round?"

"Wasn't one," the medical examiner said quite matter-of-fact.

"Had to be," Herb responded. "I didn't see an exit wound when I checked the body at the scene."

"Correct, detective, there wasn't one. But there wasn't a bullet inside him either."

"What are you telling me?" Herb questioned as he made a puzzled expression. "He was shot, wasn't he? Wound sure didn't look like it was made from a knife."

"It wasn't. Victim was definitely shot because we found powder residue on the back of his neck."

"Then where's the bullet?" Herb needed to know.

"Don't think there was one," the medical examiner stated.

"What are you talking about?"

"Ever been inside a slaughter house?"

"Can't say as I have," Herb admitted.

"Well, I have," the doctor informed, "and the only weapon I can think of that would make a wound like this would be a slaughter house pistol."

"How so?" Herb next asked.

"You see," the doctor explained, "can't have live rounds going off inside slaughter houses when they kill the animals."

"No, I guess not," Herb responded. "Just never thought much about it."

"You see, they normally fire a .22 caliber pistol with a blank round. The charge forces a metal rod out the end of the barrel which goes into the back of the animal's head killing it instantly."

William M. Jones

"Thus the powder burn on the back of the victim's neck?"

"Exactly."

"In other words, the killer actually pressed the pistol against the victim's neck when he pulled the trigger."

"I believe so," the medical examiner agreed. "It's the only scenario which makes any sense."

"I'll be damned!" Herb exclaimed. "Never heard of this before."

"And I've never seen this type of pistol used to kill a person before either," the doctor stated.

"Where do you think the killer got the pistol?"

"That I can't tell you detective. You'll have to find the answer to that yourself. Suggest you check all the slaughter houses in the region and see if any are missing a weapon."

"Good idea," Herb agreed. "Looks like our killer will become known as the Slaughter House Murderer," Herb then announced as the receptionist entered the room to talk with the doctor. When she left, Herb asked, "Something to do with this case?"

"Yes, the victim's parents are waiting to see him."

"I didn't know you'd identified the body."

"Sorry detective, thought you knew."

"No, what's his name?"

"Appears to be one Daryl Woods. Ever hear of him?"

"No, can't say as I have, but I'm new to the district. What else can you tell me about him before the parents come in?"

"Not much, just your average eighteen year old high school senior."

"Who'd want to kill him?" Herb questioned out loud.

"That's also for you to find out, detective," the medical examiner correctly pointed out. "You want to talk to the parents?"

"Yeah, guess I'd better," Herb reluctantly agreed as he proceeded outside the autopsy room to face Daryl Woods'

Murder by Memory

grieving parents. After introducing himself, he brought them into the room where they immediately made a positive identification of their son's body. Herb then escorted them back out to a vacant reception area. Daryl's mother was beside herself with grief and thus unable to answer any questions. Daryl's father, even though extremely grief stricken, was able to answer some of Herb's questions before announcing he needed to take his wife home. He promised to get back in touch at a later date, but before leaving provided Herb with the names of the crowd Daryl hung around with the most. From what the father said, his son was pretty much an average high school kid. Did confess how he was more of a follower than a leader and voiced concern over one Victor Kojan. He said that Victor, also known as Bruno, seemed like a small time punk to him and he'd confronted Daryl about hanging out with him. Herb wrote down the name and figured talking with Bruno would be his next stop.

Being late afternoon, Herb decided first to stop by the local high school and have a talk with the principal. Finding him already departed for the day, Herb was directed to the vice principal's office since he was still at work. After questioning the vice principal, he was glad he'd stopped by the school first and also realized he probably received more information from him than the principal could have provided since the vice principal had daily contact with the trouble students and Victor Kojan unequivocally fell into that category. He also learned that word of Daryl Woods murder hadn't reached the school yet. He had been counted absent for the day, but his name as the murder victim hadn't officially been released pending his official identification. Knowing the parents had just made it, Herb informed the vice principal of the fact. He then told Herb how he had agonized most of the day over the name of the individual after the news this morning had reported the murder and had reported the victim as being a white, male teenager. Fearing it could possibly be a student from this school, the vice principal admitted how he'd anguished over the absentee roster during the day and wondered if anyone on the list was in fact the victim. Not knowing for sure if the person was from his school, all he could do though was wonder and now his worst fears had come true. He knew by tomorrow morning that every student and parent would know of Daryl's murder and he openly feared for the panic and fear which would grip the school and local community. He told Herb he'd also notify the principal and school superintendent so they could plan a course of action for dealing with the situation. As to Daryl Woods himself, the vice principal confirmed Daryl's father's statements of how his son was basically a good kid but was more of a follower. Apparently he'd fallen into cahoots with Victor Kojan during this school year and had served detention a few times due to his association. The vice principal acknowledged that Victor wasn't a hoodlum or thief, simply came across as an immature punk. Said he came from a broken, lower income home and didn't have a dominant male role model in his life. Stated he had a reputation for being somewhat of a bully and figured he did so most likely for the attention. When they were done talking, Herb thanked the vice principal for all of his help, promised to keep him informed about the case and asked him to keep his eyes and ears attuned to any possible leads he might come across at school. Leaving the school, Herb proceeded to try to find Victor Kojan and have a little talk with him.

Turning onto Victor's street and looking for his address, Herb sighted two individuals standing in a driveway angrily arguing. He immediately placed his portable red siren light on top of his unmarked detective car and turned it on in hopes of drawing the duo's attention. Stopping his car, Herb promptly recognized the older of the two as Daryl Woods' father so assumed the other must be none other than the infamous Victor aka Bruno Kojan. Herb held out his

Murder by Memory

detective badge and announced himself as a police officer as he ordered the two to break it up. This part of the job he'd performed numerous times during his former duty as a uniformed patrolman. Usually individuals backed off when police arrived and Herb hoped these two would react accordingly. If not, he'd be forced to radio for backup and arrest them.

"Break it up! Break it up!" Herb yelled as he physically tried to separate the two highly vocal individuals.

"Get this SOB off of me!" Bruno ordered. "He's crazy!"

"Mr. Woods, back off." Herb demanded again as he pushed the man back with a one handed shove to the chest. "What the hell are you doing?"

"This punk got my son killed!" Woods exclaimed so emphatically that spit sprayed from his mouth.

"What's he talking about?" Bruno stated. "I don't know anything about Daryl. Haven't seen him since last night."

Finally getting Woods to back off, Herb ordered Bruno to stand over by his car. He then confronted Mr. Woods and tried to calm him down to diffuse what was quickly becoming a very volatile confrontation.

"That punk had something to do with my son getting killed!" Woods adamantly yelled.

"Calm down, Woods. You don't know that for sure."

"Give me two more minutes alone with him and we'll find out," Woods requested.

Understanding the father's anger and frustration, Herb could understand how he must feel after just losing his only son, but he couldn't let the situation get out of control. Finally talking sense into Mr. Woods, Herb suggested he get into his car and go home to his wife - she probably needed him the most right now. Herb promised he'd deal with young Bruno Kojan. After Mr. Woods departed, Herb then approached Bruno. "Okay, kid, what can you tell me?"

"I don't have to talk to you!" Bruno blurted.

Taken somewhat back by this blunt statement, Herb countered with, "Okay wise guy, you can either talk to me here or else I can haul your sorry ass down to the precinct, fingerprint you and then lock you up for awhile for hindering a homicide investigation. Your call, Bruno. How do you want this to go down? It's your call."

Quickly changing his tone, Bruno agreed to cooperate.

"Once again, what can you tell me?" Herb asked.

"Nothing. I don't know nothing." Bruno stated. "Didn't even know Daryl was dead until that maniac dad of his showed up here right before you did."

"You sure?"

"I'm telling the truth," Bruno firmly stated.

Seeing him beginning to tremble, Herb deduced he may be telling the truth. "When'd you see Daryl last?"

"I already told you."

"Oh, yeah, last night."

"Right."

"What was he doing?"

"Nothing much. Just came over here for awhile to hang out."

"What time did he leave?"

"About 10:30. Said he had to see someone before going home?"

"Who?"

"I don't know," Bruno again firmly stated as Herb could see sweat starting to form on his forehead.

"Where?"

"Don't know that either. Honest. He said he didn't want to talk about it."

"Why?"

"How do I know?" Bruno said in a slightly cocky tone.

"He was one of your good buddies, wasn't he?"

"Yeah, but he didn't tell me anymore."

"Why?"

"I said I didn't know. Maybe he was meeting a girl."

Murder by Memory

"Why'd you say that?"

"I don't know. Just a gut feeling."

"Any particular one he liked?" Herb asked.

"Sure, he liked them all, but most didn't even know he was alive."

"Like you," Herb jabbed trying to push Bruno's button.

Getting defensive, Bruno countered with, "I can have any girl I want! That's right, just any girl I want!"

"Yeah, yeah big guy. Sure you can. Now, who was Daryl going to see last night before going home?"

"For the last time, I don't know."

"Okay," Herb finally consented, "but if you know anything you'd better tell me. Understand?"

"Sure, whatever you say," Bruno half-heartily promised.

Deciding he couldn't get any additional information out of Bruno this afternoon, Herb gave him his card and told him to call if anything came up. Herb then headed back to the precinct to try to start putting the pieces to this puzzle together. Why would anyone want to kill Daryl Woods? He appeared like a harmless teenager. Now Bruno, he was a different story. Herb could understand someone wanting to get a punk like him, but a follower like Daryl just didn't make any sense - at least not right now.

When Benny Mitchell returned from the academy the next week, he praised Herb for his initial handling of the case. He also informed him how he'd help when possible, but for all practical purposes the Slaughter House Murderer was his case to solve. Herb promised he would.

CHAPTER SIX

Alvin had been awake all night. He'd tried to sleep, but his racing mind wouldn't allow it. He knew Raymond was planning to kill Daryl Woods sometime during the night and the guilt of that act was tearing him up inside. Why did he have Rita arrange the killings? Thinking hard, he realized he hadn't. Killing Victor Kojan and his cronies had been exclusively her idea, not his. Problem was, he was so weak, he'd agreed to her crazy scheme so in the end he was just as guilty of the murder as Raymond was for actually committing it. Knowing Daryl was going to be the first one killed, Alvin had seriously contemplated warning him, but resisted in the end and allowed the deed to be committed. Now looking at his clock and noticing it was almost 4 in the morning, he assumed the murder was over and Raymond was probably home snug in his bed by now feeling as if he'd committed a great personal deed by avenging his sister's virginal honor. How wrong he was since her honor hadn't been tarnished. It was all one big lie. A lie made up by his own devious sister and Alvin's one true love. Tossing and turning in bed, he knew Rita was right - the only way to put an end to all the years and probable future years of Bruno's harassment was by eliminating him. But still; murder. The thought of it made him want to vomit. Too late now to do anything about it, though. Daryl's corpse was probably propped up against some tree in the park just waiting to be discovered in the morning as planned. Alvin shuddered at the thought. He then, for the first time, thought about Daryl's family. They would be devastated. All their hopes and plans for his future had been murderously wiped out tonight. Death was so final! How Alvin wished he could take it all back; make Daryl alive again, but he couldn't! Such a shame, though. He'd actually liked Daryl. They'd talked numerous times over the years. Why did he have to get hooked up with the likes of Bruno? Rationalizing again, Alvin deduced it was all Bruno's fault. He'd caused all of this. Why couldn't he have been a decent, caring person? Why did he have to be such a bully? Why did anyone have to be a bully? Bullies couldn't be tolerated! Alvin had the right to live a peaceful life. Why couldn't all the Bruno's of this world just go away? Well, Rita's plan would certainly take care of this one and there wasn't any turning back now. Raymond had to continue and commit the next three murders. Alvin would just have to accept the fact and get on with his life. Maybe Rita was right and this was the only way to deal with the problem. Oh how he loved her. She knew what was best for him and she'd never do anything to purposely hurt him. Everything she did was for them so they could be together, forever, in peace. Noticing the time was now 5 a.m., Alvin decided to get up. He needed to get away. No way he could go to school today. He couldn't look at his classmates knowing he'd been involved in having one of them killed during the night. He had to get away by himself and think things through. He didn't even want Rita with him right now. He'd see her as soon as he came back later today. He'd need to talk with her by then and be comforted by her affection, but right now he needed to be alone. Dressing warmly, Alvin got in his car and drove to the solitude of one of his most favorite personal places. About ten miles west of his house was a small public lake which had a small campground and picnic area. Being so cold of an early spring morning, he reckoned the area would be void of anybody else. Numerous times he'd spent countless hours out there without seeing another person. He hoped that would be the case today.

Arriving at the lake shortly after 5:30, Alvin first remained inside his vehicle and kept it running so he could keep the heater on. Was still pretty dark out. Looking to the east, he could view an approaching lightness in the sky. The sun would be coming up soon. As it did, he turned off his

William M. Jones

car and slowly walked down to the small dock at the lake's edge. Shivering, he zipped his jacket up to his neck, pulled his blue watch cap firmly over his ears and tied his scarf around his neck. He knew the morning air would most likely get a few degrees cooler before eventually warming from the sun's rays as he knew the coldest time of any morning was right at sunrise. Provided with the light of the coming day, Alvin reflected on the calmness of the lake. Why couldn't life be like this - so peaceful. Sitting on the bench at the end of the dock and looking across the lake, he entered an altered state of consciousness while watching the wispy morning mist lift from the water's warmer surface and observed the morning's thick fog forming across the lake entwined among the distant trees. All would be gone in a matter of time when the sun's warming heat widened the temperature/dew point spread causing both to magically dissipate. Concentrating completely on the wonderment of the moment and blocking out the reality of Daryl Woods murder, Alvin took pencil and paper from his jacket pocket and began to write.

NATURE'S AID TO MANKIND

The morning dew, a sticky mist,
Covers the ground, not an inch does it miss.

The chirps of birds in the misty morn,
The fog is lifting, a new day is born.

The lake is calm, not yet a ripple,
To break the glassy coat, nature's wimple.

To awake to this, my, oh so great,
Some persons do miss, a grave mistake.

To arise to all this, at nature's best,

Murder by Memory

The smell of clean air, undisputed rest.

Back to bare nature, when you're in a bind,
Soul searching freedom, free to find.

Stay for awhile, let yourself free,
A new person you'll become, great relief.

The beaver's tail flaps, danger is near,
Don't be concerned, do not fear.

Nature is perfect, its balance is just,
Tis not a crime, survival's a must.

Just stay for awhile, enjoy the solitude,
Then return to society, mean and cruel.

But when once again, the desire arrives,
Return to nature, in order to survive.

The sun is setting, the day's end is near,
Keep your faith in nature, never fear.

    Finishing his poem, Alvin remained seated on the bench and blankly stared across the lake for what seemed an eternity. Slowly his mood shifted from the tranquility of the natural scene to the horrific reality of Daryl's murder. Rubbing his face with his right hand and comprehending the tragic depths he'd sunken to, he again began to express his feelings through his pencil.

SIN'S WAYS

Into a dark, damp, misty swamp did I venture,
Into a pit, darker than Hell, I am sure.

William M. Jones

    Into the damnedest, sin forbidden place in all creation,
    Where all that exist, is worthy of the gravest damnation.

    Where no one would dare, to try to humanly exist,
    Where God's creation and development, surely did miss.

    Where all that lives, are slim laden trees,
    Quick sand beds, with the unfortunate like me.

    Who by some misguidance, did happen to come,

    Suddenly removing his pencil from the paper, Alvin stopped writing. He couldn't decide what to write next. His mind had suddenly gone blank. Not wanting to force the issue, he placed the pencil and paper back inside his pocket and slowly walked back to his car. Looking at his watch, it was 2:30 in the afternoon. Where had the time gone? He needed to get home and talk to Rita. He needed to get on with his life - his and Rita's. Three more murders to go. Could he mentally survive them? Daryl's was eating him up inside. He simply had to trust Rita and have an unwavering belief that her method was the only possible solution to putting a conclusive termination to Bruno's harassment. In time he'd be able to block it all from his mind and life would be peaceful, he prayed.

CHAPTER SEVEN

Raymond had missed the last two days of school. He hated having to be absent since mid-terms were taking place, but he simply felt too fatigued to drag himself out of the house. Being someone who also enjoyed his long distance running, it was also killing him not being able to get outside and run. Damn quacks, he thought to himself. Why couldn't they find out what's wrong with him. He'd gone to the doctor again yesterday, but with the same results as last time - another test for mononucleosis came back negative. He was highly suspicious of the test results since he knew he had most of the classic mono symptoms of being constantly fatigued along with a nagging, low 100 degree temperature, but the doctor explained how he didn't have the telltale enlarged lymph nodes. The doctor also ruled out cytomegalovirus which can produce mono like symptoms. Also ruled out was chronic fatigue syndrome because again swollen lymph nodes normally accompanied that condition. The doctor still believed Raymond had a mild iron deficiency causing him to be slightly anemic so continued to prescribe lots of rest along with orally taking an iron enriched medication. Didn't the doctor realize he had to get well, and soon. He couldn't afford to miss any more school. Not if he was to get high grades in his classes. He'd never get accepted into a major university's astronomy program if he remained sick and couldn't keep his grades up. He also didn't want to have to drop his classes this semester and retake them in the fall. Oh, well, no matter how much he wanted to get back to classes, his body just wouldn't cooperate with his mind. Doctor promised he'd at least feel some better in a few days so he hoped he was right. If he wasn't, he'd find another doctor and get a second opinion. His future plans of an astronomy career depended on it.

William M. Jones

Carla had come over a few hours ago to keep him company and fix him something to eat. She'd fixed him supper consisting of chicken soup and milk toast with hot herbal tea to drink. Damn, she'd make a great mother some day. She was terrific at taking care of other people and genuinely cared for their needs. She'd hugged him when she arrived and again when she left, but they didn't engage in any oral making out. It wasn't just because she knew how bad he was feeling; was also because she was having another episode with her cold sores. Ray had a phobia of any intimate contact with her whenever she possessed one. When she was clear, he didn't give them a second thought and figured everything was okay. She'd periodically had cold sores the entire time they'd been going out and he really didn't think much of them except for not wanting to get intimate with her when one was present. He figured they were just some female, teenage thing. Anyway, after washing his supper dishes, she decided to head on home and let him get some needed rest. Once alone in his room, he turned on his planetarium light as well as his red lava lamp and then put his latest Doors album on his stereo. Laying on his back in bed, he hypnotically watched the lava flow inside the lamp and thought about his killing Daryl Woods. Been over two weeks now since he'd killed him. Sure looked like Rita was right in that nobody would ever suspect him. After reading all the reports in the paper, he felt somewhat secure that the police didn't have any connection to him. He knew they'd questioned Bruno and had been to the high school interviewing various of Daryl's friends there, but so far neither he, Rita, nor Alvin had had any contact with the police. He still couldn't figure out why Daryl had been so agreeable to meet with Rita. That part he couldn't quite figure out. Seems like if he helped sexually assaulted her that she'd be the last person he'd agree to meet with. She wouldn't tell him exactly how she'd lured him out the night he'd killed him. Said it didn't really matter. All that

Murder by Memory

mattered was that he was gone and after the next two they'd finally kill Bruno and put an end to this chapter in their lives. Raymond determined she must have threatened to turn Daryl over to the police if he didn't agree to meet with her. He decided it really didn't matter. Killing Daryl had actually been quite simple so whatever she needed to do, as long as it worked, was okay with him and then he'd methodically do his part by killing the bastards who'd dared to mess with his sister. As he got up to play the flip side of the Doors album, Rita knocked and entered his room.

"Hey, brother, how you doing?"

"Not good," he replied.

"What's the matter?"

"Still not feeling very good. Really feel tired."

"What did the doctor say? Didn't you go see him again yesterday?"

"Same old shit. Gave me more iron pills and said to rest."

"You sure it's not mental depression from killing Daryl?"

"No!" Raymond emphatically stated. "That had nothing to do with it. Been like this for over a month."

"Okay," Rita apologized. "Just checking."

"How's Alvin?" Raymond asked changing the subject.

"Pretty bummed out, but he'll get through it. He knows it's the only way to take care of the problem."

"Me, too," Ray agreed. "Who's next?"

"Tony," Rita coldly answered.

"Tony? Do I know him?"

"No. New this year."

"Hmm. Too bad for him. Shouldn't have taken up with Bruno."

"What can I say. He did. And now he'll pay the ultimate price."

"Yep," Raymond stated.

"When?" Rita then asked.

William M. Jones

"What's today's date?" Raymond questioned as he blankly thought for a few seconds before asking.

"May Day," Rita answered while giving him a puzzled look.

"May first?"

"Yep. What's the matter with you, Ray? Don't you know what day it is? You always liked May Day festivities when you were in high school."

"I did, but lately I've been getting confused a lot. Must be from being so tired all the time."

"Hope that's all it is, Ray," Rita comforted.

"Me, too," Raymond answered.

"So, when do I need to get Tony for you?"

"On the 8th."

"Why the 8th?" Rita asked.

"Cuz it's the next new moon."

"You and all your astronomy stuff."

"Got a better plan?" Raymond asked while glaring at his sister.

"No, sorry Ray. Didn't mean to make fun of you. Just think you take all this astronomy stuff a little too far sometimes."

"Whatever," he responded. "It works for me and Carla accepts it."

"You're lucky, Ray, to have her for a girlfriend."

"You're not telling me anything I don't already know," he responded.

"Oh, well, anyway, Ray, get some rest. Hope you feel better soon."

"Thanks, sis, and let me know if the cops start snooping around and want to talk with either you or Alvin."

"Okay," she promised. She then left his room and Raymond returned to watching his star constellations projected on his walls and ceiling, watching the red lava drip inside his lava lamp and listening to his new Doors album. His favorite songs were *People Are Strange*, *Break*

On Through and *Light My Fire*. He laid there in the dark singing "come on baby light my fire" over and over. Carla could definitely light his fire! He really loved her. Then thinking about the killings, he couldn't wait until they were over so he could get back to his regular life.

CHAPTER EIGHT

Detective Herbert Chalmers was exhausted. He'd been working the Daryl Woods murder case nonstop now for the better part of a month with negative results. Everywhere he looked turned into a dead end. Why did anyone want to kill a seemingly clean cut high school kid like Woods? Didn't make any sense. He didn't appear to have any known enemies. The only possibility was his connection to Bruno Kojan, but even that association led nowhere. Maybe he'd just been in the wrong place at the wrong time. Just maybe he was killed by mistake and then left in the park when the error was discovered. But if he was killed by mistake, then who was the real target? Was this mob related? Gang related? Or just a senseless murder for the hell of it? So many questions, and so far no real answers. But the mayor's office demanded answers! Not now, but yesterday! The sensationalism and fear this murder was causing in the local community demanded a quick resolution. Plus, the mayor feared it would gain unwanted national exposure the longer it went unsolved. The case consumed every second of Herb's time and kept him awake most of the nights tossing and turning as he ran various scenarios through his mind. Being a beat cop had definitely never been anything like this. Simply keep the peace at mostly domestic disturbances, squelch possible volatile situations, secure countless crime scenes plus occasionally grabbing a bad guy, but nothing like this gut wrenching agonizing he was experiencing now with his first big case as a detective. But he loved it. Gave him a positive sense of worth while trying to solve the mysteries of the case. Being a detective, while very exasperating at times, was definitely the challenge he longed for when he asked for the assignment. And true to his word, his partner and mentor, Benny Mitchell, was allowing him the latitude to perform the bulk of the

Murder by Memory

investigating on this case. Oh, sure, Benny kept fully apprised of the situation and offered Herb countless investigative suggestions, but pretty much left him alone to perform the mundane, time consuming, tedious leg work required. Fortunately for Herb, Benny also took all the heat from up the chain of command for him plus giving the daily briefings required by the Chief. This case needed to be solved, and soon. Couldn't have some nut case running amok randomly killing high school kids. Impossible for the police or even the school or parents to protect all the kids all of the time. Simply couldn't be done. The killer, or killers, had to be caught before another innocent teenager was killed. But where had the actual killing occurred? That question Herb couldn't positively answer either. The forensic crime scene investigators hadn't been able to come up with any shred of solid evidence. The crime scene was clean. No expelled .22 caliber shell casing, no fingerprints, no telltale footprints, nothing. Herb suspected that the murder, or more appropriately due to the slaughter house pistol having to be placed directly on the back of the victims neck - the assassination, had taken place somewhere else and Daryl's body had been carefully positioned in the park to be found. But why? Seemed crazy, but sure appeared like the murder had gone down like that. But if not in the park, then where had the murder taken place? No way to tell without witnesses and there simply weren't any. That was the vicious circle Herb was beating his head against - no motive, no witnesses, no evidence and thus no leads. The case seemed to be one gigantic circle of negatives which led to nowhere, but Herb knew there had to be something out there and he simply hadn't discovered it yet. He was determined he would, though. He would solve this case no matter how long it took! Murders couldn't occur without some reason or without some minute piece of evidence. He just hadn't found it yet so would just have to work harder. Grabbing another cup of hot coffee, he slouched at his desk,

William M. Jones

closed his already weary eyes and for the millionth time started running the case through his mind. Was about 6:30 in the morning when Benny Mitchell gently taped him on the shoulder bringing him out of his hypnotic trance.

"Herb, just found another one," Benny stated.

"What?" Herb questioned with a disbelieving tone.

"Just got called in. Another teenager found dead in the park."

"Slaughter house pistol?" Herb immediately asked.

"Looks that way," Benny sadly answered.

"You coming with me?" Herb asked.

"Think I'd better."

"Okay," Herb responded while gulping the last of his cup of now cold coffee. Also trembling inside from the thought of another dead, local high school kid, he silently prayed for some answers this time.

Detectives Chalmers and Mitchell arrived at the murder scene within fifteen minutes. For Herb, it was a case of deja vu - same beat cop at the scene, another dead male teenager propped against a tree, victim first discovered by an early morning jogger and an entry wound to the back of the lower head with no apparent exit wound. Only difference was this victim was found in a different section of the park.

Seeing his old classmate arriving at the scene, the beat cop commented, "See you brought out the big guns with you this time."

Thinking, Herb slowly replied, "Oh, Benny, yeah, you know, he needed something to do." Then blowing into his hands to warm them in the cool morning air and buttoning the top button of his detective's black overcoat, he continued, "Plus, the Woods' murder is still getting a lot of attention."

"And if this one makes it a serial killing, there's going to be a lot more heat from the brass."

"Something like that," Herb replied, "plus, just maybe Benny can find something I overlooked before."

Murder by Memory

"Let's hope so," the cop answered, "because if there's a serial killer running loose out here, well, we'll never get home to see our families. You know the Chief will put us all on double shifts until this thing is solved."

"Let's just hope we find the killer, then, and soon."

"I'm all for that," the cop answered.

Herb and Benny spent the next hour at the murder scene doing basically the same procedures he'd performed by himself at the first one. When they finally left, Benny went back to the precinct to start the reports and to also start briefing the chain of command since the mayor was bound to go ballistic when he heard about it. Would most likely threaten to fire the entire police force if they didn't catch the killer soon. Everyone knew he couldn't actually do it, but he could definitely make life miserable for everyone from the Chief down to the newest patrolman. After dropping Benny off, Herb proceeded to the medical examiner's office at the morgue. He wanted to be there when the body arrived so he could find out as soon as possible if the slaughter house pistol had indeed been used in this murder also. He was 99.9 percent sure it had, but needed the doctor's verification. Then he needed to learn the victim's identity. Was definitely another high school aged male, but needed a name in order to try to fit the pieces of this murderous puzzle together.

In a matter of two hours with the medical examiner, Herb had all the answers he'd come for. Yes, a .22 caliber slaughter house pistol had been the murder weapon so they positively had a serial killer on their hands. Then the victim had been identified as Tony Austin. He was another eighteen year old senior at the local high school. Herb met with Tony's parents when they arrived at the morgue for the gruesome duty of positively identifying their son. Their reactions had been similar to Daryl Woods' parents - the mother was too distraught to talk, but the father had enough composure to answer some questions. Herb learned how the Austin's had just moved to the area last fall so Tony was being forced to spend his senior year at a new school far away from his established friends back in Texas. His father admitted how this had been quite traumatic for his son. Where he'd been a rather good student and quite outgoing back at his old school, he'd withdrawn more to himself since moving here and was basically just trying to get by until graduation. Mr. Austin stated how his son's spirit had lifted recently after being accepted to a college back in Texas. He was counting the days until he could reunite with his old friends - most he'd grown up with and been together with in school since early elementary school. Tony's father stated he knew the relocation to this area for his son's senior year would be difficult for Tony, but it had been even harder than either had expected. Many times Mr. Austin said he'd regretted the move, but for financial reasons simply didn't have any choice. And now his oldest child and only son lay dead in the cold storage of the morgue. Witnessing his son laying on the gurney wrapped in a white sheet with his arms folded over his chest and his eyes pulled shut, had brought back extremely painful memories for his dad. He quickly remembered viewing the only other dead person he'd seen like this. He'd had to identify his own father after his passing. Seeing him positioned in the same manner caused him to feel the extreme loneliness of death. Seeing his father dead and laying in the viewing room by himself was an imprinted sight he'd hoped to never have to see again, but had just and this time it had been his son. In a way, a person can accept a parent's passing, but the death of a child was another matter. He didn't know what was worse, losing an infant or losing a promising youth like his son at the stage where his future plans were just starting to blossom. Tony had been really good in drafting and loved airplanes so was seriously considering a career in aircraft design or as an aeronautical engineer. Mr. Austin knew his son's grades would improve and he'd succeed once he joined his old friends back in Texas and thus emerged from his slight

Murder by Memory

depression. But now that was all over. All dreams of the future had been wiped out by his murder. Taking additional information from Mr. Austin, Herb noticed their local address. Something about it struck a nerve.

"Did your son know Victor Kojan? Goes by Bruno."

"Sure," Mr. Austin acknowledged. "Lives just down the street from us. Why?"

"I'm not sure," Herb answered. "Just that Daryl Woods was also an acquaintance of Bruno's."

"Yes, I know," Mr. Austin acknowledged. "I don't like Victor very much. He's a punk if you ask me."

"You're not the first to give me that description," Herb said. "Why did your son hang out with him?"

"I don't know. Maybe just because he was the first kid his own age he met in the neighborhood."

"You ever have any real trouble with Bruno?"

"No, not really. Just an arrogant kid. Never got into any serious trouble I know about. Just some detention at school for stuff like picking fights. Petty stuff, you know."

"Yeah, I do. Exactly what I've heard from others about him."

"Why the interest in Bruno?" Mr. Austin next asked. "Think he had something to do with Tony and Daryl's murders?"

"Not sure what to think," Herb honestly admitted, "but the only common connection in both murders seems to be both boys hung out with him." Then placing a hand on Mr. Austin's shoulder, Herb genuinely expressed his sorrow with Tony's death and promised to find the person or persons responsible for it. Saying his good-byes to both of Tony's grieving parents, Herb then left the morgue and placed a radio call back to the precinct to have a uniformed patrol squad pick Mr. Victor Bruno Kojan up at school and bring him to the precinct for questioning. Herb thought how possibly he could put a little fear into Bruno by transporting him to the precinct in the squad car and this might just get a little more cooperation and answers out of him this time. Figured the intimidation factor might just help in this case.

About forty-five minutes later, Bruno was escorted into the precinct's interrogation room. He was initially placed in the room by himself. Herb and Benny watched him through the one way glass. Since Bruno didn't have any previous police record that they could find, again, they figured a little time alone in the interrogation room might just scare old Bruno into cooperating. After another fifteen minutes of watching Bruno's endless fidgeting, Herb finally entered the room with him.

"We meet again, Mr. Kojan," Herb started.

"You again," Bruno answered.

Glad to see that Bruno at least remembered him, Herb next stated, "You know your friend Tony Austin is dead?"

Quickly looking up with an immediate startled expression which Herb sensed seemed sincere and not forced, Bruno answered, "No, I didn't!" Following about ten seconds of silence, Bruno again stated, "Honest, I didn't know anything about it. Your cops that brought me here didn't say a word about it. Just said some detective needed to see me. Figured you had something new about Daryl."

"When'd you see Tony last?" Herb asked.

"Last night. We hung out some last night at my house."

"Where'd he go when he left you?"

"I don't know. Assumed he was going home."

"He have a girlfriend?"

"Why'd you ask?"

"Well, because you said Daryl was going to meet a girl the night he was killed."

"I told you I wasn't sure. Remember? Was just a gut feeling."

"Oh, yes," Herb answered. He was hoping to trick Bruno with the question, but it didn't work so just maybe he was telling the truth and didn't know. Probing deeper, he

Murder by Memory

then flatly asked, "Were Daryl and Tony killed over the same girl?"

"Hey, man. I don't know anything." Visibly trembling, Bruno restated, "I don't. Neither had a girlfriend that I knew of. That's the truth!"

"Then who killed them and why?" Herb demanded.

Starting to cry, Bruno responded, "How should I know?"

"Because you're the only connection to both murders!" Herb stated rather matter-of-fact.

"Hey, man, I'm innocent. I don't know a thing."

"But I think you killed them both!" Herb exclaimed as he moved to within inches of Bruno's startled face and stared straight into his tearing eyes. "You're a murdering punk is what I think!"

Trying to move his chair back a few inches, Bruno again declared, "You're crazy, man. I didn't do it! I'm as puzzled as you are. Tony and Daryl were my friends. Why would I want to kill them?"

"I don't know. Tell me," Herb prodded.

"I didn't do it!" Bruno screamed as he suddenly jumped to his feet.

"Sit down!" Herb ordered. "If you know anything you'd better spill it, and now!"

"But I don't!" Bruno again proclaimed.

Convinced that just maybe he honestly didn't know anything, Herb backed off and told him he could go, but told him to keep in touch. Bruno was then driven home by the same two cops who'd picked him up earlier at school. Once safely alone at home, he took the letter out of his pocket which he'd received yesterday. Reading it again, it read, "How does it feel?" With Tony now also dead, Bruno was seriously beginning to fear for his own life and didn't have any idea who the killer was or why. Probably should have shown that prick detective Chalmers the letter, but didn't. He'd do some investigating of his own first.

CHAPTER NINE

"Damn it!" Herb Chalmers shouted while pounding his right fist on his desk spilling his fresh cup of stemming hot coffee all over the papers he was working on and dripping onto his lap causing a gigantic wet spot on his crotch area. Immediately jumping up from the hot coffee spill to his tender loins, he frantically grabbed at the front of his trousers and pulled the heated fabric from his private area. "Damn it!" he proclaimed again. "Son of a bitch!" Herb was beside himself with the announcement of another possible Slaughter House Murderer victim just being discovered. Had been about a month since Tony Austin's murder, and just like after Daryl Woods, he'd worked nonstop without gathering as much as even one tiny minuscule clue. Frustrating wasn't even a word to describe the aggravation and hopelessness he was feeling with these murders, not to mention the panic and fears they were creating within the community along with the now national press coverage they were drawing. The mayor was ballistic over the murders and the Chief was unwilling to accept any excuses for them not being solved. So far, Benny had still taken most of the verbal badgering from up the chain of command which allowed him to concentrate on the case, but he knew that arrangement couldn't last much longer. If the murders weren't solved, and soon, well, he didn't even want to think about it. But what more could he do? He'd followed every possible lead with negative results and even Benny was about out of ideas. So far whoever was committing these murders knew exactly what they were doing and had taken all the correct precautions to cover their tracks. At least that's what it looked like, but Herb knew, or at least hoped, that arrogance would eventually cause them to slip up just a tiny bit and he'd be there to find their error and finally put an end to all of this. With all the negative leads, he still believed Bruno Kojan had to be connected in some way, but couldn't figure out exactly how. Matter of fact, he'd placed a twenty-four hour surveillance on Bruno recently, so already having received word of his whereabouts last night, he positively knew he wasn't the actual killer. But he still believed there was some type of connection - if he hadn't actually pulled the trigger on the three murders, he had to be connected somehow. Just had to be. Was the only connection he'd come up with that made any sense at all. And now, if it turned out that he also knew this latest victim, well, he'd definitely haul him back in to the precinct for more questioning and this time he'd really turn up the heat. Was one difference, though, with this latest murder in that the body was found in a different park about five miles from where the first two bodies were found. Herb still believed the murders were committed somewhere else with the bodies simply left in the parks to be discovered. Why they weren't hidden was another point he couldn't understand. Didn't make any sense. Was like the killer or killers were making a statement by leaving the bodies where they could be discovered. But if they were, what was their statement? And now with three murders, a reasonable person would assume they'd made it by now and for fear of getting caught they'd stop. But then again, if it was gang or mob related, they didn't think like the rest of us. But killing teenage high school kids just wasn't their style either so Herb honestly didn't think the killings were mob related and he hadn't been able to figure in any gang connections. Had to be something completely different, but what the difference was he just couldn't seem to figure out - at least not yet. He did conclude, though, that the killer switched parks either for fear of the police most likely staking out the first one or simply to throw a new element into the game. Well, they were correct if they assumed the police would be monitoring the first park since the Chief had ordered it watched around the clock as closely as manpower levels allowed, and due to his pressure, manpower was taken from other areas to assure the park received the maximum surveillance coverage. Herb decided this fact must have been obvious to the killers. Rubbing his eyes and grabbing some paper towels to absorb the wet coffee from his pants and also to clean the mess on his desk, Herb next headed for the crime scene. Like the previous two murders, he spent the majority of the day at the crime scene, with the medical examiner and again questioning another set of emotionally distraught parents. The victim this time was Steven Watts. He was also a high school senior who attended the same school as Woods and Austin. Upon further questioning, Herb learned that Steven had been an occasional acquaintance of Bruno Kojan. His father stated how his son had first gotten mixed up with Bruno around the first of this year. Being a rather serious student, he'd quickly realized the potential trouble Bruno could cause him, so not wanting to jeopardize his future with the likes of Bruno, he'd quit associating with him over two months ago. As far as Mr. Watts knew, the two boys hadn't had any contact other than saying hello in passing at school since the split. What transpired between them, he didn't know, but figured Bruno had pushed the envelope a little too far for Steven's liking one evening so he'd separated himself from Bruno's company. Herb would just have to find out what had caused the rift between them. Just maybe there was a connection there to the other murders also. Like a month ago, Herb next had a uniformed police squad pick Bruno up and deliver him to the precinct. After he arrived, Herb, with Benny Mitchell now also present, let him stew for awhile in the interrogation room before they entered to begin questioning him.

"I didn't do it!" Bruno yelled when Herb and Benny entered the room.

"Do what?" Herb asked.

Murder by Memory

"I don't know. But whatever you guys think I've done, I didn't do it," Bruno professed while beginning to quiver.

"You know Steven Watts?" Detective Mitchell now asked.

"Stevie?" Bruno repeated while staring straight up into Benny's inquiring eyes. "Is he dead?"

"You didn't know?" Herb then asked.

"Know what?"

"That he's dead, smart guy!" Herb emphasized while raising his voice and leaning closer to Bruno's now shaking face.

"No, of course not. How could I know he's dead. I haven't hung out with him in over probably two or three months."

"Why?" Herb demanded.

"I don't know. Just don't. Nothing in particular," Bruno lied.

"Yeah, so you had him killed for leaving your little gang," Herb goaded.

"What're you talking about? You're crazy, man!" Bruno fired back.

"Am I?" Herb stated. "Then why's he dead?"

"I don't know! You tell me!" Bruno sassed with an air of cockiness to his voice.

"Don't get smart, wise guy, or we'll just lock your lying ass up right now."

"You can't do that!" Bruno hoped. "You don't have anything on me cuz I didn't do anything."

"But you'd tell us if you knew anything, wouldn't you?" Herb stated while softening his tone somewhat.

"Sure, sure. Hey, man, you think I like all this? Heck no!" Bruno proclaimed. "If I knew anything, I'd tell you, but for the millionth time, I don't!"

Knowing from the surveillance which had been on Bruno last night that he definitely didn't commit the murder, Herb finally grew exhausted with trying to get any new information out of Bruno and released him. As Bruno left the room, Herb reminded him one more time, "You better call me if you hear or remember anything, and I mean anything. You hear me, mister?"

"Yeah, I hear you," Bruno responded while shaking his head and walking away with a renewed air of cockiness to his tone and exaggerated swagger to his walk. He truly believed he was putting things over on the detectives. How stupid did he think they were?

"That son of a bitch isn't telling us the truth," Herb stated to Benny.

"I agree, Herb, but not much we can do about it right now."

Closing the interrogation room door behind them, Herb straightened his tie, grabbed his coat and called it a day. He'd been up now for almost twenty-two hours so headed home for some well deserved rest. Maybe something would come to him later after he was rested.

CHAPTER TEN

Had been almost two weeks now since Steven Watts murder and like the previous two, Herb hadn't been able to uncover any hard evidence or any new possible leads. Everything still pointed somehow to the connection which all three of the deceased boys had with Bruno Kojan. Working himself almost to the point of exhaustion and unable to sleep much at night, Herb was beginning to appear quite haggard with small, droopy bags recently appearing under his eyes and he was also beginning to fidget uncontrollably. Benny Mitchell understood Herb's motivation and desire to catch the Slaughter House Murderer and to prove his value and competence as a new detective by solving his first major case, but he also comprehended the mental and physical deterioration which was slowly eating away inside Herb. Herb refused to admit the symptoms himself and always stated he was fine, maybe just a little tired - that's all, whenever Benny tried to broach the subject, so finally Benny had to pull rank and get firm with him by ordering him home for a few days to get his mind off the case and get some rest. He'd been working now for over ten weeks without as much as an afternoon off. The case had totally consumed him and was slowly breaking him down which Benny feared might also be a factor in his not discovering any positive leads yet. He concluded that Herb was simply working too hard and had somehow lost his focus and objectivity. Benny had seen this phenomenon before when other people from all walks of life simply tried too hard at whatever their task or cause was. Seemed the harder one tried, the farther behind they'd actually get. Heck, the same scenario had even happened to him earlier in his career and after his forced time off away from the case he was vainly trying to solve, he'd come back better than ever with a renewed focus and rapidly found the

William M. Jones

obvious element of his case which he'd been unable to see before and thus promptly solved his case. He only hoped the same would work with Herb, so he basically ordered him away from the precinct to take a forced, short sabbatical to retreat for some well needed rest and relaxation.

Arriving home to his small apartment shortly after Benny exiled him from the office for at least three days, Herb felt like a caged animal. He'd put so much time and energy into the case that now with suddenly nothing to do, well, he was at a total loss with how to spend his time. He couldn't decide whether to watch TV, read a book, go to a movie, go to bed, or what. He was at a complete loss and felt utterly disoriented with himself. To him it seemed like having to go cold turkey with something such as quitting smoking or drinking. A person couldn't simply instantly quit habits like those. The human body wasn't designed for the drastic physiological affects of the sudden withdrawal. Herb's addiction had become his workaholic condition, so now he was feeling the normal withdrawal symptoms others felt from substance abuses and he felt absolutely miserable. How could he get any rest when he felt so hyper? Pacing back and forth in his apartment and chain smoking countless cigarettes, he pondered how to spend the next few days. At times like this he truly wished he had a girlfriend, wife, or even someone to call a close friend. Right now work was everything with him so Benny Mitchell was about the only person he was anywhere personally close to as a friend and Benny couldn't help him right now since he'd been the one who'd forced him to take this time off. Crushing out the last cigarette from his last pack he had on him, he decided to take a short walk and go to the local grocery store for another carton of smokes. By now it was quite dark out but with a crystal clear, brilliant sky. As he walked towards the store, he decided to stop for awhile and simply gaze at the stars. Immediately he felt the stress and tension seeping from his body. He'd forgotten the relaxation

Murder by Memory

and joy which endless stargazing had afforded him in the past. Actually, he'd spent many a night, especially during his two Vietnam tours, just watching the sky. Many nights during the war he'd taken his cot outside his tent and quietly laid alone for hours in the warm, humid Vietnam evenings entrenched in a trance like state of mystical absorption while focusing on nothing except the apparent tranquillity of the universe and then tried to forget the atrocities of the ragging war and think only about pleasant memories or dream hopefully of a happier future. Suddenly observing the brightly rising full moon whose full illuminating affect had been shrouded from his sight by the surrounding urban buildup, Herb was struck with a haunting brainstorm. Foregoing the new carton of cigarettes, he abandoned his trip to the store and sprinted the short distance back to his apartment. He must have looked like some madman or criminal to anyone who might have seen him because people in their right mind simply didn't sprint full speed at night through the neighborhood streets while still dressed in a business coat and tie. Yes, some local people were into jogging during the evening darkness, but they definitely didn't look like Herb presently did. He was a man on a mission and due to his current poor physical conditioning, he almost collapsed part way home. Finally arriving at his apartment, he came to a sudden stop, bent over and forced numerous deep breaths in order to breathe life back into his searing lungs before having the energy to proceed into his apartment. Recapturing somewhat his wind, he next found the strength to unlock his front door and then slowly dragged his now exhausted body, supported by quivering legs, into his living room. Where normally he would have collapsed onto the couch, this time he found enough hidden strength to proceed the extra distance directly to his kitchen. Ripping the calendar off his cork bulletin board where it was fastened by two colored thumb tacks, he promptly sat down at his kitchen table with it. "What were those dates?"

he muttered out loud. He couldn't remember them. His fatigued state from too much work coupled with the exhaustion from his recent running episode had clouded his mental faculties. Again trying to remember the exact dates for the three previous Slaughter House Murderer killings and unable to do so, he next raced to retrieve his briefcase which was laying on the night stand in his bedroom. Opening it and expeditiously rifling through his notes, he swiftly found the dates he was searching for. Returning to the kitchen, he quickly marked each date on his calendar and then stood back and stared at them. Suddenly a singular fact jumped out at him. His calendar was the type which listed the various phases of the moon and it suddenly dawned on him that the Slaughter House Murderer only came out with a new moon. Why? He didn't have a clue. Who? Still no closer to finding the killer's true identity, but at least he finally had something positive to go on plus he also now had a future date to focus his efforts towards if there happened to be another murder. Discovering this one little fact drastically lifted his spirits and he suddenly felt like a thousand pound weight had been lifted off his body. He was back in the game now with a renewed focus and rejuvenated spirit. Finally, something dealing with the case was starting to go his way. Sitting back down and lowering somewhat from his jubilation, he thought long and hard on this newly discovered fact. Should he tell anyone or should he keep it a secret? After a few minutes of careful deliberation, he decided for the present to keep the fact to himself. Definitely didn't want to take any chance of his new moon theory getting leaked to the media. Last thing he needed was for it to get out and then possibly scaring away the murderer. If that happened, well, then he might possibly never be able to solve this case. He even decided not to tell Benny about it either for the time being. This was going to be his big break and he would somehow now catch the guilty culprit in the act if he happened to strike again

Murder by Memory

because looking at the next month's page on his calendar, he was positive of the date when the killer might strike again if he was so inclined to. Now feeling quite relaxed and realizing there really wasn't much more he could do with the case for the next week or so, he decided to stay on the mandated break Benny had ordered him to take and now maybe he could just relax and get some of the rest and relaxation his body so desperately needed. Matter of fact, he decided to take a short trip in the morning. There was a state park about fifty miles away which he'd always wanted to visit, but simply never quite seemed to have the time to. Well, now he did. It was down along a major river and was rich in history from the early settler and Indian days of two hundred years past. He'd always been fascinated with the history from those early pioneer years. During Vietnam he'd started reading numerous historical novels dealing with the period and had become fascinated with characters such as George Rogers Clark and his brother William, Daniel Boone, Simon Butler Kenton, Tecumseh, Black Hawk, and all the countless others from that era. He'd also been captivated with the whole western expansion and how the river system of the Ohio and Mississippi, along with their numerous tributaries, had come into play. He was also attracted to how the various large cities such as Chicago, St. Louis, Detroit, Louisville and Pittsburgh, to name but a few, had been settled and by whom. Probably the most interesting town for him was Horseheads in upstate New York just north of Elmira which was named from the Revolutionary War period march through the area by General Sullivan while he and his troops pursued the area's hostile Indians. As Sullivan's troops marched south out of western New York heading back towards Tioga, Pennsylvania, their packhorses started faltering from exhaustion so each day more and more of them had to be shot to prevent them from falling into the Indians' hands. The worst occasion occurred one day when over three hundred of the horses had been killed at one time. Years later, for some peculiar reason, the Indians took all of the bleached horse bones and placed them neatly in rows along the trail. The area then became known as the Valley of the Horseheads and in 1886 became known simply as Horseheads. Yes, two days at the park was definitely in order. He'd get a room at the lodge, walk the grounds and immerse himself into whatever literature or books the gift shop might have. Deciding this, Herb proceeded to his room and threw some clothes and his hiking boots into his one mid-sized suitcase and then went to bed with a smile on his face. This night, for the first one now in over two months, he quickly fell into a deep, sound sleep and didn't wake until the alarm startled him at six in the morning. First grabbing a quick bite to eat, he then departed for the park. He hadn't felt this good in, well, he couldn't remember how long and it definitely felt good.

CHAPTER ELEVEN

Herb had a great time by himself for the couple of days he stayed at the state park. He especially enjoyed his long walks along the park's wooded trails and then spent his evenings sitting around the lodge's central fireplace engrossed in reading and discussing local historical happenings. While browsing the numerous books and pamphlets in the lodge's gift shop, he'd engaged in several enlightening conversations with other historical buffs. These were basically the first non-work related conversations he'd had in a long, long time and he found them extremely stimulating. Then before retiring to bed each evening, he'd passed his time after dinner with several additional hours of reading and conversation while seated with others around the big fireplace. Never once did he inform any of his fellow conversationalists that he was a police detective and never in any of the conversations did individual's work status ever surface. All conversations were kept strictly to historical subjects. He promised himself he'd take more trips like this in the future and privately thanked Benny for having the knowledge and then compassion to first realize that he needed the break from work and then actually giving him the time off for it. He could definitely tell he was a much more relaxed person now. He guessed he'd been forced to learn the hard way that there's more to life than just work. Stress can kill or at least ruin your health if not kept within limits. He promised himself to exercise more once he got home and also to force himself to separate himself from his work when he left the precinct after work. That appeared to be the key to a successful career as a detective - one had to be able to compartmentalize and differentiate between work and home life. He figured Benny had already discovered this fact since he usually appeared a lot calmer and happier than he did

William M. Jones

and always had cheerful stories to tell about his hobbies and family whereas recently Herb didn't have anything except work to occupy his time and thoughts.

Herb was warmly greeted by Benny when he returned to the precinct for work.

"You sure look a hell of a lot better," Benny commented.

"Thanks," Herb replied, "feel better too."

"Good. What'd you do during your time off?"

"Not much. Relaxed, like you suggested," Herb answered not feeling a need at the time to provide Benny with all the details of his trip to the state park or his new theory about the case.

"Good," Benny responded. "Ready then to get back to work?"

"Yep. What've you got for me? Anything new?"

"Come on, let's go get a cup of coffee," Benny offered.

"Okay," Herb agreed while wondering what Benny really wanted to discuss.

After several minutes in the break room of non-essential chit-chat while sipping their coffee and munching on jelly filled donuts, Benny finally stated, "Bruno Kojan called yesterday."

"What did he want?" Herb asked as his interest level peaked.

"Don't know. Wouldn't talk to me."

"Why?"

"Not sure. Said you were the only detective he'd speak to."

"You tell him I was off?"

"Yep. Said he'd wait till you got back today. He should be at his house right now. Said he'd wait there this morning for your call."

"Okay. I'll get right on it," Herb promised. He then poured out his remaining coffee, took a last bite from his messy donut and licked the jelly from his fingers while returning to his desk to call Bruno. Dialing the number, Bruno answered after only one ring.

"Hello," Bruno cautiously answered.

"This is Detective Herbert Chalmers returning your call. What's … ?"

"We need to talk!" Bruno cut in before Herb could finish his initial question.

"What's up?" Herb inquired.

"Can't talk over the phone," Bruno advised.

"Why?"

"Hey, I called you, didn't I? Isn't that enough?"

"Yeah, okay, whatever you want," Herb answered.

"Can we meet somewhere private?"

"Nothing's more private than the precinct."

"No, I don't want to come down there again."

"Okay," Herb responded while wondering what was really up with Bruno. "How about the playground at the park between here and your house?"

"Okay. When?" Bruno asked next.

"Fifteen minutes."

"I'll be there," Bruno promised while hanging up his phone.

It took Herb less than ten minutes to get out of the precinct and drive the short distance to the designated meeting location in the park. He was somewhat surprised to find Bruno already present when he arrived. He observed his anxious pacing as he approached from the parking lot. Seeing this, he figured whatever the kid had on his mind must be pretty important.

"Bruno," Herb called out as he got closer.

Startled out of the private little world his mind was currently churning in, Bruno's thought process returned to the present and he stated, "Detective."

"Aren't you supposed to be in school?" Herb asked.

"Yeah, probably. Why? You going to turn me in?"

"Depends on what you have to say," Herb answered.

William M. Jones

Not saying anything further, Bruno reached into his pant's pocket, pulled out a letter, and quietly handed it to Herb.

"What's this?" Herb asked.

"Just read it," Bruno requested.

Taking the letter from the envelope and unfolding it, Herb quickly read the short note which stated, "You're next!"

"When'd you get this?"

"Just yesterday," Bruno answered.

"What do you think it means?" Herb next asked.

"I don't know. You tell me," Bruno replied while visibly upset and beginning to tremble. Also, his normal cocky attitude was noticeably absent and Herb could sense how he was honestly troubled by the note.

"Is this the only letter you've received?"

"No," Bruno admitted.

"Well, do you have the other one with you?"

"Yes," Bruno answered while pulling it out of his other pant's pocket. "It asked me how does it feel?" Bruno then stated while handing the letter to Herb.

"How does what feel?" Herb probed.

"I guess the murders," Bruno blurted out.

"Why should they concern you?"

"Maybe because Daryl, Tony and Steven were all friends of mine."

"How long you had this letter?"

"Arrived the day Tony was killed."

"And you never told me about it?" Herb yelled.

"No, man. I'm sorry. Know I really should have, but … ,"

"No buts, Bruno. Your pal Steven might just possibly still be with us now if you'd shown it to me then."

"I realize that now," Bruno admitted as tears started rolling down his checks.

Murder by Memory

"All right. What's done is done. Can't change what's already happened," Herb tried to calm Bruno with. "So, honestly, what do you think these letters mean?"

"I think I'm next on someone's hit list!" Bruno feared.

"But what do you make of the first letter?"

"Not sure. Seems like whoever wrote them wants me to sweat out the killings."

"Some type of revenge or something?" Herb added.

"Yeah, something like that."

"Okay, so, Bruno, who's got it out for you? Or, better, who had it out against all four of you? Sure looks to me like a revenge killing, pure and simple. Appears that for some reason the killer has purposely decided to kill you last so you'd have time to agonize over the others. Is that how you see it also?"

"Yeah, yeah, that says it pretty good," Bruno agreed.

"Again, then, who would want all four of you dead?"

"I don't know!" Bruno exclaimed while sitting on the picnic table he was standing next to and also covering his face with his trembling hands.

"Think, Bruno. Really think. Would anybody have a reason to want revenge against all of you?"

"Alvin!" Bruno suddenly remembered.

"Alvin?" Herb repeated.

"Yeah, Alvin Reinhold."

"Who's he?" Herb asked.

"Another high school kid we all know."

"What did he have against you?"

Swallowing his pride, what little he had, Bruno confessed, "Well, you could kind of say I've picked on him over the years."

"You mean you bullied him?" Herb added while remembering the various descriptions he'd been given of Bruno.

"Yeah, okay, you're right. I bullied him."

"Why?"

William M. Jones

"I don't know. Maybe because he was such an easy target."

"What do you mean by that, Bruno?"

"Wimpy looking little guy with thick glasses."

"Bet he was also a good student," Herb added.

"Yeah, that to," Bruno agreed.

"He make you feel inferior? Is that why you taunted him?"

"But I never hurt him," Bruno stated. "Just called him names."

"Like what?"

"You know. 'Four eyes' or 'Alvin the chipmunk'. Harmless stuff like that."

"How long you been doing it?" Herb wanted to know.

"Since grade school," Bruno sheepishly answered.

"No wonder the kid has it in for you!" Herb declared. "Mental harassment can be worse than physical abuse. Didn't you realize that?"

"Oh, shit!" Bruno suddenly proclaimed.

"What? What's the matter?" Herb asked.

"I just remembered."

"What?"

"Alvin and I did get into one fight."

"When?"

"Little over three months ago. That's right. And Daryl, Tony and Steven were with me."

"What happened?" Herb needed to know.

"You know, the four of us were just hanging around school late one evening. Not doing much of anything. Just kind of bored."

"Kind of looking for some trouble to get into?" Herb added.

"Yeah, maybe. Anyway, we saw Alvin leaving school. He'd probably been studying late in the library."

"So you guys decided to follow him and have some fun with him?"

Murder by Memory

"Yes," Bruno admitted. "We followed him through the park over there. When we got to that dark area where the lights had been out, we started hollering at him. Called him some names. Nothing more. Just some names."

"You realize that's the same area where Daryl's body was found?"

"No!" Bruno exclaimed as his eyes got quite wide.

"Sure is. So, what happened next?"

"Instead of him running away as usual, old Alvin turned and confronted us. Said he'd had enough verbal abuse from us and then when I got close enough to him, well, he threw a punch at me."

"What happened next?"

"Well, that's when Daryl, Tony and Steven held his arms and legs and …,"

"And you beat him up," Herb finished.

"Yeah, I did, but I stopped after I'd hit him a few times because I was afraid I was really hurting him."

"So what happened next?"

"We left him there in the park and ran as fast as we could back to my house."

"Is that why Steven Watts quit hanging around with you?"

"Yes. He was really pissed about it. Wouldn't talk to me at all after that night."

"Do you remember if Alvin said anything else to you after you beat him up?"

"His face was pretty bruised and I think I may have broken his nose, but now that I think about it, yes, he did say something to the affect that he'd get even with us!"

"So he's killing all of you over this incident?"

"Well, detective, you asked if I could think of anything and that's the only incident involving all four of us I can think of."

"So, Alvin Reinhold is killing your little gang purely out of revenge." Herb stated.

"Sure looks like it and if he is, then I'm his next target!" Bruno declared. "What are you going to do about it?" he next pleaded.

"Well, now that I've got a name, I'll check it out."

"Check it out! Is that all? What about protection for me?"

"Relax, Bruno. Murder is a serious accusation. Can't just go arrest Alvin. I've got to investigate him first. As for you, well, I'll make sure you're given police protection. We'll do everything we can to protect you in return for your cooperation."

"I'm cooperating. I'm cooperating," Bruno promised.

"I know and what you've said here today is really helpful," Herb stated as he thanked Bruno and the two then left the park in their separate directions. Now Herb not only had a possible future murder attempt date, but he also had a name. With the date and name, he was positive he'd finally be able to put an end to the Slaughter House Murderer.

CHAPTER TWELVE

After leaving his meeting with Bruno, Herb proceeded directly to the vice principal's office at the high school. He needed to put a face to the name of Alvin Reinhold and figured the easiest way to do so was by looking at the school's latest yearbook. Not wanting to tip off anyone about Alvin's possible connection to the murders, he didn't tell the vice principal why he wanted to see the book and then asked for privacy while viewing it. Realizing Detective Chalmers most certainly finally had either some fresh information or at least a hunch dealing with the murders, the vice principal did him one better by giving him a copy of the yearbook to take with him. He knew better than to press Herb for any privileged information about the case even though he was personally quite curious. He did, though, offer Herb whatever future assistance he could provide and told him to feel free to contact him at any time. Herb sensed the vice principal's urge for additional information and wished he could talk openly about Alvin's possible connection, but professionally he just couldn't - would be unethical. For everyone's sake, though, Herb ascertained how this case unequivocally needed to be solved, and soon. He could only imagine the dire emotional stress the school's administers, teachers, and especially the students were feeling from the aftershock from three of their own having been killed and, therefore, the last thing he could afford to do right now was to add additional panic to the already fragile, and also highly volatile, situation by falsely accusing another of their very own. No, couldn't afford to do that. He'd definitely have to proceed cautiously with his investigation into Alvin Reinhold. Personally, he found it hard to believe how a supposedly mild mannered kid like Alvin could commit all these methodical assassination style murders simply over being called names and bullied around a little. There were bullies everywhere in our society; always had been and probably always would be - was just a sad commentary on the human race. But then as far as he knew, others hadn't committed murders just from being called a few irritating names. If Alvin was responsible for the killings, then, he must have just mentally snapped from the years of the constant, nagging harassment. He guessed stranger things had definitely happened, but he still had his doubts about this case. He also felt, though, that Bruno was finally telling him the truth and if he knew of any other possible connections he would have mentioned them. Herb could definitely tell how the last letter stating that Bruno was next had plainly rattled the kid's cage.

Leaving the school, Herb proceeded back to the precinct. Arriving there, he immediately sought out Benny.

"Hey, you've been gone quite awhile. What's up with Bruno? He have anything new for you?" Benny asked.

"He's pretty scared."

"Why?"

"Someone just sent him a threatening letter. Said he was next."

"Next? Why?" Benny questioned.

Herb then filled him in on all the details of both letters and of Bruno's confrontation with Alvin. When he was finished, he stated, "Guess I'd better get these letters to the lab for analysis."

"Probably won't help, but sure, give it a try," Benny agreed. "Let me see those envelopes again." Studying them for a second, he then stated, "You see the post marks on them?"

"Yeah, out of state," Herb answered.

"Someone's gone to a hell of a lot of trouble not to be traced," Benny offered.

"How about searching Alvin's house anyway? Can't hurt and might just get lucky and find something."

Murder by Memory

"My exact thoughts, Herb. I'll get a search warrant for you within the hour. Take a uniformed team along with you. Try not to tip your hand about the murders when you go there, though."

"You mean make something up?"

"Like I said, don't give away anything. Last thing we need is for you to scare Alvin away if in fact he is the real killer. Did you know the governor is now putting political pressure on the mayor to get this case solved?"

"Figured as much from what I've read in the papers."

"So, unless you want to be unemployed soon, don't screw anything up!"

"Gotz ya," Herb responded and then returned to his desk to wait for the search warrant. As promised, within the hour Benny procured the required document granting court approval to search the Reinhold's property and especially Alvin's bedroom.

Upon arrival at the Reinhold home, Herb was struck by its classic appearance. It was definitely upper middle class and well taken care of. Probably another reason Bruno felt a need to verbally harass Alvin - he appeared to possess all the material goods which he lacked. Also from the appearance, it looked like Alvin came from a highly successful, stable family. If so, why then would he commit all the murders? Plus, if being a small, wimpish kid like Bruno described, how could he have possibly carried out the three murders in the obvious assassination style in which they were committed? All the deceased were definitely larger and stronger boys than Alvin. Plus, with the previous run in they'd all had, didn't make any sense how any of them would let Alvin get close enough to them to actually place the barrel of the weapon right on the back of their heads when pulling the trigger. Nothing made sense to him about this Reinhold kid, but it was still the only lead he had. Ringing the door bell, Mrs. Reinhold appeared at the door within a few seconds.

William M. Jones

"Detective Chalmers," Herb immediately stated while flashing his badge and also introducing the two uniformed cops accompanying him.

"What's this all about, detective?" Mrs. Reinhold quizzed.

"Ma'am, we have a search warrant for your house. May we come in?"

"Why?" Alvin's mother demanded. "No one here's ever been in trouble with the police."

"Yes, ma'am, but we still need to come in. Is your son Alvin here?"

"Alvin?" Mrs. Reinhold questioned with a shocked tone. "What's he done?"

"Nothing, ma'am. Is he home?"

"No. Hasn't come home from school yet."

"Are you alone, ma'am?"

"Yes, my husband's away on business," she stated before realizing she probably shouldn't have offered that information in case these people weren't who they claimed to be.

"Ma'am, please, we have a search warrant. Would you please show us to your son's room?"

"Do I really have any choice?"

"Not really. Definitely make things easier on us all if you cooperate."

"Certainly, but what are you looking for?"

"Can't tell you exactly. All I can say is an informant told us how your son may have some evidence in a juvenile case we've been working over at the school."

"Drugs?" Mrs. Reinhold questioned. "If it is, Alvin's not involved. He's a good boy. Never been in any sort of trouble. Gets good grades at school and loves listening to music and reading and writing poetry. He's never given us any trouble. Been accepted to the university in the fall. Going to major in English, you know," she further stated while beginning to cry.

Murder by Memory

"Yes, ma'am, but we still need to check. Now, which way to his room?"

"Follow me," she finally consented while allowing them in and personally leading them to Alvin's room. "We have nothing to hide," she added.

"Beautiful home," Herb remarked while wishing his own place looked this nice. Everything was in its place, not cluttered, and everything appeared spotless. He figured the Reinhold's had paid maid service to keep this place looking like this. Mrs. Reinhold's meticulous personal appearance, coupled with her expensive clothes and sparkling jewelry, didn't give the impression of someone used to performing menial household laundry or cleaning chores.

"Here it is," she informed while opening the door to Alvin's bedroom.

Herb was rather surprised when he first looked into the room. Wasn't anything like the rest of the house in that it was extremely bare. Just a basic bed, plain looking dresser and small desk along with a limited number of clothes hanging in the closet. "This is your son's room?" Herb remarked while giving Mrs. Reinhold a quizzical look.

"Yes, he likes it like this. He's not into material possessions. Like I said, his major interests are his music and poetry. He's a very sensitive boy, detective. Wouldn't hurt a fly. Likes to spend his time alone. Always has."

"Doesn't he have any close friends?" Herb inquired.

"Not really. No. No one I'd really say he was particularily close to. Just normal acquaintances from school," she fibbed not wanting to involve Rita since she considered her a godsend for Alvin. She knew how special they were to each other and expected her to become her daughter-in-law some day. No, she couldn't afford doing anything which might cause a rift between them. If the police were to find out about Rita, it wouldn't be from her.

"You know, I've never seen a teenager's room look this neat before," Herb then remarked.

William M. Jones

"Like I said, detective, Alvin's a good boy and has never given anyone any trouble."

"Yes, ma'am, but we'll still have to have a look around," Herb said before he and the two policemen then thoroughly searched the room plus walked through the remainder of the house without finding anything. Satisfied that he wasn't going to find anything in the house, Herb then asked, "Does Alvin have a car?"

"Yes," Mrs. Reinhold acknowledged. "Would you like to see it?" she openly offered.

"Definitely. He didn't take it to school?" Herb asked.

"No, was having some type of mechanical problem so I dropped him off at school this morning and he said he'd call if he needed a ride home or else he'd walk if the weather was nice. Probably walking by the looks of the weather." Mrs. Reinhold then led them to the detached garage and opened the door.

Herb and his helpers spent only a few minutes looking over the car before becoming satisfied that they weren't going to find anything in it either. Oh, well, was worth a shot. Herb then thanked Mrs. Reinhold for her cooperation and advised her that his information about her son must have been wrong. He again thanked her for her time and stated he was sorry for any inconvenience they may have caused.

Watching the police back out of her driveway, she felt slightly ashamed that she hadn't been completely honest with them. She'd showed them Alvin's room in the house because they'd asked to see it. She'd failed to inform them, though, how he didn't use his old room any longer and actually resided in the spare room above the detached garage. They hadn't asked, so she simply hadn't offered the additional information. Not that she was afraid Alvin was actually involved in anything mischievous, though, but there was always that nagging parent's doubt regardless of how good they believed their own child to be. Sadly, she'd

Murder by Memory

heard others talk of hidden things their kids had gotten into before eventually getting caught. So she figured - why take the chance. Satisfied she'd performed her civic responsibility as well as look out for her son's best interest, she returned to the house. She then decided not to even mention the episode to Alvin. No sense upsetting him. She knew how sensitive he was. No sense getting him upset over nothing. Must have been a mistake like the detective said and she was positive the police now also realized the fact and wouldn't be back.

As Herb turned the corner some two blocks from the Reinhold residence, he spotted a teenage male slowly walking along the sidewalk. Passing the individual, he quickly identified the youth as Alvin. Then watching the slightly built youth through his rearview mirror while he continued driving on down the street, Herb was hit by the nagging feeling of how this innocent, clean cut looking kid just couldn't be the elusive Slaughter House Murderer. No way. But then Alvin was the only lead he had, so regardless of appearances and his own doubting thoughts, he'd still have to keep a careful eye on Mr. Alvin Reinhold. At least for a few more days until the next new moon passed.

CHAPTER THIRTEEN

"Rita, I can't take this much longer," Alvin sobbingly admitted while clutching his loving girlfriend's hands. "My nerves are shot and my stomach's in knots. Look," he next stated while unbuttoning his shirt and lifting the front of his white t-shirt, "my stomach's all broken out in a rash. My god, Rita. What have we done? All the murders! Rita, what are we going to do? If we get caught, we'll spend the rest of our lives apart in prison. I'm really scared. Can't sleep or eat." Beginning to cry, he then genuinely requested, "Hold me, Rita."

Tenderly kissing her beloved while amorously caressing him, she calmly stated, "It'll be all right, Alvin. I promise. Be over in a few days and then we'll be left alone forever like I promised."

"I hope so!" Alvin declared while leaning his head back a few inches and fixing his sight directly into her reassuring eyes.

"It will, Alvin, it will. Nobody suspects any of us. We're not going to get caught. You know the police are completely baffled so far. From what I hear, all they know is that Bruno knew all of the others. That's all. There's absolutely no connection to any of us. Raymond and I have taken every possible precaution. Everything will be fine. Just have faith in me."

"I do," Alvin pledged, "but still, I'm really scared, Rita."

"Yeah, I know. You've just got to have faith in me," she again calmly stressed in her attempt to reassure and settle Alvin's fears. "Why don't you go out to the lake for the next few days?" Rita next suggested. "Take your tent and camp out for awhile. Try to get your mind off of things."

"Good idea. Thanks, Rita. Will you come with me?"

"Maybe Raymond and I will drive out and see you, but I think it's best if you go by yourself."

Murder by Memory

Leaning his head forward, Alvin again gave Rita a tender kiss which she passionately reciprocated. Reassured that she was right, as usual, his body temporarily stopped trembling. Biding her good-bye, he gathered his camping gear, left his parents a note, and headed for the lake for a few days. As he pulled out of his driveway, he didn't notice the unmarked police car which had just parked a short distance down the street from his house. Having just arrived to start their surveillance of him, they didn't realize when they saw Rita walking down the sidewalk how she'd just come from Alvin's or the fact that she was his girlfriend and the real mastermind behind the Slaughter House Murderer. Not knowing either of these facts, they didn't give her much official attention at all. Matter-of-fact, about the only attention they accorded her was the normal male ogling afforded any young, pretty girl.

Was early evening by the time Alvin got his camp all set up. With the pleasant, warm weather, he wasn't alone this time at the lake. He did, though, find his favorite campsite slightly isolated from the other campers, so he felt personally secure and settled in to enjoying an evening campfire while trying to forget the horrid consequences of his and Rita's murderous deeds. Gazing into the now small, blazing campfire and affixing two additional marshmallows to his pointed cooking stick, he proceeded with making yet another chocolate dripping, messy, graham cracker sandwiched s'more. His belly satisfied when his bag of marshmallows was empty, he then sat into the wee hours of the night simply gazing into the mystical, dancing flames of his fire. Other than occasionally poking at the fire to keep it from going out, his mind was blank as he watched the flames slowly burn down eventually becoming a bed of red hot embers. When the lighted color from the embers finally faded into a mess of smoldering ashes, Alvin retreated to his tent and went to sleep.

William M. Jones

Not waking until late morning when the rising sun solar heated the inside of his tent and the brightly shining rays disturbed his sleeping eyes, Alvin finally got up. After a quick breakfast, he proceeded, with pencil and paper in hand, down to the bench on the end of the lake's solitary dock. Staring around at the tranquility of the scene for numerous minutes, he eventually put pencil to paper and thoughtfully formulated his latest poetic composition.

A DAY IN THE WILDERNESS

Wilderness, five miles from civilization, would you believe?
Tis true, solitude of a lake and nature, free for the asking.
A short ten minute drive, you're back with the rest,
Pick up supplies, back to the woods, wildernesses quest.

The very early morning, the break through of the light,
All of nature's elements, start their daily fight.
The early morning dew, the grass is oh so wet,
The misty fog on the lake, woven like a net.
The birds start to chirp, the frogs at their croaking,
I'm up with the dawn, for the early morn, no joking.
The silence and stillness, the innocence of the new day,
Will surely bring new experiences, the shinning of a new ray.

During the day, the sun's glare through the woods,
The sun's glare on the water and God's answer to what should.
The glossy coat on the glittering lake,
The unpredictable jump of a fish, the surface it breaks.
The glide of a boat, through the enchanted calm,
The sight on the shore, a deer, or mother and fawn.
The occasional strike, of a trout or bass,

Murder by Memory

 Fighting for its freedom, with the deepest augment and sharpest sass.
 Or simply your own enjoyment, which nature has brought,
  To you for the seeking, you'll find yourself caught.
  Caught in nature's, unreleasing hold,
  For you this is the life, others just to be told.

  Dusk is setting, darkness is near,
  Soon the night will overcome us, many noises to hear.
  Total black all around, keenness of ear, many a sound,
  To keep your nerves, tensely wound.
  The slightest noise, how alert you become,
  Just a tree or wind, how welcome will be the sun.
  Sleep comes so hard, being so alert,
  Humidity is high, mosquito bites hurt.
  The only thing to do, is to lie absolutely still,
  Think about the day tomorrow, the fish that will.

  Soon the sun is shinning, the alarm is ringing,
  Time to get up, breakfast to begin preparing.
  Now a new day has started, in this still solitude,
  Who would believe civilization is so near, how rude!

 Finishing the poem and proofing it several times, Alvin folded it up, put it into his pocket and then sat for the next few hours seated on the dock's bench doing nothing much more than absorbing the afternoon's warming sunlight. Staring across the lake and blocking out all sounds from others present around him at the lake or engaged in other activities within the small park and campground, Alvin passed the time until near sunset in reflecting thought. As hard as he tried, he couldn't keep from thinking about the lives of Daryl, Tony and Steven. Bruno had always been the main aggressor, not them. But too late now. They were gone and hopefully he'd also be rid of Bruno in a few days. Then

William M. Jones

he thought on the devastation and humiliation his parents and Rita's mom would feel if the truth were ever known. Rita seemed so sure it wouldn't; so for their parent's sake he hoped she was right. But, then, could he live with himself for the rest of his life knowing what he'd been a part of? Again, Rita had assured him how in time everything would be forgotten by the police and how eventually he'd also personally displace the murders from his mind. Certainly he, and even she and Raymond, would always think of them at various future moments, but slowly they'd, even the sensitive Alvin, block them from their minds the majority of the time and be able to mentally function unimpeded through their daily lives. Furthermore, their new lives, without the fear of future harassment, would be filled with peacefulness and contentment so they'd believe forever how their dastardly murders had been absolutely just and morally right. In their own minds, they'd believe for eternity that they were the real victims in all of this and how the murders were simply a form of justifiable self-defense. They'd simply taken, for self-preservation, matters into their own hands and eliminated the source of their mental torture. Yes, that's what Rita had desperately been trying to convince him of through all these agonizing months - he was a victim, not a murderer. Finally satisfied she was correct, he left the dock and proceeded back to his campsite with the thought of how he couldn't wait until Bruno was dead and he'd be able to get on with his life - one which most definitely included Rita.

Unbeknownst to Alvin, Rita and Raymond drove out to the park about thirty minutes later to visit him. Raymond wasn't feeling very good, so he rested while Rita drove his car. He'd had a splitting headache on and off for the last week or so. Seemed to come and go for no particular reason. Usually popping a few aspirin relieved the pain somewhat, but today nothing seemed to work. He'd even laid with a cold compress applied to his feverish forehead

Murder by Memory

without relief earlier in the day. He'd also, around noon today, felt quite nauseous and had actually vomited twice. The nauseous feeling had subsided, but from the headache and probably slight dehydration, he now also felt extremely drowsy and was having a hard time keeping his eyes open. Rita was quite concerned about her brother's condition; at least that's what she told him where the truth of the matter was she was more afraid he'd be too sick or weak to kill Bruno in a few short days. He couldn't afford going to see a doctor now. Couldn't take a chance of him being hospitalized or confined to bed at home. He'd just have to tough it out for another couple days and then once Bruno was finally eliminated she'd be the first to force her brother to consult a doctor. Rita also decided that Alvin couldn't be informed of Ray's condition. He had enough doubts on his mind and she simply felt that telling him of Ray's sickness might just be too much for him to handle. Couldn't afford doing anything which might stress him any more than he already was. No, couldn't afford that. She was afraid he might then do something stupid which might possibly draw attention to their involvement in the killings if he felt any more stressed over the situation. Since Raymond was feeling so bad right now, he'd have to stay in the car while she talked to Alvin. Couldn't take a chance of him seeing her brother. As they drove down the park's dirt road leading to the parking area by the lake and campground, Raymond caught sight of a suspicious looking car parked along the side of the road just before the normal parking lot.

"You see that car?" Ray softly asked his sister after they passed it.

"What about it?" she returned.

"I don't know. Just didn't look right."

"Why?" Rita questioned.

"Looked like two guys inside it."

"So," Rita commented.

"Well, why would two guys be parked out here at this time of the night? Just doesn't feel right."

"What're you thinking, Ray?"

"I think it's a stake out," he stated.

"A stake out?"

"Yeah, didn't you say the police had been talking with Bruno?"

"Yeah."

"Well, maybe, just maybe he somehow put things together and suspects Alvin and then squealed to the police."

"But they haven't questioned me," Rita said.

"I know. Seems like if he gave them Alvin's name then he would've also told them about you."

"I know," Rita lied since she knew Bruno didn't know anything about the fabricated story she'd fed her trusting brother in order to enlist his aid in committing the murders. "What do you suggest?"

"Rita, we can't take any chances. May just be imagining things, but can't risk being seen with Alvin right now if in fact there are police in that car."

"Should we just turn around and leave then?" Rita suggested.

"No, that might also look suspicious. If cops are out here watching Alvin, they might sense we suspect them by immediately leaving."

"So we just stay here for awhile?"

"Yeah. Alvin's not expecting us, is he?"

"No, not really. Mentioned we'd try to come out, but never gave him a time."

"Good. Then if we just stay in the car and park over there for awhile before leaving, Alvin won't see us and the police shouldn't suspect anything either."

"Okay," Rita agreed.

Murder by Memory

After parking, then, for a little over thirty minutes, Rita and Raymond cautiously left the park. Leaving, they still observed the two men seated inside the suspicious vehicle.

Inside the unmarked police car, the two plain clothed policemen grumbled about their surveillance assignment. Watching the two teenagers who'd driven in about thirty minutes earlier now leave, they commented how they were probably just two hormonal crazed teenagers who came out to the lake to park and spark, they laughed, for awhile. How wrong they were. Two serial killers had been in their sights and they didn't even know it. They could have become heroes tonight, but instead, they continued being two highly frustrated and presently, cold cops.

CHAPTER FOURTEEN

Herbert Chalmers tossed and turned all night. Couldn't sleep. He was too keyed up. Figured he'd seen every agonizing minute throughout the entire night so far so around 4 a.m. finally just gave up trying to fall asleep and got up. Nothing to do at home, so he got dressed, had a quick bite to eat and headed for the precinct. This day he'd finally put an end to the elusive Slaughter House Murderer. He just knew it; could feel it in his bones. The next new moon would finally arrive tonight. He knew his theory was correct. Had to be. Was the only pattern linked to the three previous murders which made any logical sense. Couldn't have been just a coincidence. The murderer had to have some twisted, cultist fixation with the new moon phenomenon. But why? He didn't have a clue. He'd heard tales of cultist's full moon rituals, but didn't know of any dealing with a new moon. But, again, there was always a first time for everything. Right now he just needed to catch the SOB and then all the psychologists and psychiatrists in the country could psychoanalyze the crap out of it with whoever figured it out first becoming world renowned from their synopsis and then probably making a fortune out of it on the lecture circuit. Even that was okay with Herb. All he really wanted to do was to get the responsible bastard or bastards off the street and return normalcy to the school and community as well as divert its negative national press attention on to some other happening hopefully far, far away from the local area. But he also knew how that was most likely an improbability since if the murderer was captured alive tonight and then went to trial, well, the publicity it would create would probably cause an even larger media circus. At least then the local citizens wouldn't be forced to live in constant fear for their or their children's safety plus the governor and mayor would most likely get off the Chief's case thus making life one hell of a lot easier on the average police cop or detective like himself. This case had taken on a personality of its own and needed to be stopped, and Detective Herbert Chalmers was positive he was the individual to do just that - and tonight! Disregarding certain minor nagging doubts, Herb believed Alvin Reinhold had to be involved in some manner with the murders and most likely was himself the actual killer. His surveillance teams had kept him under constant surveillance now for a couple of days. The kid seemed to be a reclusive loner. Definitely the classic personality type who could commit these types of crimes. Shunned by society, they blamed everyone else for their problems and then suddenly one day just crack and take matters into their own hands. Classic textbook description of a serial killer was how Herb rationalized Alvin the more he thought about him and lately that was all he did - focus in on catching him in the act. For the last few days Alvin had remained camped in solitude at the local park lake. Herb had even gone so intense with his surveillance that he had two young policemen pose as campers and actually pitch a tent close to Alvin's. They didn't initiate any personal contact with him, but it afforded them the ability to monitor his every move and also canceled out the possibility of any of his cohorts sneaking in to the campground to talk with him without being seen. So far that hadn't happened. Alvin had remained totally by himself. They hadn't even observed him talking with any of the other campers. He basically either stayed around his tent and campfire or sat alone at the dock. He'd been observed sitting alone out there for hours at a time. Sometimes he'd do some writing, but mostly he'd just sit and stare out across the lake. He most likely was plotting his next move, they figured. The only time he'd left the campground had been for about an hour. A mobile surveillance team had then followed him while the campground duo looked inside his tent. Didn't find anything other than a nature oriented poem.

William M. Jones

Poetry! Was the kid simply sitting on the dock dreaming up poetic thoughts? Herb Chalmers didn't think so when the fact was repeated to him. In the hour Alvin was away from the campground, he'd only driven back to his house and then to a store to pick up some more supplies. Nowhere else. Just to his house, the store, and then straight back to the campground. Maybe he suspected he was being followed, but Herb discounted that knowing how discreet his surveillance teams were being. For the remainder of the day until he'd hopefully catch the devious Mr. Reinhold in the act later tonight, surveillance of him would continue at the campground as well as at his house. His every movement would be carefully scrutinized. He wouldn't be able to fart without Herb first knowing about it. Then, as to Bruno Kojan, Herb would personally get with him later in the morning. He never told him why he figured today was the day. Simply told him he had a hunch. Old Bruno was so scared by now that all he wanted was for the day to pass with him still being alive in the morning with the real murderer captured and securely confined behind bars. Out of fear, he threatened to leave the state, but Herb expertly convinced him to stay and cooperate. Convinced him it was the only possible way to catch the killer. If Bruno ran, well, he'd live in fear for the rest of his life and would most certainly be reduced to constantly looking over his shoulder with every unknown sound. No, wasn't worth living like that. Herb eventually convinced him to face his fears and cooperate. Yes, Bruno was somewhat to fault if in fact the murders had resulted from his verbal harassment toward Alvin, but calling Alvin names definitely wasn't a crime. Not a very nice thing to do, but from all the information Herb had of Bruno's verbal harassment, not a crime. At least not in the eyes of the law. But in Alvin's eyes, well, that was possibly a different matter entirely. Apparently he viewed it as greater than any crime and was willing to commit the ultimate crime himself over it. Herb knew that something had to have just snapped inside the kid's brain housing group. Normal people didn't just go out and commit murder over a few harassing names, but then Alvin probably wasn't your normal teenage kid. His mind had to be operating on a completely different level from the norm. Herb promised Bruno how his cops would be with him every second of the day and night and pledged his personal assurance that he wouldn't allow anything to happen to him. Just still needed him for bait. Since he didn't know where or exactly how the other three boys had been lured to their killing sites, Herb had Bruno fitted with a wire so the police could closely monitor any telephone or personal conversations he might have. With all his surveillance teams in place for the day, Herb would act as their overall coordinator and then through his boss, Benny Mitchell, would call in additional help whenever the time came. Herb and Benny had gotten the Chief's approval to have additional manpower standing by for the night. They promised the Chief that every possible contingency had been accounted for. All they needed now was participation out of the Slaughter House Murderer and then they'd finally arrest him. Herb didn't even want to think of the scenario of the killer not striking tonight. That wasn't even an option for him. He knew he would and he knew he'd get him - plain and simple.

About eleven in the morning, unbeknownst to the police meticulously watching Alvin and guarding Bruno, Rita knocked on her brother's bedroom door to finalize tonight's plans for finally putting an end to their main nemesis - Bruno Kojan. Not receiving a response to her knocking, she opened his door and peered inside.

"Raymond!" she screamed upon seeing him trying to lift himself off the floor.

"Rita," he feebly stuttered while trying to hold a hand out to his shocked sister.

"Raymond, what's wrong with you?" she begged while tears began streaming down her face. Her concern for her brother's health was genuine and for a short moment she totally blanked out her devious plot to eliminate Bruno from her's and Alvin's future life together. Seeing her brother struggling to speak while also hopelessly trying to lift himself from the floor was a sight she wasn't prepared for. His speech was slurred when he spoke her name and she could see how the entire left side of his face was drooping. Looked like all the elasticity in the muscles on that side of his face had just collapsed. Raymond looked like he was a hundred years old. Rita hurriedly grabbed her brother's outstretched hand and tried to help him to his feet, but it was a futile effort. In attempting to do so, Raymond's eyes suddenly rolled back in their sockets and he pulled Rita over on top of him as they both collapsed to the floor in the middle of his room. Forcing herself off of him, she immediately stood, placed both hands over her mouth and froze in place simply horrified at the pitiful sight of her now unconscious brother. She desperately tried to revive him, but nothing worked. He was out cold. Her only prayer now was that he was still alive. Being alone in the house with him, she quickly gathered her wits enough to have the presence of mind to phone for help.

A few blocks away over by Alvin's guarded house, that surveillance team sat in their vehicle and watched as an ambulance suddenly raced by with its siren blasting. Never in their wildest thoughts could they have known that it was racing to the rescue of the Slaughter House Murderer.

Herb was exhausted by the time the next morning arrived. No, exhausted wasn't the word; he was mortified. Nothing had happened last night! He hadn't caught the killer! Alvin was still alone at the campground and Bruno was happy to be alive, but with many questions of why and what next? What happened? What had gone wrong? Was Bruno actually on the killer's agenda? Did the letters really mean what they thought they did? If Bruno wasn't involved, why had the other three boys been murdered? Nothing made

Murder by Memory

any sense to Herb right now. This case was supposed to be solved by now. What had he missed? He swore he'd get the killer regardless of how long it took. This case had suddenly turned into a personal vendetta and obsession for him. Realizing how he was emotionally distraught over the night's zero results, Benny ordered Herb home. He needed to give it a rest. They'd figure something out in a day or two. Benny then tried to lift Herb's spirits as he got up to head out of the precinct by telling him that at least no other murder had occurred last night. They needed to look on the bright side. Case would definitely be worse right now if they were actually having to investigate another dead corpse right now. Herb understood how Benny was trying to cheer him up some, but right now he felt too depleted for that. Maybe in a day or two, but not right now. No, he was supposed to have apprehended the Slaughter House Murderer last night and he'd failed.

CHAPTER FIFTEEN

By the time Raymond's mother, Betty Powers, arrived at the hospital, her son had already been moved from the emergency room to the intensive care ward. Rita was nervously waiting in the small waiting room outside Raymond's ward for their mother to arrive.

"Mom," she hollered upon finally seeing her mother getting out of the hospital's pitifully slow elevator. Sobbing, she then ran to her mother and, with tears streaming down her face, hugged her mother.

"How's he doing?" Betty bravely requested while trying to calm her obviously upset daughter.

"He's really bad," Rita replied while sniffing back the dripping snot from her reddened nose.

"What happened?" Betty demanded.

"I don't know, mom. I don't know. I went to his room and found him laying unconscious on his floor," she lightly fibbed.

"Has he regained consciousness yet?" Betty needed to know.

"No. He's still in a coma," Rita informed her mother as she began to cry harder and tears also formed in her mother's eyes. Gathering herself somewhat, Rita continued, "Mom, he looks horrible. Absolutely horrible."

"Why do you say that, Rita?"

"You've got to prepare yourself before seeing him," Rita warned. "His face muscles have sagged and he's hooked up to all sorts of tubes and monitors."

Then guiding her daughter with her right arm gently pressed behind her daughter's lower back, Betty led Rita to the chairs in the waiting area where they next sat down. Betty decided she needed to collect herself before seeing her only son. "Have the doctors told you anything yet?" she next asked Rita.

Murder by Memory

"No, nurses said they wanted to wait until you got here."

Coming out of intensive care and seeing the older woman seated in the waiting room with Rita who he already recognized, Doctor Stanley Bratt assumed her to be his patient's mother. Rita had informed him earlier how she was on her way and also how their father had passed away years earlier.

"Mrs. Powers?" Doctor Bratt asked while holding out a hand.

"Yes," Betty responded while looking up through her tears at the handsome, middle-aged doctor standing before her.

"Hi, I'm Doctor Stanley Bratt …,"

"How's my son doing?" Betty rapidly interrupted before the doctor could even finish his introduction.

"Mrs. Powers, to be honest, I'm not sure."

"What do you mean by that?" Betty frantically asked as she gave a horrified look at the doctor and then over to her daughter before returning her attention back to Raymond's doctor.

"Well, your son's in a coma."

"I already know that. The real question, is why?"

"We don't know. Cases like this are more complicated than they look."

"Why?" Betty Powers demanded.

"Because there are just so many different things that can cause a person to fall into a coma. And right now we simply haven't had enough time with your son to start to sort out all of the possibilities."

"I see," Betty responded as she calmed slightly. "Can I see my son?"

"Certainly. I'll go with you and then if you feel like it we can talk."

"Okay," Betty agreed.

William M. Jones

Even though Rita had warned her of Raymond's extreme appearance, she was still mortified when she finally saw her son for herself laying in his hospital bed all hooked up to all the various monitors with tubes going everywhere. Seeing Raymond brought back tearful memories of her dying grandfather. He'd been in his mid eighties when he'd passed away many years ago, but the memory of how old he looked flashed back into her mind when she suddenly saw the aged appearance of her son. Definitely didn't look like the nineteen year old she'd last talked to.

"Is he in any pain?" Betty asked Doctor Bratt as she turned towards him and stared straight at him with her pleading eyes.

"No, I don't think so. If he was, he'd be restless and so far he's been exceptionally calm."

"What do you suspect?"

"Like I said earlier, we haven't had enough time to thoroughly examine your son's condition. So far we've been more concerned with stabilizing him and keeping him calm, which you can see we've successfully accomplished."

"Are you giving him any medications?"

"Yes, he's on penicillin right now."

"Why?"

"Because we feel he's got some sort of swelling in his brain."

"And the penicillin will help?"

"Well, let's just say right now that it won't hurt."

"What do you mean by that?" Betty needed to know.

"Well, Mrs. Powers, there are a lot of different things which can cause the brain to swell. Eventually we'll probably perform a spinal tap, but right now we've got to eliminate other possibilities first."

"Why?"

"Because in certain conditions a spinal tap can actually be harmful. Mrs. Powers, can I get you a cup of coffee?"

"Yes, please," she answered, "I'd really like that."

Murder by Memory

"Good, then if you feel up to it, let's go back to my office where we can talk in private. There are a lot of questions I need to ask you."

"Sure, fine. Can Rita come?"

"If you think that's best."

"I do," Betty stated while grabbing her daughter's hands and smiling at her. "She's really close to her brother, you know, so she can probably answer some questions better than I can."

"Okay. Would you like a soda?" Doctor Bratt then asked Rita.

"No thanks, coffee's fine with me too."

Telling the intensive care nurses where he'd be just in case something came up with Raymond, Doctor Bratt led the two women to the privacy of his personal office. Once there, he directed them to have seat on the plush couch positioned directly in front of his large, mahogany desk and then he poured each a cup of fresh brewed coffee before fixing one for himself also.

"What can we tell you?" Raymond's mother first asked after relaxing somewhat, taking a sip from her coffee, and then sitting comfortably back on the couch.

"Has your son been experiencing any problems lately?"

"Yeah, he hasn't been feeling very well lately."

"How so?" Doctor Bratt inquired.

"Been tired a lot."

"Has he seen a doctor?"

"Yes, went to our family doctor."

"And what did he say?"

"Thought he was anemic and gave him some iron medication and told him to get some rest and not to exert himself."

"Is that all?"

"No, I believe they tested him for mono, but that test came back negative."

"Good, that helps," Doctor Bratt assured. "What other specific symptoms can you remember?"

"Oh, I don't know, just tired. Oh, yeah, complained of a stiff neck some time ago and has felt sick to his stomach a lot recently. Can you think of anything else?" she then directed towards her daughter.

"He's been having some really bad headaches lately," Rita stated.

"Did he take anything for them?" the doctor asked while scribbling notes of all the symptoms he was being provided with.

"Yes, took a lot of aspirin."

"Did they help?"

"Yes, at first, but lately nothing seemed to help much."

"Good, this really helps," Doctor Bratt thanked. "What about a fever?"

"Sure," Rita again answered. "He's complained about that also."

"Now, I can see how he's lost facial muscle strength, did you ever notice any slurred speech?"

"Yes," Rita confirmed, "just in the last day or two."

"Good. How about any sensitivity to light?"

"He hasn't said anything," Betty Powers added, "but he's been wearing sunglasses a lot lately."

"And previously he didn't usually wear them?"

"No. Just in the last six weeks or so."

"Is he really close with anybody else. Say, a girlfriend?"

"Yes," Betty answered. "He and Carla Travis have been going together for, what Rita, almost four years?"

"Yeah, mom. Think they met back in tenth grade."

"Has she been notified?" Doctor Bratt asked.

"No, should we call her?" Betty then asked.

"I think so. She might just know something more that you two may have missed."

"Can I use your phone?" Rita asked.

"Certainly."

Murder by Memory

Betty Powers tried to relax and think of anything else she could remember about her son while Rita placed the call. Finishing her cup of coffee, she asked for a second.

"She's on her way," Rita reported while handing the phone back to the doctor. "Be here within half an hour."

"Good," Betty responded. "Doctor Bratt," she next directed, "while we're waiting for Carla, please be honest with us and tell us what you suspect."

"Okay. And I'll try to be as non-technical as possible."

"That would be appreciated."

Doctor Stanley Bratt then decided to provide the family with the most honest estimation of Raymond's condition as he possibly could. From the short time he'd spent with the mother and sister, he'd determined they could withstand the discussion and if things did happen to get too much for them, he'd request that they ask him to stop. "First, I need to ask a few more questions."

"Okay."

"Has your son ever had the measles, chickenpox or rubella?"

"Yes, had chickenpox when he was a child. Is that important?"

"Could be. How about any tooth aches lately?"

Showing a very puzzled expression, Betty Powers answered that her son hadn't. At least none that she was aware of. Rita also shook her head indicating no.

"What about ear infections or any other type of infection to his head?"

"Again, none that I can think of," Betty honestly replied.

"Any bad insect bites or mosquito bites?"

"No," again Betty and Rita both responded.

"Has your son gone out of the country in the last few years? Especially, did he go to any third world countries?"

"No," Betty again answered, "I don't think he's even left the state."

"Okay, thanks, this all really helps."

"So, again, what do you think?" Betty Powers requested.

Taking a deep breath and leaning slightly forward in his chair, Doctor Stanley Bratt stared straight at Betty Powers and started explaining. "Like I said earlier, your son has some swelling in his brain. Why? Well, that's what we don't know right now. Lots of different things can cause that."

"Such as?" Betty interrupted.

"A tumor."

"Oh my god!" Betty gasped as she put both of her hands over her mouth and started to cry again.

"That's just a possibility. I'm not saying he has one for sure. Are you sure you want me to continue?"

"Yes, please. I'm sorry. It's just…,"

"I know. Conditions like this are sometimes harder on the family than on the patient. I guarantee you, doctors don't like it either. We're here to make our patients well and it's very frustrating for us at times also. You see, what we're going through right now is the really tough part. Once we finally determine the cause of the problem we can treat it. But finding the cause isn't always easy."

"I realize that."

Continuing, Doctor Bratt stated, "Like I said, a brain tumor is only a possibility. If we narrow it down to one of our options then we'll perform a CT scan to further evaluate it. Problem with tumors is there are so many different kinds, both benign and cancerous. From what you've said, I definitely don't think Raymond's got a benign Schwannoma tumor. That can be either good or bad depending on your view. Yes, they're benign, but they can cause a lot of neurological damage. They're extremely rare in the brain or cervical neck section and you didn't mention any tingling or numbness in your son's right index finger."

"No, he never complained about that," Betty said.

Murder by Memory

"Good, because that was the deciding clue in a case I just read about in my recent medical journal. Swelling in the brain can also be caused by a brain abscess. It's a localized collection of pus in the brain. Patients have a lot of the same symptoms you've described in your son such as headaches, nausea, vomiting and drowsiness, but since you can't remember him having any tooth or ear infections or other type of head injury I doubt this is what's causing Raymond's swelling. You see, in those cases, the infection can be carried to the brain by the blood. They can be extremely critical and even fatal if not treated quickly with antibiotics."

"Is that why you're giving Raymond the penicillin?"

"Yes, exactly. We can also perform a CT scan, but lots of times a brain abscess will resemble a brain tumor on the scan so even that isn't always conclusive. Next, we've got to consider a subdural empyema."

"A what?" Betty asked.

"Subdural empyema. It's a collection of pus which develops between the brain and its surrounding tissue instead of inside the brain like the abscess. This condition can be caused by the same kind of bacteria as the brain abscess. It's just that the pus collects in a different area," Doctor Bratt explained while viewing the squeamish expressions on Mrs. Powers and her daughter's faces. "Are you two okay?" he then stopped and asked.

"Yes, we'll be okay. I promise. For Raymond's sake, continue. We've got to hear this."

"I agree," Bratt concurred. "Problem with the subdural empyema is that it can evolve over a long period and without treatment can rapidly cause a total lose of consciousness and possibly death. This condition is also why we haven't performed a spinal tap yet. You see, with this condition, the tap can be quite dangerous so we've got to rule it completely out before administering one to Raymond to check for other possible causes for his brain swelling. Then we've also got to check for parasitic infections."

"What are those?" Rita asked.

"Well, to be blunt, worms can infest the brain."

Rita almost vomited with that explanation.

"Sorry," Doctor Bratt immediately apologized upon recognizing her involuntary gesture. "Normally occurs in third world countries after eating contaminated food. You see, contaminated foods can contain Cysticercus eggs which our stomach juices then harvest and allow to hatch becoming larvae. The larvae then enter the bloodstream and are distributed to all parts of the body including the brain. Violent headaches and then seizures are major symptoms from the parasite infections, but they can be successfully treated with certain drugs or in some cases where the infections develop into cysts, they can be surgically removed."

"So that's why you asked if Raymond had been to any third world countries?" Betty stated.

"Yes, so since he hasn't, we can probably rule this condition out, but we'll still have to check some more since it is possible to get from foods around here if they aren't prepared correctly."

"Is that it, or are there any other possible causes?" Betty fearfully asked since she'd already heard more than she really cared to know.

"Afraid we're just getting started," Doctor Bratt acknowledged much to Betty's chagrin. "We've also got to check for meningitis and encephalitis. By the way, did Raymond happen to have a tick bite lately?"

"No, not that I know of," Betty again answered.

"Good," the doctor responded. "You see, meningitis and encephalitis can both be caused by a virus. Encephalitis is an actual inflammation of the brain whereas encephalomyelitis is an inflammation of the brain and spinal cord and then aseptic meningitis is an inflammation of the

Murder by Memory

lining around the brain and the spinal cord. Sometimes brain inflammations don't occur until weeks or even months after the actual viral infection."

"What causes them?" Betty wanted to know.

"That's the problem. Lots of things. Insect bites such as mosquitoes or ticks or the tsetse fly which as far as I know is confined to Africa."

"Good."

"But also can be caused from viruses following diseases such as measles, chickenpox or rubella. This type is called postinfectious encephalitis. Other viruses which can invade the brain can also be caused from the mumps or herpes. To be honest, I really believe Raymond's condition has been caused by one of these viral infections which has infected his brain and caused all the swelling."

"Why do you say that?" Betty now asked.

"Because of the symptoms. Fever, headaches, vomiting, stiff neck, fatigued, muscle weakness, sensitivity to light, blurred speech, loss of consciousness and how he's now in a coma. He has all the classic symptoms. Now it's a matter of discovering his actual cause and then administering the correct treatment," he stated, cutting himself off short before saying "it's too late." The distraught mother and sister sitting before him didn't need to hear that remark right now. They needed to have hope, not despair. "Well, I think that's finally about it. Any questions?"

Before either could answer, there was a knock on Doctor Bratt's door. "Yes," he stated as a nurse stuck her head in.

"Sorry to disturb you doctor, but the young lady had a telephone call. Said it was urgent."

"Me?" Rita questioned.

"Yes," the nurse confirmed while handing Rita the piece of paper with the number written on it. Viewing the unfamiliar number, she was quite perplexed. "There's a pay phone down the hall," the nurse added.

"Thanks," Rita returned.

"Use my phone," Doctor Bratt offered. "More private here. Your mother and I will check on your brother. Meet us there when you're done."

"Thanks, I will," Rita agreed. After her mother and the doctor left, she sat in the doctor's comfortable chair and dialed the mysterious number.

"Rita, what happened?" came Alvin's panicked voice on the other end of the line when he answered.

"How did you know it was me?" Rita asked.

"Because this is a pay phone so you're the only one who'd call."

"Why are you at a pay phone, Alvin?"

"Because the cops are outside my house and I also think they've been watching me at the lake."

"I know," Rita said.

"You know! What do you mean, you know?"

"Raymond and I saw a suspicious looking car with two guys sitting in it at the lake when we drove out the other night."

"You came out?"

"Yes."

"I didn't see you."

"I know. After we suspected the cops were out there, well, we decided it was best for us to leave."

"Did you know about them at my house?"

"No, didn't know about them. Haven't gone near there in a few days."

"What happened, Rita?"

"Raymond's in a coma, Alvin," she stated quite matter-of-fact.

"From what?"

"We don't know. Really looks serious though."

"What about Bruno? How are we going to take care of him?"

Murder by Memory

"Nothing we can do, Alvin. Without Raymond we can't do anything."

"So he gets to live?"

"Looks like it unless you're going to kill him yourself."

"No way, plus the cops are watching me."

"Okay, then, relax. Where are you, anyway?"

"Went home to check on some things. That's when I first suspected the cops. No one was home, but mom had left a note on the kitchen table. She'd picked up Raymond's emergency call on her emergency scanner. You know how she likes to listen to that noisy thing. She'd heard how he was unconscious and was being transported to the hospital. I was afraid the cops might have bugged the phone at the house, so I stopped by this store on my way back to the lake since I knew it had an inside pay phone so nobody would be able to see me using it from out in the parking lot."

"Okay, good. Get on back to the campground and stay there until tomorrow. Then just pack your gear and go home."

"Should I come to the hospital?"

"No, positively not!" Rita emphasized. "The cops don't suspect anything between you, me, and Raymond. My guess is Bruno gave them your name when he was being questioned. They're just grasping for straws. You know they don't have any hard evidence. Can't, because you didn't do anything."

"You're right, Rita," Alvin admitted.

"Of course I am. You just do like I said and this will all blow over. Anyway, if Bruno actually suspects you, you can rest assured he'll leave you alone in the future. Just think of it - he'll go through life always looking back over his shoulder. Always afraid you might just be lurking out there somewhere."

"Haven't thought about it like that. I love you, Rita."

William M. Jones

"I love you too, Alvin. Now, just relax and get back to the lake. I'll see you in a few days when Raymond's better and things settle down a little. We'll talk more then."

"Okay, thanks," Alvin stated as he quickly purchased some supplies and drove straight back to his campsite.

After she hung up, Rita proceeded to Raymond's room in intensive care. Leaving Doctor Bratt's office, she almost ran into Carla who was just arriving to see Raymond.

"How is he?" Carla asked while bursting into tears upon seeing Rita.

Hugging her brother's girlfriend, she stated, "Not very good right now. Mom and the doctor are in with him right now. Let's join them, okay?"

"Okay," Carla agreed.

Temporarily forgetting about Alvin, Rita led Carla to her brother's bedside. Arriving there, she was somewhat shocked to see more tubes coming out of him than when they'd left his side just a short thirty minutes earlier. "What are all those for?" she demanded from the doctor.

"It's okay," Doctor Bratt stated with a calming voice. "Due to his coma, we've put him on a ventilator to help his breathing and then he's also got a nasogastric tube so we can feed him. I promise, he hasn't gotten any worse. This is all just to help him until we can get him to come out of the coma." Then looking at the girl with Rita, he asked, "Is this the girlfriend?"

"Yes. Carla Travis," Rita introduced.

Looking at her while extending his hand, Doctor Bratt quickly noticed Carla's reddened cold sore. Not saying anything at first, he engaged her in idle small talk before leaving her alone with Raymond and his family for a few minutes. When he returned, he requested to speak privately with Carla.

"Certainly," she agreed. "Mrs. Powers said you'd probably still have some questions for me."

"Good. Then let's go down to my office."

Murder by Memory

"Lead the way, doc," she said before releasing her loving grip on Raymond's still, cold hand.

On their way out of the intensive care ward, Doctor Bratt stopped at the nurse's station and placed a quick call. When he was finished, he smiled at Carla and then led her down the corridor to his office. Once inside his office, he inquired if she'd like a soda and when she indicated she would, he reached into the small refrigerator located in the corner of his office and handed her a cold Coke. As she was opening it, a knock came at his office door.

"Come on in, it's open," he ordered. "Please be seated," he then directed the slightly plump nurse dressed in the customary white nurse's uniform.

"Carla, this is Nurse Jenkins. I asked her to sit in with us."

"Why?" Carla asked seemingly somewhat confused.

"Well, it's hospital policy whenever I have someone of your age alone with me in my office."

"You mean of my sex," Carla prudently stated.

"Yes. It's simply policy both for your protection as well as mine. I promise you that anything you tell me will be held in the strictest confidence. Okay?"

"Sure, doc, I don't have a problem with that. Plus, I don't have anything to tell you about Raymond that's a big secret anyway."

"This meeting isn't about Raymond," Doctor Bratt shocked Carla with.

"Not about Ray? Then what's it all about?"

"You, Carla. I have some very personal questions to ask you about."

"Me?" Carla stated now more confused than ever. "What's Ray's condition got to do with me?"

"That's what I'm trying to find out. May I continue?"

"I guess. Can't imagine what Ray's condition has to do with me," she again proclaimed while looking at Doctor Bratt with her questioning eyes and then also viewing Nurse

William M. Jones

Jenkins sitting stoically off to the side in a chair with her arms folded in her lap.

"How long have you had that cold sore on your mouth?"

"Couple of days. Why? It's no big deal."

"Is this the first one you've ever had?"

"No," Carla slowly answered.

"How long have you been getting them?" Doctor Bratt next needed to know.

"I'm not sure. On and off for a couple of years probably. Why?"

"You ever been treated for herpes?"

"Herpes!" Carla blurted out rather loudly. "What are you getting at? That's some type of venereal disease isn't it? What's this got to do with Ray?"

"Please settle down. I assure you this discussion is for medical purposes only. I'm not here to lecture you or even judge you for your sexual activities. I'm simply trying to find out what's wrong with Raymond."

"I'm a virgin, doc," Carla admitted as she started to cry. "I've never even had sex."

"Okay, okay Carla. Please let me explain. Herpes isn't always caused by having sex with another infected person."

"Oh," Carla said seeming to settle down somewhat now.

"Carla, actually there are two kinds of herpes. Technically, one is Herpes Simplex Type 1 and the other is Type 2."

"What's the difference?" Carla asked.

"Both are viral infections and actually look the same when viewed under the microscope. The difference is Type 1 normally affects the body above the waist whereas Type 2 generally affects the genital area."

"Okay, I understand that. But what are the symptoms?"

"That's why we're having this discussion, Carla. Herpes Type 1 shows up as a cold sore or fever blister on the lips or mouth whereas Type 2 causes sores on the genital area.

Murder by Memory

Carla, there's another very important question I have to ask you. You must be honest with me. Raymond's life depends on your honesty. Understand?"

"Yes, sir."

"Have you and Raymond ever engaged in oral sex?"

"Definitely not!" Carla emphatically stated while suddenly feeling quite warm with embarrassment. "Why do you even ask that?"

"Because a person with Type 1 Herpes on their mouth can pass herpes to the genital area of their partner through oral sex. I need you to tell me the absolute truth about this, Carla."

"I did!" she almost screamed. "I'm a virgin and Raymond and I never had oral sex, period!" Carla bluntly stated. "I swear! We never did anything other than make out a lot and some touching," she now nervously confessed to with her face suddenly turning flushed from her blushing. "I still don't understand what's this all got to do with Ray's condition."

"Because one of the ways to contract encephalitis is through a herpes simplex infection. You see, the herpes virus can enter the bloodstream and then localize in the brain which causes the swelling."

"So you think I may have caused Ray's sickness?"

"Yes, I'm afraid so," Doctor Bratt acknowledged as Carla suddenly burst into tears. "I was really puzzled about his condition until I saw you. Carla, I'm really glad you came here today."

"Why?"

"Because now we can most likely save Raymond's life."

"Thank god, but I still don't understand."

"Understand what?"

"Ray and I never kissed whenever I had an active sore. He always said everything was all right whenever my sores were gone."

"I'm sorry, Carla, but he was wrong. That's the problem with diseases like this. There are a lot of false myths floating around out there and sadly that's one of them. So you see, anyone who has herpes can transmit it without even knowing it or can spread it between outbreaks when there's no visible signs or symptoms. That's apparently what happened between you and Raymond. It's called asymptomatic transmission."

"But how did I get it in the first place?" Carla needed to know.

"Did you have a boyfriend before Raymond?"

"Nobody serious."

"But you did make out with other boys?"

"Of course. What teenage girl hasn't?"

"You're right, Carla, but hopefully now you can see how possibly one of those other boys inadvertently passed the virus to you. Also, have you ever heard you parents talking about herpes?"

"My parents. Heavens no! Why?"

"Because it can be passed from one generation to the next."

"Oh," Carla slowly said as she settled back on the couch.

"Carla, I promise you this isn't something to be ashamed of. Probably one out of every six adults in this country has some form of herpes."

"You're kidding."

"No, that's the truth. So, you see, it doesn't really matter how you got it. The important thing now is to test you to see if you really have herpes. Then, if you do, well, through education and medication we can treat it. But the important thing right now is we'll probably know exactly what's causing Raymond's brain swelling."

"Okay. Can I get tested right now?"

"Certainly. I'll personally take you to the lab for the test. It won't take very long, either."

Murder by Memory

Saying that, Doctor Bratt and Nurse Jenkins escorted the emotionally drained Carla to the hospital's lab. It only took a matter of minutes to take a culture and then view it under the microscope to verify the presence of the herpes simplex virus in Carla's sample.

Hearing the official results, Carla looked at Doctor Bratt and asked, "What do I do now?"

"Well, first I'll prescribe some acyclovir which is an antiviral cream to put on the sores or blisters whenever you have the outbreaks. Then you'll need to make sure you follow good hygiene procedures. Then always keep the infected area dry and clean during your outbreaks. Try not to touch the sores, but if you do, make sure you immediately wash your hands with soap and water. Also, try to keep yourself in the best possible general health condition you can and also try to keep stress to a minimum. And then, most importantly, make sure you tell anyone you're with in the future that you're infected with the herpes virus. Any questions?"

"No, but I feel so very foolish," Carla admitted.

"No reason to, Carla," Doctor Bratt stated as he placed a reassuring arm around her trembling shoulder. "You simply didn't know. Now you see the importance of better health education both in schools and at home about unpleasant subjects like this. People's health depend on it."

"That I do. Can we go back and see Ray now?"

"Certainly. I think we need to have a talk with his mother and then I need to get some tests done on Raymond."

Without saying a word, Nurse Jenkins returned to her normal work station as Doctor Bratt and Carla left the lab and headed to the intensive care ward. Arriving there, Betty Powers and Rita were still holding their bedside vigil with Raymond.

"You sure were gone for quite a long time," Betty pronounced as Carla and Doctor Bratt returned. "Is everything okay?"

Without initially saying a word, Carla ran over and tightly hugged Mrs. Powers. With tears uncontrollably flowing from her eyes, she eventually cried, "I'm sorry, I'm so sorry. This is all my fault!"

Looking with a stunned expression at Doctor Bratt, Betty promptly asked, "What's this all about?"

Pulling Carla away from Mrs. Powers and trying to calm her, he then coolly announced, "Through Carla's help I think we've discovered what's causing your son's condition."

"What?" Betty demanded.

"I'm so sorry!" Carla this time screamed.

"What's she babbling about?"

"Mrs. Powers, did you ever notice the cold sores around Carla's mouth?"

"Sure, many times. What of it? Just a normal teenage problem caused by pimples. Right?"

"No, I'm afraid not."

"Then what?" Betty demanded.

"Her sores are caused by a herpes virus."

"Herpes?"

"Yes, but please listen. Carla and your son didn't do anything wrong, I promise you. Carla's type of herpes isn't associated with a venereal disease. It's called Type 1 and is the same type of virus as that which attaches to the genital area, but this virus attaches itself mainly to the body above the waist and when it flares up the outbreak shows up as cold sores or fever blisters to the mouth or lips."

"I didn't know that," Betty displayed her ignorance of the subject by acknowledging and Rita also admitted how she was also unaware of the fact.

Murder by Memory

"Either did Carla or your son," Doctor Bratt interjected, "so you see, it's not really their fault. It's simply one of those unfortunate medical things that happens."

"So you're telling me my son's condition is herpes?"

"Not exactly."

"Then what?"

"Please let me finish. I believe Raymond has encephalitis. You see, one of the ways to contract it is through the herpes simplex virus."

"Okay, so what do you do next?" Betty Powers needed to know.

"Well, now I know what test to perform. We'll get a blood test done as soon as possible. You see, herpes simplex encephalitis contains red blood cells in addition to white blood cells so we should be able to confirm our suspicions rather quickly. Mrs. Powers, I've got to again mention how it's not really Carla's fault. Matter of fact, she probably saved your son's life by coming here today and being totally honest with me."

"Thank you," Betty said as she turned toward her son's frightened girlfriend and hugged the trembling girl.

CHAPTER SIXTEEN

1999

Herbert Chalmers trembled with anticipation as he checked his watch and decided it was finally time to head to the old precinct. Hadn't been there since his quasi forced retirement over three months earlier. Hard to believe how just some short eight to ten hours earlier he'd been wallowing in his deplorable state of self pity and hopelessness and now, for the first time in years, he enthusiastically had something to look forward to. Wasn't sure which excited him the most; being needed again to work the Slaughter House Murderer case or the juvenile tingling he felt from the anticipation of seeing and also getting to work with his new partner - the mysteriously intriguing Detective Elizabeth without an E, Lizabeth Barcay. Just the slightest thought of her made his cold heart warm again. He'd have to play it cool with her, of course. Couldn't let her see the emotions she stirred inside of him, at least not yet. Right now she was just his newly assigned partner, nothing more. Just another detective to work with, but oh how his heartbeat raced every time he thought about her. Checking himself one last time in the mirror before leaving his apartment, he thought to himself, "Damn, but I sure look good!" Definitely didn't look like the same poor slob Benny Mitchell and Lizabeth had visited last night. He was definitely sober now and he also made sure to pop a few breath mints after brushing his teeth this morning. He'd also shaved again this morning even though he'd done it twice last night before taking his shower - this was a trick learned back in his basic training days in the military to assure the smoothest possible face for inspections. He'd also trimmed his scraggly hair, or what was left of it, this morning with a pair of scissors and his razor. He'd get a

Murder by Memory

regular haircut later, but his self trim job definitely made him look a lot better. Thinking back, he realized he hadn't had a regular haircut now in over four months. Had been about a month before he'd agreed to retire. Hadn't really grown that much in those four months, though; mainly because it was so thin and fine now with balding definitely settling in on the top. Was mainly shaggy around the ears and on the back of the neck so his effort this morning had mainly erased the roughness from his appearance. With his week's growth of his whitish coarse beard now also gone, looking in the mirror he questimated he looked a good ten to twenty years younger than he'd appeared to Benny and Lizabeth late last night. And then he couldn't remember the last time his appearance had looked as spiffy as it did today with his being all decked out in his freshly pressed best suit and wearing his highly polished pair of seldom used dress shoes. Only thing he couldn't totally hide today was his recently acquired pot belly, well, he'd just have to work on that one. At least his good suit made it appear somewhat smaller than the old pair of sweat pants and sweat shirt did which he'd been attired in last night when Lizabeth, and Benny to be honest, had been repulsed by his personal hygiene and slovenly appearance. Checking himself one last time, Herb took a deep breath and headed for the precinct. Arriving there, he parked in the visitor's parking place. He made a mental note to ask Benny for an assigned spot when he saw him later. Entering the precinct building, he headed directly for Benny's office and especially hoped to find Lizabeth already there hard at work on the case. Walking towards Benny's space, many of the old gang were surprised to see him and let out greetings and whistles of approval when they witnessed the now dapper appearing Detective Chalmers passing through the area. He didn't know if any of them had been informed yet of his being recalled to work this case or not, but seeing him in his present attire certainly got their attention and raised his personal feeling of self worth. He'd never looked this good, at least not in the recent memory of any of those who happened to see him today. Finally arriving outside Benny's office, he was somewhat disappointed to find him presently alone. Since his back was turned to the door as Herb viewed him through the office's outer window, he knocked loudly before entering.

"Can I help you?" Benny first questioned as he rotated and viewed the eloquently attired person standing before him.

"It's me, Benny," Herb declared.

Then staring closely at the face currently positioned before him, Benny was flabbergasted. "Jesus, Herb, is that really you?" He then told whoever he was talking to on the phone how he needed to go and promptly put the receiver down.

"Yep, it's really me," Herb affirmed.

"Holy shit! Wouldn't have believed it if I hadn't of seen it with my own eyes. What did you do?"

"To be honest, I think you just gave me a new lease on life," Herb honestly proclaimed.

"I'd say," Benny stated while still rather shell shocked from Herb's apparent physical transformation. "I guess it's fair to say, then, that you're ready to get to work?"

"More than ready, Benny. Anyway, where's my new partner? What's her name again?" Herb asked trying to hide his deep burning desire to see Lizabeth again this morning.

"Um, Lizabeth will be in in a few minutes."

"Lizabeth, oh yes. She always this late?" Herb asked while looking at his watch to reinforce his punctuality with Benny.

"No, actually she's been here since six this morning," Benny stated rather matter-of-fact.

"Good," Herb responded, "don't want to work with a slacker."

"Oh, you won't, Herb. I can promise you that."

Murder by Memory

Before Herb could respond to Benny's glowing praise of Lizabeth, she suddenly appeared at the door. Seeing only Herb's backside, she didn't initially really know who Benny was talking with. She'd actually been keeping a look out for the crusty old geezer she'd so crudely been introduced to last night. Whereas Herb had spent the night in amorous anticipation of her, Lizabeth had fretted her night away worrying about Benny's sanity in teaming her up with some overweight, highly depressed loser - and a retired loser to boot. Just the thought of one Herbert Chalmers sent creeping chills shooting through her body. Yes, she'd put up a good front last night by being cordial and stating how she had faith in him, but the truth of the matter was she considered Herb to be one of the most disgusting individuals she'd ever had the misfortune of laying her eyes on. She seriously hoped he'd fall flat on his face in some filthy gutter during the night and then from his inebriated state completely forget the visit she and Benny had had with him. She fully understood Benny's motive in trying to help his old friend, but her initial impression of the wretched bum was how he was a lost cause and she'd definitely be better off working the case by herself rather than having this drunken has-been tagging along. Realizing the time was now 8:10, and knowing Detective Chalmers had emphasized he'd be here at 8 sharp this morning, she felt somewhat secure now that he wouldn't show and she'd simply be able to get on with her work.

"Lizabeth," Benny announced upon suddenly seeing her at the door. "Herb's been asking where you were this morning."

"Herb?" she questioned while still wondering where he was.

"That's right. I never like to be late," Herb declared as he turned and faced the obviously startled female detective. Feeling warm all over from the mere sight of this mysteriously attractive woman again, he continued, "You ready to get to work or are you just going to stand there with that dumb expression on your face?"

"This some kind of a joke, Benny?" Lizabeth stated while now staring at the eloquently attired and rather well groomed individual standing before her.

"No, why?"

"This isn't the same Herbert Chalmers I met last night?"

"Yes I am!" Herb declared. "Now, can we please get to work," he stated while trying to hide his racing heart and shear desire to be near this woman again.

"Benny?" Lizabeth again questioned.

"Hey, don't look at me. I was just as surprised as you to see how he looks today. Cleans up pretty good, doesn't he?"

"Yeah, that he does," she conceded while shaking her disbelieving head. "Okay, then, I guess we're ready to get to work," she then agreed while still in a somewhat confused state of mind. Maybe she'd misjudged this guy some how.

"Where we working out of?" Herb asked with a smile.

"My office, it's just over there," she pointed.

"You mean my old office," Herb stated.

"Your old office?"

"Yep. Spent over twenty years in there."

"I didn't know."

"Doesn't matter. It's yours now."

"Right. So, let's get to work."

"That's what I'm here for Elizabeth without an E," Herb smiled as he looked right into her dreamy eyes and almost wet himself on the spot. So hard to act cool around her when he was melting inside from desire.

Entering his old office, he noticed it still only had one desk. "Thought you'd at least fix me up with another desk in here," he lightly offered. "You didn't really think I'd show up this morning, did you?" Herb prodded. "Well, if I were you and I'd met me last night, well, I'd hope I wouldn't show either," Herb next laughed trying to break Lizabeth's obvious tension. "Come on, let's forget about last night and

Murder by Memory

chalk it up to a bad dream. The important thing is I am here and I'm ready to get to work. Now, what have you got so far?"

"Nothing more than what we told you last night," she offered.

"Well, that's nothing!" Herb disappointedly stated.

"I'm sorry, but that's all we know right now," she apologized. "That's why Benny brought you back," she acknowledged while swallowing her pride a little.

"Yes, he did, didn't he?" Herb boasted while feeling useful again for the first time in years. Man, it felt good and then working with this deliciously looking woman simply made the whole situation all the more gratifying. "What do you know about Alvin Reinhold?" he next asked.

"Not much, yet. Just how you always suspected him."

"Correct. You know why?"

"No, not really. Just got assigned this case last night right before we came over to your place." She then shuddered from thinking about his filthy apartment. Her skin had felt like creepy things had been crawling all over her body the entire time she'd been in that disgusting place.

"Okay, then I'll get you up to speed," Herb offered.

"I'm all ears," she informed him while sitting at his old desk and pulling out a pen to take notes in her field notebook.

"First, have you had time to read my old file?" Herb asked.

"No, can't say as I have. Where is it?"

"Good question. Haven't seen it in years, but must still be filed somewhere in the archives. We'll check later."

"Good idea."

"Anyway, old Alvin Reinhold was the only, and I must repeat, the only suspect I had, but couldn't ever pin anything on him."

"That's pretty hard to believe."

William M. Jones

"Yeah, I know, but we followed him for over a year without anything before Benny officially ordered the surveillance stopped. But since then I've personally kept an eye on him, or should I say, kept an eye on him until I volunteered to retire, without seeing any suspicious behavior."

"But why did you suspect him?"

"Because he's the only name Bruno could think of who held a grudge against him and all the others."

"Who was Bruno again?" Lizbeth wanted to confirm.

"Victor Kojan. A small time punk. Apparently back then he was the neighborhood bully. One night he and the three other boys who were killed kind of beat poor old Alvin up. Bruno remembered Alvin swearing how he'd get them when they finally quit beating on him and left him right there in the park where two of the three boys were eventually found, or should I say placed, after they were killed. The third body was placed in a different park."

"Why'd you think they were placed in the parks?"

"Never found one minute piece of physical evidence in either park, that's why. Murders were conducted assassination style at close range and as far as I'm concerned they most likely took place somewhere else."

"Could Bruno have been wrong? What I mean is, maybe someone else had a grudge against him and the others."

"Yeah, that's haunted me all these years, but couldn't ever prove it. But the biggest mystery of all is why didn't the killer try to kill Bruno when he was definitely the main perpetrator. Didn't make any sense to kill the others and then let Bruno go, especially after the letters."

"What letters?" Lizbeth questioned.

"Benny didn't tell you about them?"

"No, really didn't give me much yet. Said you'd fill me in with all the particulars. I got the distinct impression that right now he's more concerned with public relations damage

Murder by Memory

control and in helping the Chief answer questions than with the specific details of the case. Said that was our job."

"Okay, then let's do it."

"What kind of person was Alvin?" Lizabeth next asked Herb.

"Solid citizen. At the time of the original murders over twenty-four years ago I thought maybe he possessed a disturbed personality."

"Why'd you think that?"

"Because he was a loner. Liked to camp out alone and wrote a lot of poetry. Not your normal teenage activities, don't you think?

"Maybe he was just a sensitive kid," Lizabeth added.

"Now days I think you're right, but back then sure seemed to fit the profile of a serial killer, or at least I liked to think it did."

"So why did you continue watching him all those years?"

"Because it was my first big case. You see, had only been a detective for a few weeks when Benny let me work it. Looking back, guess I took it too personal. But I just couldn't let it go."

"What about Bruno?"

"What about him?"

"Why didn't you suspect him? You know, he could've been lying to you all those years."

"You mean, was he the real killer and then falsely concocted the story about Alvin threatening him?"

"Sure, why not? If it's true, it worked, didn't it? I mean, he's still out there alive and living the good life."

"Yeah, the thought had crossed my mind more than once, but then I just couldn't believe it."

"Why?"

"Because I saw the fear in his eyes when he thought he was going to be killed. Just can't fake the look he had. He was absolutely terrified."

"Okay, back to Alvin, tell me more about him," Lizabeth requested.

"Like I said. Solid citizen. Ended up becoming an English professor at the local community college."

"No, don't tell me. He taught poetry!"

"Sure did. Actually published a couple books of them also. From everything I know about him, he was well thought of in the academia world."

"What about his personal life?"

"Married a local girl while still in college. No children, though. Had a good marriage as far as I could tell. Enough of that, Lizabeth. What do we know so far from last night's killing?"

"Well, Alvin's wife found him in their driveway."

"Driveway?" Herb repeated.

"Got a problem with that?" Lizabeth asked while giving Herb a funny look.

"No, go ahead," Herb prompted.

"Yeah, apparently she'd been out late shopping or something and when she pulled into their driveway she found him spread out in front of his car which was still parked in the driveway."

"Where was he shot?"

"Back of the neck, just like the original murders."

"Get the medical examiner's report yet?" Herb needed to know.

"Yep. That's where I was before I came to Benny's office."

"And?"

"And it confirms a slaughter house pistol was used, just like before, Herb."

"But the killer wasn't the Slaughter House Murderer!" Herb boldly proclaimed.

"How can you say that?" Lizabeth dared to ask.

"Two things, really. First, the original killer wouldn't have left him in the driveway. He would have toyed with us

Murder by Memory

and left Alvin's body in the park to be found just like he did with the others. But that's not the real reason."

"Then what is?" Lizabeth asked while getting rather frustrated with Herb's analysis.

"You bother to look at the sky last night?"

"Sure, was a beautiful night."

"And quite bright, wasn't it?" Herb reminded.

"Yeah, it was. Wasn't there a full moon?" Lizabeth now remembered.

"That's right," Herb confirmed.

"So what of it?" she demanded.

"The Slaughter House Murderer only killed during a new moon!" Herb vigorously declared.

"He what?"

"You heard me. All the murders occurred with a new moon. Whoever killed Alvin Reinhold last night didn't know that."

"So who did know it?"

"Only me and the real killer!" Herb positively pointed out. "You see, I never told anyone about this. Didn't want it leaked to the press. I was positive Alvin would try to kill Bruno at the next new moon after Steven Watts murder. Surveillance was tight as a drum on Alvin and we had Bruno wired and guarded round the clock, but nothing happened. Damned old Alvin just sat out at the lake and wrote poetry! To be honest, I kept tabs on him for years during new moon nights and nothing ever happened. When Benny forced me years later to officially close the file, I finally included it then, but no one has seen the file since it was sent directly to the archives. As far as everyone else was concerned, the case was dead, but not for me."

"And that's why Benny brought you back," Lizabeth proclaimed.

"Damn right!" Herb proudly stated.

"So, Herb, if Alvin wasn't killed by the Slaughter House Murderer, then who do you think killed him?"

"I'm not sure, but I think it's certainly worth having a talk with my old buddy, Bruno Kojan."

"You know where to find him?"

"How long have you been in town?" Herb quizzed Lizabeth.

"Not quite a month," she replied.

"Watch much TV?"

"Sure. Why?"

"Haven't you seen the commercials for Kojan's Used Cars?"

"Yeah, that's Bruno?"

"The same! Rich as hell now, but I wouldn't trust him any farther than I could throw him. He's still a punk as far as I'm concerned. Guess he quit bullying people, but he's still a con artist in my book. Old Big Bruno and his top of the line used cars. What a line of crap! Probably stole half of the cars he sells."

"Then why's he still in business?"

"Cause the people love him. He's like a local celebrity around these parts with all his cute car commercials."

"Glad to see you two are such good buddies," Lizabeth joked. "So, we going to go see him or not?"

"You bet we are!" Herb replied as he tightened the knot on his tie and headed for the door. Lizabeth had to practically run to keep up with him. Passing Benny's office, Herb stuck his head in and asked, "You got a car for me or what?"

Surprised to see Herb was departing the precinct so soon, he replied, "Sure, here, take mine," as he threw Herb his keys. "I'll make sure you have one assigned to you by this afternoon."

"Thanks, that would be nice," Herb stated rather sarcastically as he and Lizabeth left to go and have a friendly little chat with good old boy Victor "Bruno" Kojan. Arriving at his used car lot, they were happy to see him walking the lot apparently surveying his merchandise. Herb

Murder by Memory

pulled his car right up beside him, stopped, and honked the horn. Bruno jumped from being startled while Herb laughed for the first time in a long, long time.

"What the hell?" Bruno shouted while glaring at Herb's car.

"Remember me?" Herb stated with a smile on his face as he rolled down his window and grinned at Bruno.

Looking hard, Bruno finally realized who he was now talking with. "Detective Chalmers?" he questioned.

"The same," Herb replied as he got out of the car.

"Well, I'll be. Haven't seen you in years. Thought I heard where you retired."

"You must have heard wrong, Bruno, because here I am and this is my new partner, Detective Lizabeth Barcay."

"Nice to meet you, ma'am," Bruno politely greeted displaying all the good old boy charm from his used car commercials. "You need a good car, detective?" Bruno then asked Herb while glaring at Benny's relic.

"Not from you, big guy," Herb firmly stated.

"Big guy. Hmm. Looks like you've put on quite a few pounds of your own over the years, detective."

"So what?" Herb fired back. "Anyway, we're here on official business You remember Alvin Reinhold?"

"Remember him! You don't forget someone who tried to kill you."

"But we never proved that," Herb responded.

"But you sure thought he was the killer, didn't you?"

"I did," Herb accurately replied, "but that was a long time ago and by the looks of things, you've done okay for yourself in spite of it all," he then added while turning and looking over Bruno's vast used car lot.

"But my three friend's killer wasn't ever caught, was he?"

"No, he wasn't, so maybe we just had things figured all wrong over all those years," Herb admitted while smiling at Bruno.

William M. Jones

"And what do you mean by that, detective?" Bruno questioned implying he didn't appreciate the insinuation.

"Where were you last night, Bruno?" Herb then asked starting to get to the heart of the matter.

"Home with my family. Why?"

"Read the paper yet this morning?" Herb next asked.

"No, haven't had time yet."

"Well, I'll tell you then."

"Tell me what?"

"Alvin Reinhold was killed last night."

"Son of a bitch!" Bruno exclaimed as a definite sigh of relief spread through his body from the years of worrying about that little SOB. "So what's that got to do with me?" Bruno then asked.

"Well, you two do have quite a long history, Bruno. Plus, he was killed with a slaughter house pistol so who else knew about his connection to the old days?"

"Hey man, I didn't kill that little weasel. May have wanted to over the years, but I never laid a hand on him."

"You mean since the time you and your buds beat the crap out of him in the park?"

"Yeah, yeah, you're right. Not since that night."

"Good," Herb then stated, "then you won't mind coming down to the precinct to take a polygraph test?"

"The precinct?"

"That's right. You do remember the way don't you? I seem to recall you've been there before."

"Very funny, Chalmers. Sure, I'll go. I don't have anything to hide. Just let me tell my people I'll be gone for awhile."

"Sure, no problem. We'll be waiting right here for you," Herb promised as Bruno walked off towards his showroom.

"Wow," Lizabeth stated. "You really don't like him very much, do you?"

"It's that obvious?"

Murder by Memory

"You bet, but I like your style, detective," she approvingly stated while also flashing him a slight smile which absolutely set his heart on fire.

Within a few minutes, Bruno returned and hopped into the back seat of Herb's car. As they drove the short distance back to the precinct, Herb placed a radio call requesting a polygraph operator be standing by when they got there. Arriving at the precinct, they proceeded to the same interrogation room Bruno had hated so much over twenty-four years earlier. They all went in and sat at the rectangular wooden table. Herb sat at the top with Bruno off to his side. The polygraph operator positioned himself directly across from Bruno with Lizabeth to Bruno's other side. Benny Mitchell also observed the proceedings from the other side of the one way window mirror. He figured he'd better since this was Herb's first morning back on the job.

"Ready to start?" Herb asked after Bruno had time to get reacquainted with his environment and was provided with a hot cup of coffee and two raspberry filled jelly donuts.

"You not going to have any?" Bruno asked while looking directly at Herb's pot belly.

"I'll be asking the questions, big guy," Herb angrily replied.

"Great. Fire away."

"State your name," Herb began.

"Victor Kojan," he replied as the polygraph needle showed a small movement back and forth indicating a correct response.

"Did you kill Alvin Reinhold?" Herb asked getting right to the point.

"Absolutely not!" Bruno replied as the polygraph needle didn't waver one iota from the norm.

Starting to get agitated, Herb continued. "What's your wife's name?"

"Stella."

"How long you been married?"
"Twenty-two years."
"How many kids do you have?"
"One."
"Boy or girl?"
"Boy."
"What's his name?"
"Victor junior."
"What's he called?"
"Little Bruno."
"Did you kill Alvin Reinhold?"
"No," Bruno still replied while the polygraph needle confirmed his response.
"Did you ever harm Alvin Reinhold?"
"Yes."
"When?"
"We got into a fight back in 1975."
"Ever bully him?"
"Yes, used to call him names."
"Did you kill or have killed Daryl Woods?"
"No."
"Did you kill or have killed Tony Austin?"
"No."
"Did you kill or have killed Steven Watts?"
"No."
"Did you kill Alvin Reinhold last night?"
"No," Bruno again stated while the polygraph needle still confirmed how he was apparently telling the truth.
"Did you or anyone in your family ever own a slaughter house pistol?"
"No."
"Did you kill or have killed Alvin Reinhold last night?" Herb decided to ask one last time.
"No," Bruno still answered.
"Are you glad Alvin's dead?"
"Yes," Bruno honestly stated, "but I didn't do it."

Murder by Memory

"Okay, that's all for now," Herb finally allowed.

"Then I'm free to go?" Bruno asked as the polygraph operator unhooked his equipment's attachments from him.

"Yeah, but stay close. Don't leave town without letting me know."

"I won't, I promise," Bruno stated as he got up.

"I'll arrange a ride for you back to your car lot," Herb offered.

"Just like the old days," Bruno smiled. He then got up and left the room.

"What do you think, Herb?" Lizabeth inquired after Bruno left.

"Either he's telling the truth or he's the coolest SOB I've ever seen. Either way, just like in '75, I know he's connected somehow to all this. Just don't know how."

"We'll just have to find out then, won't we?" Lizabeth stated with a smile as she emphasized the word - we.

The next two weeks were like deja vu for Herb as he and Lizabeth relentlessly worked the case. Like before, lots of work with negative results. They checked and triple checked any and all connections to Bruno. Was he part of the mob? Was he related to the mob in any way? Was any member of his family connected to the mob? They tried to think of any possible illegal connection he might have and in all cases he came up squeaky clean. He may be a wealthy schlockmeister used car salesman, but they couldn't pin any illegal operations on him. If he did have any illegal connections, they were totally discreet. No, as far as Herb and Lizabeth could determine, Bruno was just a big schmuck who could bull shit a bull shitter and schmooze with the best of them. Herb decided he was perfectly suited to the persona of the classic used car salesman. But that wasn't a crime. Then as to Alvin, they'd drawn a blank there also. He had a superb reputation as a college professor, and from all indications, had a good rapport with his students and fellow workers. Again, couldn't find anyone who held a grudge against him except for Bruno, and for all Herb knew, he could have been wrong about that over all these years. Basically, investigating Alvin and Bruno was like beating your head against a brick wall. Nothing seemed to fit. Then who killed Alvin and why? Had to be something they'd missed. But what? After almost two weeks of working practically around the clock, Herb and Lizabeth decided to take a short break last night and regroup in the morning. Returning to his apartment around six, he'd fixed himself a quick bite to eat and then basically collapsed on his couch with his clothes still on.

"What's that banging?" Herb thought to himself as he ever so slowly became cognizant of his surroundings. Slowly waking and realizing he'd fallen asleep on the couch, he quickly noticed it was already seven in the morning while the loud knocking at his door continued.

"You in there, Herb?" He recognized Lizabeth's voice frantically calling out.

"Yeah, yeah, I'm coming," he finally hollered back as he rubbed his sleepy eyes and slowly strolled toward his front door.

"Your phone off the hook?" she asked when he opened the door.

"Why?"

"Been calling for half an hour. Just kept getting a busy signal."

"I don't know," he responded.

"Doesn't matter. Get your coat, we're leaving," she ordered.

"What?" he asked not fully comprehending what was taking place.

"Herb, a body was just discovered in the park!"

"Slaughter House Murderer?" Herb quickly questioned.

"Very possible. Let's go."

"Okay, okay, I'm right behind you," he promised as he rapidly grabbed his keys, badge and wallet and then tried to

Murder by Memory

smooth his hair and rumpled appearance from his night on the couch. Stopping outside his apartment, he saw how Lizabeth was already in her car with the engine running. As soon as he was most of the way in on the passenger side, she turned on her portable red flashing light and sped off. Within five minutes they arrived at the crime scene. Flashing their badges to the uniformed cops securing the area, they headed straight for the dead body.

"Bruno!" Herb declared as soon as he was close enough to clearly see the victim. "My god, it's Bruno!" he again stated while giving Lizabeth a most startling expression. "I knew the SOB was connected somehow to all this. Just knew it!"

"And you know what last night was?" Lizabeth added.

"Sure do. A new moon!" Herb emphasized. "We've really got a dilemma on our hands now, Lizabeth," he next stated.

"What's that, Herb?"

"Just look. Alvin's dead and now so is Bruno. Killed on a new moon with what looks to be a shot to the back of the head fired from a slaughter house pistol. You know what this all means?" he questioned her.

"Afraid I do, Herb. Means the real Slaughter House Murderer is still out there," she proclaimed.

"And even worse than that, Lizabeth. We don't have any idea at all who it is! That's the really scary part, Lizabeth. We don't have the foggiest idea who it is," he reinforced as he let out an audible sigh of despair. "Not the foggiest idea," he again stated as he turned and slowly headed back to the car.

William M. Jones

CHAPTER SEVENTEEN

Bruno's funeral was attended by one of the largest crowds ever assembled for a local funeral and, for traffic control purposes, the following procession to the cemetery required a rather large police escort. More out of curiosity than anything, Herb and Lizabeth attended and Herb was flabbergasted at the number of citizens who obviously adored the one time school bully and was disgusted at the police support the event required after everything he suspected Bruno of. Unbelievable, he thought. From bully to local folk hero as a lovable character bigger than life to most of the local citizens. Almost made Herb puke. If they only understood the real Victor Kojan. Well, maybe when this whole ordeal was solved the truth would finally come out about him. But again, didn't really matter because Bruno was dead. Word had it his wife was selling their home and moving out of state and their only son, Little Bruno, didn't want anything to do with the family car business and was planning on quitting college and joining the service. So, if Herb and Lizabeth could eventually connect the Slaughter House Murderer to Bruno, it really didn't matter since he, and now his family, would be gone. Herb also reflected on the glaring differences between Bruno's and Alvin Reinhold's funerals. Whereas Alvin had been a quiet college professor and solid citizen as compared to Bruno's ever present loud mouth and used car showboating, his funeral had only been attended by a small gathering of family, colleagues and students which hadn't required any police support for the trip from the church to Alvin's final resting place. Leaving the church following Bruno's excruciating long service, Herb suddenly caught a glimpse of a couple which made him do a double take. What was Alvin Reinhold's widow doing here and who was that older man she was with? He couldn't figure this one out and also

Murder by Memory

couldn't place the gentleman she was tightly clutching as they left the church without paying their final respects to Mrs. Kojan or her only son. The whole scene really seemed strange.

A few days after the funeral, Herb was in Benny's office discussing television's renewed interest in the Slaughter House Murderer. *60 Minutes* and *Dateline* had both contacted the mayor's office about doing a feature for their shows. The Chief wasn't really thrilled about the idea, but his hands were tied in the matter and he'd promised the mayor the police department would cooperate. What the Chief really wanted before the TV crews arrived was the real Slaughter House Murderer. Needed to have a positive angle televised on the department instead of one where they'd been unable to catch the notorious serial killer now for over twenty-four years. To Herb and Benny, the current crisis was all too familiar as the same pressures had been applied all those many years ago by the previous Chief and mayor.

"What are you smiling about?" Benny said with a scowl when he noticed Herb's sudden expression.

"Oh, I don't know," he began, "maybe just that I don't have to put up with all this crap if I don't want to."

"What do you mean by that?"

"You forget, I'm retired. I can leave anytime I want to. Simply go back to my apartment and leave you all alone to deal with all this."

"Well, maybe I'll just up and retire and move in with you."

"Yeah, right," Herb returned, "you think you could stand living in my place?"

"No, guess not. And you'd better not leave me either."

Laughing now, Herb promised, "Oh, I won't. Plus, I'm having too much fun this time."

"Thought you were frustrated."

William M. Jones

"I am, but knowing how I can walk away if I want to makes it okay. You know, Benny, doing something because you want to instead of because you have to gives someone a whole different perspective on things."

"Working with Lizabeth wouldn't have anything to do with it, would it?" Benny winked.

"Maybe," Herb acknowledged to his old friend. Taking a deep breath and thinking about her, he realized how his life had drastically changed for the better because of her. Just hoped she was beginning to feel the same about him.

"Lizabeth, speak of the devil, come on in," Benny stated upon seeing her appear at the door.

"You boys talking about me?" she kidded.

"Who, us? Would we do that?" Herb jokingly returned.

"Well, if you were, hope it was good."

"Definitely. What's up?" Benny requested.

"Rita Reinhold just called."

"Rita!" Herb exclaimed. "I told you I saw her at Bruno's funeral."

"Exactly. Said she saw you there also."

"What does she want?"

"To talk to you, Herb."

"Me?"

"Yep. Said you're the only one she'll talk to."

"About what?"

"Said she had some information about who killed Bruno."

"She coming here?"

"No, she's expecting you at her house. I told her we'd be there within the hour."

"She okay with you coming along?"

"Yeah, no problem. I explained how I was your partner now."

"Take some backup with you Herb," Benny ordered.

"Why, you suspect something?"

Murder by Memory

"I don't know what I think. Just can't hurt to have some uniformed backup."

"Okay."

Within fifteen minutes, Herb and Lizabeth pulled into the Reinhold's driveway. Two marked police cars accompanied them and positioned themselves along the road to both sides of the Reinhold home.

Ringing the doorbell, Herb was courteously greeted by Rita Reinhold. "Nice to see you, detective."

"Mrs. Reinhold," Herb returned, "have we met before?" he questioned because he was surprised she seemed to know him so well. He knew her fairly well from all the years of watching Alvin, but thought he'd been extremely discreet with his presence undetectable to Alvin or his family.

"You're right, detective, we haven't. But I've known about you for years."

"How so?" Herb inquired.

"Well, I know it was you who searched Alvin's house back in '75 and then had him followed. I also know how you've kept tabs on him and Bruno over all these years."

Somewhat embarrassed, Herb replied, "I'm impressed. Didn't think anyone ever noticed."

"Oh, Alvin didn't. Very sensitive person, you know. Wouldn't hurt a fly, but I guess you finally figured that out. He was also a terrific husband, detective."

"Mrs. Reinhold, I've got to ask then, why did you go to Victor Kojan's funeral?"

"Because that SOB terrorized my husband years ago, and then killed him, so I wanted to finally see the bastard go to hell where he belongs."

"That's what you wanted to tell us, that Bruno killed Alvin?"

"No, I can tell you who killed Daryl, Tony, Steven and finally Bruno," she calmly stated.

"You know who the Slaughter House Murderer is?" Herb demanded.

"Yes, detective, I do," she again stated rather calmly. "And he's upstairs right now."

"Here, in your house?" Herb questioned suddenly getting quite nervous while at the same time excited as he turned and also stared at Lizabeth.

"Don't be afraid, detective. Please, sit down. He's harmless now. He won't even come down until I bring him."

Thinking back to Bruno's funeral, Herb next asked, "Was he with you at Bruno's funeral?"

"Yes, he was."

"Who is he?"

"My brother, detective."

"Your brother!" Herb exclaimed not even knowing she had one and even more surprised that she was willing to turn in her own flesh and blood. "I'm afraid I don't understand, Mrs. Reinhold," he next stated.

"It's really quite simple. Alvin and Bruno are gone. Nothing we can do about them now, so it's time to put the whole thing to rest for everyone's sake."

"Mrs. Reinhold, I must ask two questions first."

"Sure, go ahead."

"Does your brother know that you're about to turn him in for committing four murders. You must realize he'll be facing the death penalty."

"Yes, but I don't seriously believe any court would award him that."

"Why, after four premeditated murders?"

"You'll see. Now, what's your second question?"

"Are you involved?"

"Yes," she again calmly stated.

Taken aback by her bluntness, Herb next asked, "So why are you confessing? I don't understand?"

"Like I said. It's time to put an end to all this. Guess my conscious is getting the better of me."

"Herb," Lizabeth added.

"What?" he questioned as he looked at his partner.

Murder by Memory

"She needs a lawyer before she says anything more," she reminded him.

"You're right, of course," he positively agreed. Sure glad Lizabeth was with him. He was getting so enthralled with Mrs. Reinhold's unbelievable confession that he was forgetting about proper police procedures. Last thing he needed was to blow this case on a technicality. Turning then to Mrs. Reinhold, he asked, "Do you have a lawyer?"

"No, afraid I don't. Can't we just proceed and get through with this before I lose my nerve?"

"No, really can't. We need to do this by the book."

"Can we at least do everything here? I think it's really best for my brother."

Looking at Lizabeth for her agreement, Herb consented.

"I'll make the call," Lizabeth offered.

"Thanks," Herb said. "Also get the District Attorney here and give Benny a heads up call."

"How long until they can be here?" Rita asked.

"Not long," Herb promised as he remained with Rita while Lizabeth excused herself to go use her cell phone. As she turned to leave, Herb requested, "Lizabeth, I'd feel a lot better if one of the uniformed cops came in here."

"I agree. I'll see to it," she promised.

Lizabeth returned to the room about a half hour later. "I think one of the lawyers just arrived. I'll stay in here with Mrs. Reinhold while you brief the lawyers outside."

"Good idea," Herb agreed as he turned the watching of Rita Reinhold over to Lizabeth and headed outside. Opening the front door, he immediately recognized the first lawyer. "Wyatt Barfield, you old son of a bitch," Herb greeted the elderly and portly lawyer from the County Public Defender's office.

"Nice to see you again too, Chalmers. Thought you were kicked off the force months ago," Barfield jabbed Herb with.

"Retired, Wyatt, I retired, but Benny Mitchell needed the best back to handle this case."

"And you're the best?" Barfield laughed.

"Cut the crap, Wyatt. You know why you're here?"

"Not exactly."

"You do know about the Slaughter House Murderer case, don't you?" Herb questioned his old nemesis who over the years seemed to get off more petty criminals than Herb cared to remember. Had been kind of a standing joke for years: Chalmers would catch um; and Barfield would release um. In Herb's mind, Wyatt Barfield had done more to hinder justice than to help it, but being a good law officer he had to abide by the due process of the law - and he certainly didn't want anything to get fouled up with this case.

"You telling me you've caught the notorious murderer?" Barfield commented.

"Not exactly."

"Then what?" he stated starting to get impatient.

"The killer's sister is ready to confess and then turn her brother over to us."

"Just like that?" Barfield questioned not believing what he was hearing.

"That's right. That's why you're here and hopefully the DA will show up soon."

"Whatever you say, Chalmers. Never seen anything quite like this before," Barfield professed.

"Me either," Herb acknowledged as another car slowly pulled into the driveway. Herb figured it must be the DA, but was startled to see an extremely young woman getting out of the car. Leaving Wyatt Barfield by the door, Herb walked out to meet the young lady. "I'm Detective Herbert Chalmers, and you are?"

"Marilyn Sparks," the pretty woman returned.

"You out of college yet?" Herb joked.

"Very funny, detective. Got out last year."

Murder by Memory

"Oh great, the biggest case of the century and the District Attorney sends his least experienced deputy."

"Sorry to disappoint you, detective, but I was the only one available on such short notice."

"Hey, Chalmers, quit harassing the young lady," Barfield demanded as he approached the car.

"You know her, Wyatt?"

"Sure I do. Really smart young lawyer," he expressed as he passed a good old boy smile Marilyn's way which reminded Herb of Bruno's sickening charm. In his book, Barfield and Bruno could've been brothers.

"All right, all right, let's go inside and get on with this," Herb said while leading the opposing lawyers inside the house. Once inside, Herb made all the introductions and explained to Rita Reinhold why everyone was present and also explained the process to her. He also informed her how the conversation would be taped.

"She has nothing to say!" Barfield suddenly announced. "If you want my client and her brother you'll just have to find your own evidence since I'm advising them not to say another word."

"Wyatt, you...," Herb started to say when Rita quickly jumped in.

"No!" she exclaimed. "I called Detective Chalmers here and I want to get on with this. We've waited long enough already," she declared as Herb flashed a satisfying smile Wyatt's way.

"Good," Herb then said. "First, I don't understand why your brother's letting you do this or why he's agreed to stay upstairs for now."

"Any of you ever hear of Wernicke-Korsakoff syndrome?" Rita then asked.

"Amnesia, isn't it?" Marilyn Sparks immediately answered much to Herb's amazement.

"Exactly," Rita replied.

William M. Jones

"You telling us he can't remember anything?" Herb jumped in.

"Basically," Rita replied.

"How'd he get it?" Herb then wanted to know.

"Well, you see, years ago he got a severe case of encephalitis."

"And this caused the amnesia?" Herb asked.

"Exactly," Rita answered. "You see, Korsakoff's amnesia can be caused by an acute case of encephalitis. In Raymond's case, he's lost all of his intermediate memory."

"What do yo mean by that?"

"Can't remember anything from the time he went into the coma from the encephalitis until the present."

"Nothing?" Herb questioned.

"Not really. His immediate memory last only for a minute or two."

"You mean he forgets what he's doing or saying after only a minute or two?" Herb then asked.

"Exactly. That's why he's not a threat to anyone here right now because he doesn't remember that he killed Bruno."

"Then how do you know he did it?" Marilyn Sparks added.

"Because I helped him," Rita confessed.

"Again, I must demand that you don't say anything else, Mrs. Reinhold," Barfield again demanded.

"No, I must. Can't live with this any longer."

"When did your brother have the encephalitis?" Herb needed to know.

After Rita provided the date, Herb was dumbfounded because that was the exact date he thought Alvin was going to try to kill Bruno. "Then he remembers killing the other three?" Herb asked.

"Yes, when questioned directly," Rita answered.

"And what do you mean by that?" Marilyn asked.

Murder by Memory

"Well, when confronted with events prior to getting sick, he can remember certain things. It's kind of like his mind processes quick flashes from his past. He can't really think about the past like a normal person, just responds to specific events."

"How did he get encephalitis?" Herb next inquired.

"From his girlfriend's cold sores."

"Cold sores?"

"Yeah, herpes simplex virus from cold sores can cause it."

"I'll be," Herb stated.

"That's right. And if you don't believe me, Ray's old doctor is still over at the hospital."

"No, that's okay, I believe you. But, now, from what you've just said, your brother can remember killing the others?"

"Yes, if asked specifically about them."

"And you're telling us that Bruno would've been killed back in '75 if your brother hadn't of gotten sick?"

"Yes, it was all planned," Rita acknowledged.

"But why?" Herb asked.

"Because Bruno and his gang threatened to kill Alvin!" Rita lied.

"That's not what Bruno told me," Herb rapidly countered.

"And you believed him?"

"Well, at the time I didn't have any reason not to. He was really scared about it. Those letters he got really shook him up."

"Good!" Rita replied with a satisfying smile. "But you see, Bruno and the others beat Alvin up real bad one night and then threatened to kill him if he told anyone. Well, Alvin wasn't a violent person so when he feared for his life he asked my brother to help him."

"Why did he ask your brother?"

William M. Jones

"Because I was his girlfriend as well as the only true friend he had."

"I didn't know that," Herb acknowledged.

"I know," Rita said. "We purposely kept it that way after the murders were agreed upon. You see, for months we didn't see much of each other so you wouldn't have any connection between Alvin and us. And apparently it worked."

"Then you helped with the other murders also?" Herb added.

"Yes," Rita lowered her voice and confessed. "Had to. Bruno and his bunch had threatened to kill my true love," she now proclaimed while starting to cry.

"What did you do?" Herb needed to know.

"Let's just say I kind of lured them to Ray," she admitted while Herb remembered how Bruno had thought Daryl was going to meet a girl the night he was murdered.

"Still don't understand," Herb stated.

"What, detective?" Rita asked.

"If you were Alvin's girlfriend back then, why weren't there any pictures of you in his bedroom. All teenage boys keep pictures of their girlfriends."

"That's easy, detective. You searched his bedroom and not his room."

"Explain that."

"You asked to search his bedroom so that's what Alvin's mother showed you. What she didn't tell you was how he'd moved out of it months earlier and was actually living in the room above the garage. You see, detective, you didn't ask the correct question that day and then assumed a lot. You do know what assume means?" she questioned having a little fun with Herb.

"Yeah, yeah, makes an ass out of me," he sheepishly acknowledged while now beating himself up for being so stupid back then. "Anyway, where's your brother been all these years?"

Murder by Memory

"In a special hospital for the mentally challenged. You see, when he finally came out of his coma, he had severe speech problems besides the memory issues. Was just too much for our mother to deal with so he was sent where he could receive special help."

"How long did he stay there?" Herb next asked.

"Well, about twenty-three years," Rita correctly answered. "You see, the place closed last year and since our mom died a few years ago, well, Raymond came to live with Alvin and me. He's really no trouble. Can take care of his own daily needs and knows us. Mainly stays up in his room or goes places with me."

"What ever happened to his old girlfriend who gave him the encephalitis in the first place?"

"Oh, Carla, she visited him for six months or so, but finally split when she realized he'd never get any better. Haven't heard from her since the late 70's. Really don't know any more than that."

"Did she know about the murders?" Herb questioned.

"No, Ray kept them from her. She never suspected a thing."

"Okay," Herb responded, "so tell us, Rita, why did your brother kill Bruno after all these years?" Herb finally asked.

"Well, you see, after Bruno killed Alvin…,"

"We're not positive of that," Herb interjected.

"I am!" Rita firmly stated. "Like I was saying, after Bruno killed Alvin, well, it kind of triggered the old times inside Raymond's mind and he unexpectedly remembered how he was supposed to have killed Bruno back in '75."

"But you said he can't remember things now for more than a minute or two. How did he remember he wanted to kill Bruno now?" Marilyn Sparks added.

"If you're ready to see Raymond, I'll show you," Rita claimed.

William M. Jones

"Okay, I think we'd all like that," Herb answered as Rita, with Lizabeth accompanying her, went upstairs to get Raymond.

Returning within a matter of a minute or two, they returned with a well groomed individual probably in his early forties. Still with an athletic build with just a hint of gray hair, walking down the stairs with his sister, Raymond Powers looked like any family's kindly uncle - not a notorious serial killer. To prove her point about Ray's memory loss, Rita introduced him first only to Herb.

"Ray, this is Detective Herbert Chalmers. He wants to ask you some questions."

"Herbert, nice to meet you," Ray said with a smile as he extended his hand with a firm handshake.

"Nice to finally meet you, Ray. Been looking forward to this for years."

"Really, why?" Raymond returned.

"Because I've heard so much about you."

"That's nice," Raymond responded showing Herb how he was competent enough to carry on a normal conversation.

Getting right to the point, Herb callously asked, "Did you kill Bruno Kojan?"

Jumping right into the conversation, Rita asked her brother, "Ray, who are you talking to?"

Pondering the question for a few seconds, Ray slowly answered, "I can't remember."

"What question did the man just ask you, Ray?" Rita then asked.

"I don't remember. Sorry, sis."

"Nothing to be sorry for, Ray. It's okay," she comforted while placing her arm around his sagging shoulder.

"Can I go back upstairs now?" he wanted to know.

"No, not yet. Detective Chalmers has some more questions he'd like to ask you."

Murder by Memory

"Detective Chalmers, nice to met you," Raymond stated while extending his hand again. Herb was initially startled since they'd just done this a few minutes ago, but then quickly deduced how Raymond most likely couldn't remember that first greeting. What a horrible way to go through life, he thought.

"Raymond, can I ask you a few questions?"

"Sure, go ahead."

"Thanks, Ray," Herb continued. "Did you kill Daryl Woods back in 1975?"

"Yes," Ray honestly answered.

"Did you also kill Tony Austin?"

"Yes."

"What about Steven Watts?"

"Yes," Ray again confessed much to the astonishment of all present. Was almost unbelievable how calmly and directly he answered those questions. Was like he knew he'd committed the murders, but didn't understand what murder was. All present found it quite erie.

"Raymond, did you kill Bruno Kojan?"

"Bruno," Ray repeated, "no, I didn't kill him."

"Did you ever plan to kill him?"

"Yes, but then I got sick."

"Raymond, do you remember my name?" Herb then asked.

"No, have we met?" Raymond answered.

"Ray, do you remember what we were just talking about?"

"No, were we having a conversation?"

"Been like this since '75," Rita interrupted.

"Then how was he capable of killing Bruno?" Herb asked not being able to figure that one out.

"Watch," Rita instructed. "Ray, what do you have in your left pants pocket?"

"I don't know," he replied while pulling out a few small pieces of folded paper.

William M. Jones

"Can you read one of the notes, Ray?"

"Sure," he agreed. "Bruno killed Alvin," he immediately read.

"Read another one Ray."

"Kill Bruno at next new moon," he next read much to everyone's amazement.

"Read the last one, Ray," Rita finally instructed.

"Get old pistol."

"Any questions, detective?" Rita now asked Herb while also looking at the others.

"You mean to tell me he wrote himself notes to remind himself to commit Bruno's murder?" Herb stated.

"Exactly, detective. He was really upset when Alvin was killed. You see, he understands his amnesia problem, so he figured out this method to carry out his revenge and to complete what he was supposed to do back in '75 in order to protect Alvin."

"Where'd he get the pistol?" Herb then needed to know.

"Originally was our dad's," Rita admitted. "He'd worked in a slaughter house years ago and had kept the pistol in a trunk in our attic. Raymond remembered it from when dad had showed it to him when he was a kid, so since it was the only weapon he had access to, well, that was how he came up with the plan we used. That's also why I had to help him because he needed to be able to walk right up to each victim without being noticed."

"So you distracted each boy while Ray snuck up, placed the pistol to the back of their heads and pulled the trigger?"

"Yes, I'm ashamed to say, but it was the only way to protect Alvin. You've got to believe me," she now said while starting to cry again. "We did it for self-defense. Can't you see that?"

"Why didn't you go to the police?" Marilyn Sparks now asked.

"Oh, sure, you honestly think they would've helped us. No way, they would've laughed us out of their precinct.

Murder by Memory

They don't take teenage threats very seriously. Telling them probably would have just made things worse if Bruno would have ever found out," she proclaimed while Herb and the others silently had to agree with her reasoning.

"Why did Raymond do the murders on new moon nights?" Herb asked. "You realize I was the only investigator who figured that connection out. That's why surveillance was so tight on Alvin and Bruno the day Raymond was originally planning to kill Bruno."

"I'm not sure, detective," Rita honestly answered. "Ray's always been intrigued with the universe. He was planning to become an astronomer, you know, but Carla changed all that."

"Carla?" Herb questioned.

"Sure, defending Alvin didn't have anything to do with Ray's encephalitis. Messing around with Carla caused it so he'd still be like this regardless of the murders. Sad, isn't it?"

"Certainly is," Herb agreed beginning to feel sorry for Raymond Powers and his sister, Rita, where previously over all those long years he'd pictured the killer as some crazed monster - what a different view he was getting today. "Where's the pistol now?" he thought to ask.

"Don't know," Rita lied.

"Why?"

"Quite simple. Ray disposed of it after he killed Bruno and can't remember what he did with it," she stated rather matter-of-fact.

"Didn't write himself a little note for that one?" Marilyn Sparks quipped.

"Apparently not," Rita replied while shooting Marilyn a disapproving cold stare which could have frozen time.

"I think we're done here now," Wyatt Barfield quickly stated trying to change the mood from Marilyn's snide little comment. Also, from all that had been said, he was mentally beginning to formulate his defense strategy.

"Okay," Herb also agreed. "I think we've got about all we're going to get right now. Where do we go from here?"

"Detective Barcay, would you mind escorting Mrs. Reinhold and her brother back upstairs?" Barfield politely asked.

"No problem," she said before leading the two back upstairs.

"Well, Marilyn, how far do you plan to take this?" Barfield asked the young Deputy District Attorney. "Looks to me like self-defense, mental anguish and lastly a simple case of mental deficiency. No jury in the state will convict those two," he emphasized.

"I totally disagree," Marilyn promptly stated. "I plan to take this case to the grand jury and ask for an indictment for murder in the first degree for all four murders!"

"For both of them?" Barfield questioned. "No way you can charge Mrs. Reinhold with first degree murder."

"Maybe not, but she's definitely culpable of second degree murder."

"How do you see that?" Barfield demanded.

"Well, she admits to being present when the murders were committed and she did aid her brother, didn't she?"

"Agreed, but she was under a severe mental handicap at the time. Remember, her future husband's life was being threatened and she honestly feared for his life."

"What are you getting at, Wyatt?" Marilyn adeptly questioned knowing full well that the crusty old defense attorney had something up his sleeve.

"Well, Mrs. Reinhold did volunteer everything, didn't she?"

"Yes, I'll give her that."

"So, without her testimony there's no case and also without it I believe the police are out of any other leads. Correct, detective?" Barfield then directed to Herb with his good old boy shit eating grin.

Murder by Memory

"Afraid so," he answered while wishing he could respond differently, but knowing full well how Wyatt Barfield was absolutely correct - without Rita's testimony the Slaughter House Murderer case would remain unsolved.

"So, what do you want then?" Marilyn again asked.

"A deal for Mrs. Reinhold."

"I'm listening."

"Well, how about one to three years in a minimum security facility for being an accessory in return for turning her brother in and also being allowed to testify in his defense."

"And what about Mr. Powers?" Marilyn wanted to know.

"I'll take my chances with a jury with him."

"All right," Marilyn agreed.

"One more thing," Barfield now added.

"What now?"

"No jail time for either before the trial."

"Are you crazy, Wyatt? Mr. Powers is a serial killer!"

"No, you saw him, Marilyn. He's harmless right now. I think his special mental capacity rightfully justifies a house arrest order instead of jail time right now and since the only person he can currently relate to is his sister, well, it's only right that they stay together for the time being. What do you think, Herb?"

As much as he wanted to disagree with his old nemesis, he couldn't after what he'd just seen and heard. "In this case, I think Wyatt's right," much to his chagrin, he was then forced to agree.

"So be it," Marilyn reluctantly conceded. "I'll take it up with my boss as soon as I get back to the office."

With everything basically agreed upon, additional police were brought to the Reinhold home to guard it, the opposing lawyers headed off to prepare their respective cases, and Herb and Lizabeth, both extremely exhausted right now, returned to his apartment to relax. Much to

William M. Jones

Herb's shear delight, the case was definitely bringing them personally much closer together.

CHAPTER EIGHTEEN

Lizabeth tiptoed softly past the lightly snoring Herb as she proceeded from his bedroom toward the kitchen to prepare a hot cup of coffee. Not having any additional clothes with her when they'd spontaneously returned to his apartment following their startling discovery at Rita Reinhold's home late yesterday, Lizabeth was now wearing an old set of his worn, but clean sweat pants and shirt which she'd slept in and for comforts sake, now preferred to remain in to lounge around the apartment this morning. Smiling at Herb as she walked past him while he remained asleep on the living room couch, she thought to herself how improbable it was that she was currently here with this man after their offensive introduction just three short weeks earlier. Leaving his apartment with Benny Mitchell that first night, she sincerely hoped she'd never see the filthy, depressing and discourteous Herbert Chalmers ever again in her life, but here she was, of her own free will, enjoying life to its fullest with him in the very same apartment where she vowed that night she'd never set foot inside of again. Continuing to smile to herself as she reached the kitchen, she found it incredible how circumstances had surprisingly changed in the last few weeks. The true Herbert Chalmers was definitely not the rude, crude, obnoxious slob she'd first met. He had actually turned out to be extremely polite and charming and was certainly a dedicated professional detective. Why the change? Was it from the pride he obviously felt from being asked back to the force to work the case, or did she have an influence on his immediate character reversal? He hadn't come right out and admitted anything to her, but she sensed that he was smitten with her and how that attraction had been the major element in his sudden revival. He'd been trying to act so nonchalant around her as they worked the case, but the little things had

William M. Jones

given his true feelings away. From their first work day together, she'd caught him staring at her when he thought she wasn't looking. At first this had bothered her greatly due to her initial repugnance toward him, but by the end of their first day together, well, things just changed. She now found herself highly attracted to Herb and had even given serious thought to a shared future with him. She'd also given careful consideration to the ethical problems involved by becoming emotionally and physically attracted with one's working partner, but after careful consideration had rejected that dilemma. Theirs wasn't the normal working relationship. She was only temporarily assigned to this police force for six months for the exchange program and Herb wasn't actually on the force any longer - he was retired and had only been recalled for the singular purpose of catching the Slaughter House Murderer. Therefore, through all her rationalizing, she couldn't determine any moral improprieties from being with him. It was also surprising how they'd come back to his place from the Reinhold home last night. After other work days, they'd departed to their respective residences like any normal working partners, but last night, while initially heading back to the precinct, they'd basically just looked at each other without speaking and both had intuitively understood what the other desired. Then without discussing the matter, Herb had driven to his apartment where Lizabeth had freely agreed to stay. Once inside, he'd been the utmost gentleman. In actuality, Lizabeth had made the first physical move by grabbing his hand when they entered through the front door. Throughout the course of the evening they had talked endlessly, hugged, and finally kissed a few times, but nothing more and Lizabeth had been perfectly content with that level of initial physical attention. When it came time to finally call it a night, Herb had graciously offered her his bed while he'd retired to the living room couch where he was still peacefully resting. Turning from the kitchen and looking

Murder by Memory

back at Herb, Lizabeth continued smiling and shook her head. All this was so uncharacteristic for her. Fifteen years earlier she'd had a one year disastrous marriage and since that divorce she'd immersed herself in her work and hadn't allowed anyone to get personally close to her again. Back on her own detective force, she had the reputation of being the ultimate professional but also of being personally aloof and socially unapproachable. Maybe was from a deep, hidden fear of not wanting to get hurt again. Certainly she'd been on a few arranged dates over the years, but never allowed any to proceed into anything serious. Had mainly agreed to most in order to appease her few well-wishing close friends or relatives who thought she needed a man in her life. Wow, would they all be shocked with her now! And Herbert Chalmers. Why? He was probably a good twelve to fifteen years older than her and face it, his portly appearance still needed some trimming. So what was it about him? She wasn't sure, but one thing was - she was physically attracted to him for better or worse and after last night she was certain he felt the same about her. She also knew how the separate sleeping arrangement from last night wouldn't last much longer. Yes, it was totally appropriate then, and probably helped cement their mutual attraction and respect for each other, but today was a whole new day with a completely different set of rules to go by. The ice had been broken and hopefully future good times would flow.

While Lizabeth stood in the kitchen pouring her second cup of coffee of the young morning, she viewed Herb's sleepy head slowly rising above the couch cushions. "Good morning," she cheerfully greeted.

"Pinch me, quick," he responded.

"What?" Lizabeth returned.

"Pinch me because I must be dreaming."

"Why?" she asked.

"Because I see Lizabeth Barcay standing in my kitchen drinking a hot cup of coffee dressed in my old gym clothes!"

"You're not dreaming, silly, it's really me," she professed while putting down her coffee cup and proceeding back to the living room to give him a morning hug and kiss.

"Wow!" he proclaimed after they released their embrace. "I haven't felt like this in years."

"Me either," Lizabeth honestly stated.

"So, where do we go from here?" Herb questioned.

"I don't know," Lizabeth returned. "Let's just go slow and see what happens. No promises, just go with the moment. Okay?"

"Sounds good to me," Herb acknowledged.

"Now," Lizabeth said while changing the subject, "how about a big stack of pancakes for breakfast? I'm cooking."

"Sounds good, but...,"

"But what, Herb?" she questioned with a dejected tone to her lowering voice.

"Believe it or not, but I've dropped seven pounds since we first met."

"That's great, Herb. But what's that got to do with pancakes?"

"Too many carbs," he answered.

"Okay, I understand. What can I fix for you then?" she then requested with a renewed cheerfulness to her tone.

"Scrambled eggs with extra cheese and four or five slices of bacon with a big glass of water to drink."

"No coffee?" she surprisingly asked.

"Maybe later," he agreed. "Been starting my day with two big glasses of water. Want to drop another thirty pounds and when I do, I promise I'll never put them back on."

"Good for you, Herb," Lizabeth applauded as she opened his recently well stocked refrigerator and happily prepared their breakfast.

Murder by Memory

"Been a long time since I cooked for anyone other than myself," Lizabeth admitted while they sat at his small kitchen table and enjoyed their first home-cooked breakfast together. "Think I could really get used to this."

"Yeah, me too," Herb returned as he flashed her an agreeing smile.

After they finished cleaning the breakfast dishes, Lizabeth was the first to bring up a work related topic. "Herb," she slowly gained his attention with.

"What?" he asked while inwardly still finding it hard to believe she was actually here with him.

"We've still got one big problem with the case."

"I know. Who really killed Alvin?" he surprised her with.

"Exactly."

"So you're not sure Bruno did it either?"

"No, not really. I know Rita Reinhold thinks he did, and he still seems like the obvious killer, but the lie detector test."

"I know," Herb agreed, "that bothers me too. I know the polygraph isn't foolproof, but Bruno was so cool when he passed it."

"So what do we do?" she asked.

"I think we need to search Bruno's property. Maybe, just maybe, we'll get lucky and find something."

"Good idea. I can be ready in fifteen minutes," she promised.

"Take your time. You can have the shower first. Clean towels are in the hall closet. I'll call Benny and get him busy getting us a search warrant. I'll tell him I've got to swing around your place to pick you up and we'll see him at the precinct in an hour or so."

"Good plan. Also,"

"What?"

"Thanks for not telling him I was here."

"Don't think he'd believe it if I did," Herb laughed.

William M. Jones

"Yeah, you're probably right. Does seem pretty strange, doesn't it?" Lizabeth teased with a wink before pulling off the sweat shirt as she headed towards the bathroom.

Catching a glimpse of her exposed breasts as she turned the corner into the hall, Herb almost ejaculated on the spot. Not able to resist his natural urges, he decided to join Lizabeth in the shower. The once mysterious Lizabeth Barcay wasn't quite so mysterious any longer. Fate had brought them together and Herb intended to keep it that way. Benny Mitchell would simply have to wait a little longer before they came in for the search warrant. Shouldn't matter. Bruno was dead and buried and Rita Reinhold and her murderous brother, Raymond Powers, were under a heavy police guard awaiting trial. The only thing the search warrant might do is answer the question of who actually killed Alvin and since there was about a 99.9 percent chance that it had been Bruno, well, another half hour or so wouldn't make any difference - at least not in the case, but the extra time with Lizabeth in the shower might just make all the difference in the world with their future possibilities. Herb hadn't been this aroused, well, probably never. Right now he was at the ultimate peak of his sexual excitement and he sincerely hoped it would last for many, many joyous years to come.

Finally arriving at the precinct later in the morning, Herb and Lizabeth appeared more as the odd couple than as two individuals suddenly finding themselves hopelessly attracted to each other. Acting as the professional detective team they were as they walked through the precinct, no one would have ever suspected the loving rendezvous they'd just completed in Herb's shower. No way. Not with her alluring, statuesque grace and beauty compared to his balding, portly exterior. But looks can be deceiving and in this case they certainly were. Lizabeth had simply uncovered Herb's hidden charm which others had failed to witness during his recent years of personal tribulation caused by his failed

Murder by Memory

marriage to Irene coupled then with his obsession with the Slaughter House Murderer case. With the case now nearing its end, and with his sudden involvement with Lizabeth, well, Herb had transformed during the recent three weeks into a born again soul. Where he'd been despondently lost and destitute, he now had purpose and love in his life. What a difference they'd made.

"There you are. What took you so long?" Benny questioned Herb and Lizabeth as they entered his office.

"You get the warrant?" Herb returned without even addressing Benny's intrusive question.

"Yeah, it's right here. You sure you need to do this? You know, with Mrs. Reinhold's admission and all?" Benny stated.

"I think so, Benny. I know it looks more and more like Bruno killed Alvin, but we really need to find out for sure."

"Okay, then, have at it. But if you don't find anything…,"

"Yeah, I know, Benny. If we don't find anything the case will be considered closed with Bruno listed as Alvin's killer just like we suspect and Rita Reinhold reinforced."

"You got it. Any problems with that, old buddy?"

"No, not really. Would really just like to know for sure, though."

"Then get out of here and find out," Benny ordered.

Within fifteen minutes, Lizabeth and Herb arrived at Bruno's rather large estate. "Used car business must be pretty good," Lizabeth quipped upon seeing the Kojan residence for the first time.

"What's that all about?" Herb questioned upon seeing a moving truck backed into the tree lined driveway. Parking their police car, Herb and Lizabeth expeditiously approached the house. Immediately sighting Bruno's widow, Herb headed straight for her.

"Stop!" he startled Stella Kojan with. "Don't let the movers touch anything!" he ordered while flashing his detective shield. "Mrs. Kojan, I'm Detective… ,"

"I know who you are," Stella surprised him with. "I saw you and your partner at my husband's funeral, plus Bruno had talked about you after you questioned him a few weeks ago."

"Yes, ma'am. So sorry for your loss."

"Yeah, well, nothing I can do about it now," she dejectedly professed. "He was a good husband, you know?"

"I'm sure he was," Herb politely agreed before asking, "What's with the moving truck? You leaving town?"

"Just want to get on with my life, detective. Nothing left around here for me any longer."

"What about Bruno's car dealership?"

"I don't want it," she surprisingly admitted.

"Your son doesn't want it either?"

"No, and he left town right after the funeral."

"I didn't know that. Where'd he go?" Herb asked.

"Quit college about a week before his dad was killed. We thought he was doing okay, so were both dumbfounded when he suddenly dropped out."

"Where's he going?" Herb again asked.

"Joined the Army. Said he wanted to get out of these parts and see the world. Packed his car and left from the funeral for one of his college friend's house down in Texas. Said he'd stay there until reporting for basic training next month."

"I can see why you're ready to leave, then. Did you sell out already?"

"Yes. Buyers were lining up as soon as word of Bruno's death got out. He had quite a lucrative business, you know?"

"Yes, I noticed. Hope you got a fair price for the place," Herb then sincerely stated as he honestly empathized with her sudden plight.

Murder by Memory

"You won't have to worry about me, detective. I'll be okay."

"Good," Herb replied.

"Now, what's this all about?" Stella questioned.

"Ma'am, we have a search warrant for your residence and the dealership."

"What for?"

"Well, to be honest, we still think Bruno had something to do with Alvin's death."

"That's ridiculous!" Stella Kojan firmly stated. "My husband was a lot of things, but he definitely wasn't a murderer."

"Then you don't have any objection to us having a look around?"

"No, be my guest. Please by quick, though. The movers are being paid by the hour."

"Won't take very long, I promise," Herb informed Mrs. Kojan as two uniformed patrol units turned into the driveway to assist with the search. Handing the four man moving crew $40, Herb informed them to take an extended lunch break which they cheerfully agreed to.

Luckily for Herb, the movers had only arrived about ten minutes before he and Lizabeth did so nothing had been packed up yet or removed from the house. It took Herb's team about an hour of searching before Herb was satisfied they wouldn't find anything at the house. After thanking Stella Kojan for her cooperation and wishing her well, Herb and his assistants departed for Bruno's old used car dealership. There they met with the same results - they didn't find anything suspicious in his private office. Bruno's old assistant, who was running the place until the new owners took over, did provide Herb with one interesting bit of information though - Bruno had a hunting cabin on a lake about an hour or so away. Needing to know more about it, and to learn if he had any other property, Herb and Lizabeth returned to the Kojan residence.

"Sorry to trouble you again, Mrs. Kojan," Herb interrupted Stella with when they arrived and found her observing the moving events from the comfort of a lawn chair placed under a shade tree in the front yard next to the driveway.

"Didn't expect to see you again, detective."

"Yes, ma'am. One more question we need to ask, though."

"Sure, what is it?" she inquired without hesitation.

"Did your husband own any other property besides this house and the dealership?"

"Oh, yes, the hunting cabin. I'd forgotten about it."

"He go up there very much?"

"Used to. Don't think he's been there in two or three years, though."

"Anybody else use the property?"

"No, not any more. Bruno had some hunting buddies years ago, but they all kind of lost interest. Was a great place to go on a nice summer day, though. Fishing was pretty good. But after Victor Jr. grew up and had other interests… ,"

"Like girls?" Herb added.

"Yes," Stella smiled, "definitely. Once he got into high school he didn't seem to want to go up there with his dad any longer so Bruno quit going also. As far as I know the place is all boarded up. Not much up there, really. Pretty primitive cabin with a small storage shed. Place doesn't even have electricity or running water. Used a hand-pumped well for water and Bruno kept a portable generator in the shed for small electrical needs whenever I was up there. Over the years we talked about fixing the place up and using it more, but never seemed to do anything about it."

"I understand," Herb consoled. "Thanks again Mrs. Kojan. We shouldn't have to bother you again," he stated before departing and leaving her to the uncertainty of her future.

Murder by Memory

Herb and Lizabeth then proceeded back to the precinct to brief Benny. They also needed him to make arrangements for a new search warrant and to coordinate with the local sheriff's office up by Bruno's cabin to meet them and assist with the search since the cabin was outside the city's jurisdiction. Benny assured Herb and Lizabeth all arrangements would be coordinated during the time it would take them to drive to the cabin. They were then happily surprised to find the local sheriff and his deputy waiting at the cabin when they arrived. After briefing them on the case and the purpose for the search, they decided to take a look inside the storage shed first. It was about a 12 by 15 rickety wooden structure with two small windows and a two sided opening door locked with a rusty pad lock. A pair of bolt cutters from the sheriff's trunk had the shed opened in no time. Inside was the generator Mrs. Kojan had mentioned along with assorted fishing and yard instruments. Lifting an old tarp in the back of the shed, Herb discovered an old trunk. Using the bolt cutters again to open it, he at first found only some old clothing. Lifting the clothes from the trunk, Herb suddenly came across a dark green plastic trash bag with something heavy inside it.

"Bring the flashlight over here," Herb directed the sheriff since he needed better lighting.

Wearing plastic gloves, Herb carefully opened the bag and lifted out a pistol.

"That what you're looking for, detective?" the sheriff asked.

"I think so," Herb replied while staring straight at Lizabeth.

"I'll be!" she proclaimed. "It is a slaughter house pistol, isn't it?"

"That it is, Lizabeth. That it is. Sure looks like Rita Reinhold was right."

William M. Jones

"Guess Bruno suddenly snapped from all the mental pressure of worrying about Alvin over all those years and finally decided to do something about it."

"But he killed the wrong person," Herb reminded her.

"I know. That's the sad part in all of this."

"He really had us all fooled when he took the lie detector test."

"Best I'd ever seen," Lizabeth declared.

"Better get this to forensics to check for prints before briefing Benny," Herb then announced.

"Hey, detective, look at these," the sheriff's deputy suddenly stated.

"What is it?" Herb asked.

"Latex gloves. Found them in this garbage pile over here."

"What do you make of it, Herb?" Lizabeth asked.

"Not sure. If there's no prints on the pistol could be that Bruno wore the gloves when he killed Alvin. Better take them to the lab also."

"Good idea," Lizabeth agreed.

After searching the cabin with negative results, Herb thanked the local sheriff and his deputy for their assistance and he and Lizabeth then headed straight back to the city with their newfound evidence. Once at the police lab, it only took a matter of minutes to discover the pistol was covered with Bruno's prints; and only Bruno's prints. Forensics didn't find anything additional with the latex gloves so Herb decided they'd been used for other purposes at the cabin and weren't connected to the pistol. Didn't make any sense to wear the gloves and also leave prints all over the pistol. So, as far as Herb and Lizabeth were now concerned, they'd inform Benny that Bruno had indeed killed Alvin so now the only thing left with the case was the trial of Raymond Powers for the four murders of Daryl Woods, Tony Austin, Steven Watts and Victor Bruno Kojan. Since he was known to be the Slaughter House Murderer, the only remaining

Murder by Memory

variable actually was how culpable would a jury find him due to mitigating circumstances surrounding the first three murders and then with his diminished mental capacity while killing Bruno. Whatever the outcome, Herb and Lizabeth knew it would be an exciting trial and couldn't wait for it to begin, but in the meantime they'd head on back to his place to resume where they'd left off earlier this morning when they had to leave the shower to go to work.

William M. Jones

CHAPTER NINETEEN

Judge Sandra Heath sat alone in her chambers, elbows on her mahogany desk, hands clasped together on the top of her head and contemplated her recent assignment - trial judge for the Slaughter House Murderer Case. Of all the available judges in the district, it was unequivocally a testament to her creditability that she was singled out to preside over what most likely was the biggest case the local area had witnessed in probably a quarter of a century. On the other hand, though, the case could possibly prove catastrophic for her political aspirations if handled incorrectly. To put it simply, the case would either make or break her future. Forty-eight and still single, she was a workaholic with an eye set on the governor's mansion. If things progressed as she planned, then next year she'd win election as the state's new attorney general and then four years later would make a run for governor. Her whole adult life had been geared in that direction and she'd purposely avoided any serious personal relationships along the way for fear of interfering in her ability to achieve her lofty goal. But being single and extremely attractive, many of her political rivals hinted that she was a lesbian, but couldn't ever produce one iota of reliable evidence. She fully understood, though, how even the appearance of lesbianism could be detrimental to her political ambitions so she was planning on making a concerted effort to appear at public social events with numerous high profile male companions. Having been celibate since her adventurous college years, she didn't desire any new romantic commitments, but fully understood how for appearances sake she positively needed to dispel all the ugly lesbian connotations if her master plan was to succeed. Being a former highly successful prosecuting attorney, coupled with her current notoriety from her ten year judgeship, she knew all the right

Murder by Memory

influential men who would be more than willing to subject themselves to public scrutiny and viewing for the honor of being her escort. Her ambitions weren't a secret to those in the political arena, so any male helping her would most definitely be improving his own political or business future by doing so. In the dog-eat-dog world she lived in, the unwritten rule was always of how if you scratch my back, then I'll scratch yours - go against me and I'll bury you when I succeed! What a conniving jungle politics revolved in, but to forego it was pure professional suicide. And now the Slaughter House Murderer Case. Come across to the public as the fair and impartial judge she knew she was and she might as well head straight for the governor's mansion, but let this case get out of hand and be seen as a media frenzy and circus event like the O.J. Simpson trial out in California and she might as well retire right now. She held her future in her own hands and was determined not to let it slip away. She would run a tight ship with this case; no doubt about it. And even if she wasn't paranoid about her own political future, she'd be forced to walk a straight line with this case - any judge in their right mind would have to due to the case's unusual nature. It was like none other she nor any of her colleagues could think of. Actually, it was unlike any they'd studied during their law school years, either. This wasn't a case about guilt or not, it boiled down to how guilty was Raymond Powers and not just for one murder, but for the three murders all those years ago for which there wasn't any statute of limitation, and now for the murder of Victor Kojan. Normally when someone confessed to a murder, the assigned judge would pronounce sentencing or agree to the plea bargaining arrangement struck between the defense and prosecuting attorneys, but this case was oh so different. The only plea bargain allowed was to Rita Reinhold for confessing her brother's guilt and for her testimony against him and also for admitting her assistance with the first three murders - these facts alone were highly unprecedented. The grand jury had returned an indictment against Mr. Powers for criminal homicide for all four murders due to the confession, but had ordered the court to conduct the trial to determine the defendant's culpability with each due to possible mental anguish and helping a friend with his right for self-defense with the first three and then the question of mental competency dealing with the last murder due to Mr. Powers' altered mental thought capacity. No doubt about it, this was definitely going to become a landmark case and Sandra Heath's future would plainly be determined by the outcome. She'd be under the microscope and scrutinized like she'd never been before and as witnessed during the Simpson trial, the press would analyze everything from the clothes she wore to her hair style to the fact that she was still single at age forty-eight - none of which held any relevance with the outcome of the trial, but details she all too well knew the press would dwell on and would thus have a tremendous affect on her political goals. One week to go before the trial was to begin and already network and cable news groups were setting up shop outside the courthouse. How she hoped for a speedy trial. Needed to put closure to this case, and quick. Removing her hands from the top of her head, Judge Heath got up and walked to the window at the back of her office. Through it she had a panoramic view of a small city park located directly behind the courthouse and she greatly enjoyed just peering out her window on pretty days like today and simply watching the birds or squirrels as they scampered among the century old trees. Their only thought being of where their next nut or seed would come from, not the great moral issues of the frail human race which she was faced with. Many times she wished she could simply trade places with them, but realistically knew that was out of the question. She actually lived for the law; it consumed her and was her total life - for good or bad. Hearing a knock at her door, she responded, "Come in. it's open."

Murder by Memory

"Staring at the birds again, Sandra?" Public Defender Wyatt Barfield asked his old friend as he and Assistant District Attorney Marilyn Sparks entered Judge Heath's office. "Do you know Miss Sparks, Judge?" he next formally inquired.

"Not officially, Wyatt," Sandra answered as she approached and greeted the young prosecutor who was visibly nervous from being called into the legendary judge's office for the first time. "Let's get right to the point, shall we?" she next declared.

"What do you mean?" Wyatt asked.

"You know exactly what I mean, Wyatt," Judge Heath pronounced while she looked straight at the cantankerous old defense attorney. "We've known each other too long to play games."

"Agreed," Wyatt stated. "What are you looking for?"

"Facts, and facts only. Understand?"

"I get your drift. You want this trial to be over quickly."

"Exactly. The sooner the better for all of us."

"No argument about that."

"Wyatt, that means no showboating."

"Who, me?" he sheepishly returned. "What are you really trying to tell us, Sandra?" he next asked his old compadre sensing her apprehension with this case.

"I want just the facts from both of you. Understand?" she directed while looking directly at both attorneys individually for a few intense seconds. "I've declared a closed courtroom," she next announced.

"You what?" Wyatt almost exploded.

"You heard me. It's fully within my right to do so. I won't allow any cameras inside for the trial and I plan to personally screen the limited press I'll allow inside. Also, I'm ordering both of you and your associates not to speak with the press for the duration of the trial."

"Why?" Wyatt demanded.

"I think you know why, Wyatt? You saw what happened at the Simpson trial. Well, that's not going to happen here. No way. I won't allow this trial to become a media circus and ruin careers like that one did. Too much is at stake with this one."

"For who? Powers or you?" Wyatt bantered.

"That's not fair, Wyatt, and you know it," Sandra fired back.

"Sorry," he apologized while realizing how right he was in knowing how this case would most likely determine the political future of his old friend. Knowing this and really wanting to see her succeed, he then continued, "Okay, I'll agree to play by your rules with this one, Sandra. I'll simply present my case as best I can without my normal, as you call it, showboating, and let the jury do their job."

"That's all I'm asking for. Want to keep things as unemotional as possible. Just present your facts and let's get on with it. If there was any doubt about the defendant's guilt I wouldn't ask, but there isn't. This case is only about the defendant's degree of guilt, not whether or not he is or isn't, so let's allow the jury to decide the facts for what they are and not complicate the situation by playing on their emotions. Any questions?"

"None from me," Wyatt said. "I actually agree with you on this one, Sandra."

"Thanks, how about you Miss Sparks? You haven't said much."

"You won't have any problems from me, either. I think you'll find I'm a rather cut and dry individual as it is. I like to get right to the heart of an issue so I also agree that it's in the best interest of the court, the city and everyone involved that we conduct a swift and unbiased trial. This case needs closure and if anyone's to get publicity from it, let it be the jury for whatever they decide since that's the real issue here since no one has ever been tried for murder before with Mr. Powers' mental condition."

Murder by Memory

"Good," Judge Heath returned, "then I guess I'll see you both in a week." After the two lawyers left her office, she returned to staring out the window and dreaming about her future. She wasn't about to let one Raymond Powers stand between her and the governor's mansion. No way. If anything, she'd make sure this case accelerated her timeline. Governor Heath - sure had a nice sound to it and the first female governor of the state also. Yes, if everything went as she hoped, well, the governor's mansion might just only be a stepping stone to even bigger things. Crazier things had happened.

CHAPTER TWENTY

Judge Sandra Heath stood by the window at the back of her office and smiled as she watched two playful squirrels performing tag as they leaped from bending branch to bending branch among the city park's massive old trees. What a life they had, she thought. Not a care in the world except to chase each other among the trees and most likely hassle each other for the rights to the best nest or biggest cache of buried nuts. Little did they know, nor did they care, that the biggest trial in years was about to start inside the massive courthouse building adjoining their small world inside their protective park. But Sandra Heath sure knew. She was glad the trial was finally going to start and was also excited at the future possibilities it could open for her, but on the other hand she was quite nervous and her sweaty palms attested to that fact. Not wanting to take any chances of getting caught up in the publicity of the trial, and especially not wanting to get cornered by the over zealous press before the trial started, she'd remained sequestered inside the courthouse for the last two days and her only contact to the outside world had been through the TV and conversations with co-workers during normal working hours. Having a small microwave and refrigerator in her office, along with a private bath equipped with a shower, she'd subsisted quite comfortably while waiting for the trial to begin. Having spent countless other nights in her office during her tenure as a judge, she found her couch quite adequate as a bed and didn't view the few days of holing up inside her office as a major inconvenience. Looking at her watch, she took one last look in the mirror, buttoned and straightened her judge's robe, took a deep breath and excitedly headed for the courtroom. The court clerk would be calling the court to session in a matter of minutes. She'd

Murder by Memory

been informed that all concerned were properly assembled and simply awaiting her arrival.

"All rise, this court is now in session. The Honorable Sandra Heath presiding," the clerk loudly bellowed as Sandra made her way to her judge's bench and quickly sat down. Scanning the courtroom, she first observed the fourteen person jury and could sense the nervous anxiety they must be feeling. She'd been extremely pleased with the voir dire to pick this jury. Many times that was an excruciating long and drawn out process, but for a trial of this magnitude it had progressed rather easily. Fifty prospective jurors had initially been summoned to appear for possible jury duty. One by one each prospective juror had been questioned with the same query as to if they knew, personally or professionally, any of the witnesses, parties involved in the case or either of the attorneys. They were also questioned concerning if they had a past criminal record or negative feelings toward the criminal justice system and lastly if they'd ever served as a member of a court before. The pool of fifty was swiftly reduced to twenty-seven. Most had been excused due to previous business dealings with Victor Kojan at his used car dealership. Two had used Wyatt Barfield as their personal lawyer before and a few were released for minor prior criminal records. Lastly, one retired military man was excused since he'd conducted numerous summary court-martials during his later years of active duty in the service. The remaining twenty-seven were then subjected to individual questioning by the defense and prosecution and either through their challenge for cause or right of pre-emptory challenge, the number was eventually reduced to fourteen. The jury now sitting before Judge Heath consisted of eight women and six men. Average age was around forty-five and ten of the fourteen had at least a high school education. The racial mix of the jury was eight whites, four African Americans, and two orientals. The final voting jury would consist of twelve members only, so two of the jurors sitting before the court today would only serve as alternates. The two alternates hadn't been notified yet because it was important for them to pay close attention during the trial in case their status was upgraded to regular member due to release of one of the others for medical or other reasons. Judge Heath also understood how the members of the jury also hoped for a speedy trial since they'd been ordered sequestered for the trial's duration. Sandra next glanced at the defense and prosecuting attorneys and saw the anticipation visibly present in their facial expressions. Raymond Powers sat quietly with Wyatt Barfield to his one side and his sister, Rita Reinhold, on his other. Two sheriff's deputies would stand off to their side at all times. Marilyn Sparks sat alone at the prosecution table and Sandra was somewhat surprised that she wasn't flanked by more experienced members from the District Attorney's office. Either she was extremely competent or else assistance would arrive at a later time. Detectives Herbert Chalmers and Lizabeth Barcay had been allowed inside for the trial and were seated one row behind the defense. The Chief of Police and the mayor had both decided to stay away in order to avoid any possible problems with the swarming press. Benny Mitchell would be allowed inside whenever he was available and felt like observing. Seated directly behind Marilyn Sparks were various surviving members from the Woods, Austin and Watts families. They'd all assembled to hopefully see justice served and then to finally put closure to the death of their loved ones. Conspicuously absent from the audience were Stella and Victor Jr. Kojan. Stella had informed the court she was content with her new life far removed from here and also stated how she'd suffered enough grief with the loss of her husband and didn't feel she'd be able to mentally stand up to actually observing the trial. Victor Jr. was absent because he'd left the area while waiting to start basic training with the Army.

Murder by Memory

Representation for the Kojan family was then relegated to one of Bruno's male second cousins who resided in the local area and had also previously been a minor business partner at Bruno's car dealership. Seated a few rows behind the family members was the small press corps Sandra had reluctantly allowed access to the proceedings. Completing her survey of the courtroom, she ordered, "Be seated."

"Case number 27-322024 of the state V. Raymond Powers," the court clerk clearly read before sitting down.

"Are counsel ready to proceed?" Judge Heath then inquired of both attorneys. When both acknowledged they were, she then directed the prosecution to begin her opening statement.

Marilyn Sparks, impeccably dressed and giving the appearance of being ten years older than she actually was, got up, walked to the front of her table where she first addressed the judge, and then addressed the jury. "Your Honor, members of the jury. My name is Marilyn Sparks and I will be representing the people of this state in the prosecution of Mr. Raymond Powers for the murders of Daryl Woods, Tony Austin, Steven Watts and Victor Kojan. All present understand the uniqueness of this case as it is unlike any other murder case ever tried in this court before. Mr. Powers is guilty of all four murders and that is a given fact. The prosecution will show that Mr. Powers willingly committed all four murders and should be held accountable as such regardless of his current mental condition. Murder does not have a statute of limitations and when all is said and done, for the families seated behind me and for the memory of the deceased, I know you'll do the right thing and find the defendant responsible for the murders he did commit." Finishing her statement, Marilyn slowly looked each juror directly in the eyes, then stared at Raymond Powers and his sister, Rita Reinhold, for a good five seconds before turning towards the deceased's relatives, closed her eyes and nodded, and then returned to her seat.

William M. Jones

After the prosecution took her seat, Wyatt Barfield got up to present the defense's side of the story. "Your Honor, and ladies and gentlemen of the jury, I'm Wyatt Barfield. The prosecutor, Miss Sparks, wants you to believe that the defendant, Raymond Powers," Wyatt stated as he turned and pointed his right hand towards Raymond who was quietly sitting erect dressed in a new suit and groomed with a fresh haircut, "is a cold blooded killer. Quite the contrary. I'll show how he committed the first three murders in self-defense. Not for himself, but for his sister's dear friend and future husband, Alvin Reinhold. You see, Alvin Reinhold had been unmercifully harassed for years by the school bully, Victor Bruno Kojan. Unable to act on his own, and fearing for his safety as well as his own life, Mr. Reinhold did the only thing he possibly could do when he felt the police wouldn't protect him - he enlisted the aid of his girlfriend's brother to act on his behalf. What Mr. Powers actually committed when he killed Daryl Woods, Tony Austin and Steven Watts was third party self-defense. Therefore, due to his friend's and then his own mental anguish over the unresolvable situation, Mr. Powers isn't guilty of murder. The real guilty person in all of this was actually Victor Kojan. If he hadn't of been a bully, none of this would have ever occurred. So you see, if anyone is really responsible for the murders, and in the end for his own also, it was Victor Kojan, not Raymond Powers. Mr. Powers was just defending his friend and in his own mind was also still defending him when he killed Victor Kojan some twenty-four years later. Mr. Powers doesn't belong in jail, he belongs in a special care facility until his sister serves the term of her plea bargain agreement and then should be remanded to her care. That's how justice would best be served and would also put the other Victor Kojan like bullies of the world on notice. Thank you."

Murder by Memory

After Wyatt Barfield returned to his seat, Judge Heath informed the prosecution, "You may call your first witness now."

Standing, Marilyn announced, "The prosecution calls the defendant, Mr. Raymond Powers."

"I object!" Wyatt quickly shouted while jumping up and giving Marilyn a startled look.

"What do you object to?" Judge Heath demanded. "You know he's on the witness list, don't you?"

"Yes, Your Honor, but I didn't expect him to be first."

"I feel it's important for the jury to hear from the defendant right away," Marilyn added knowing she needed to go for the jugular and set the tone early with the jury. She realized they understood how he was guilty, but wanted them to hear it from him right up front so it would leave a better lasting impression throughout the trial.

"You're overruled, Mr. Barfield. It shouldn't matter when the prosecution calls the defendant. You may continue, Miss Sparks."

"Thank you, Your Honor."

Rita Reinhold then told her brother it was okay and, as previously agreed, accompanied him to the witness stand.

After Raymond was sworn in, Marilyn began. "Please state your full name for the record," she requested.

"Raymond Edward Powers."

"Did you kill Daryl Woods in 1975?" she directly questioned without beating around the bush with any unnecessary preliminary questions.

Thinking to himself for second as his mind clicked back in time some twenty-four years, Ray finally answered in a soft tone, "Yes."

Marilyn Sparks then surveyed the expressions on the juror's faces and realized she had their undivided attention. She then continued. "Did you also kill Tony Austin?"

"Yes," Ray again softly admitted.

"And did you also kill Steven Watts?"

"Yes."

"Did you plan to kill Victor Kojan back in 1975?"

"Yes," Ray again admitted.

"Why didn't you?"

"Because I got sick the day I was supposed to kill him."

"Please explain, Mr. Powers."

"I went into a coma from encephalitis."

"So you admit that if you wouldn't have gotten sick that you would have also killed Victor Kojan back in 1975?"

"Yes, that's true."

"Did you then finally kill Victor Kojan this year?"

"Is he dead?"

"Yes, Mr. Powers, he is. Did you kill him?"

"No, I don't think so."

"Thank you, Mr. Powers, that's all," Prosecutor Sparks stated as she turned toward the defense. "Your witness," she then allowed.

"Nothing at this time," Wyatt Barfield informed the judge as he watched Rita lead her brother from the stand back to his seat. Once they were seated back beside him, Wyatt then requested, "Sorry, Your Honor, but I do have some questions for the witness. With your permission, I request he retake the stand."

Shooting Wyatt a disapproving stare since he'd promised no showboating with this case, Judge Heath reluctantly agreed. "Okay. The witness will retake the stand. But let me warn you, though, Mr. Barfield. The next time you state you don't have any questions, that will be your finally answer. Understand?"

"Yes, Your Honor. I promise the court it won't happen again."

"Good, then you may proceed."

Wyatt had purposely used this delaying tactic to gain affect with the jury. He fully understood Marilyn's reasoning for calling Ray to the stand first and the reason for her blunt, direct questioning. He could tell it had a

Murder by Memory

dramatic affect with the jury so he also needed to make points with them, and fast.

"Good morning, Mr. Powers," Wyatt began.

"Good morning."

"Do you know my name?"

"No, can't say as I do," Ray declared while the entire jury looked puzzled from the fact that the defendant didn't know his own lawyer's name.

"Do you know that pretty, young lady sitting over there?" Wyatt next asked while pointing at Marilyn Sparks.

"No, can't say as I do," Ray responded.

"You haven't ever talked with her?"

"No, not that I can recall."

"Ray, have you ever been on this witness stand before?" Wyatt next asked.

"No, don't believe so."

"Can you tell this court the medical ramifications from the encephalitis you had back in 1975?"

"My memory since then isn't any longer than a minute or two," Ray honestly answered.

"Just since you fell sick?"

"Yes."

"What about prior to becoming sick?"

"No major problem there."

"How so?"

"If I concentrate really hard I can recall facts from that period in my life."

"Did you recently kill Victor Kojan?"

"I don't remember."

"Thank you, Mr. Powers. That's all."

Rita then led Raymond back to his seat at the defense table.

"You may call your next witness, Miss Sparks," Judge Heath then continued.

"The prosecution calls Rita Reinhold."

Patting Ray on his hand to comfort him, Rita left his side and took the witness stand. Once sworn in and seated, Marilyn Sparks began questioning her.

"For the record, please state your name."

"Rita Marie Powers Reinhold."

"And what is your relationship to the defendant?"

"His sister."

"And your relationship with Alvin Reinhold?"

"First his girlfriend and later his wife."

"Did you help your brother commit the three murders back in 1975?"

"Yes."

"Did you also help him kill Victor Kojan this year?"

"Yes," Rita again admitted.

"Did you turn your brother into the police as the notorious Slaughter House Murderer?"

"Yes, I did."

"For the record, Mrs. Reinhold, did you agree to a plea bargain in exchange for admitting your part in the murders and for your testimony?"

"Yes," Rita simply stated.

"And what are the terms of that plea bargain?"

"As soon as the trial's over, I'll be spending eighteen months in a minimum security facility."

"So you admit that your brother committed four murders known as the Slaughter House Murderer Case and that you were an accessory to all four murders."

"Yes," Rita again affirmed while tenderly looking at her brother.

"One last question, Mrs. Reinhold. With your brother's short term memory problem, how did he remember he wanted to kill Victor Kojan? I mean, the defense has skillfully demonstrated to this court here today that Raymond's short term memory doesn't last more than a minute or two. Seems quite odd, then, that he could hold his

Murder by Memory

thought about wanting to kill Mr. Kojan long enough to actually do it. How was that possible?"

"He wrote himself notes."

"Notes?"

"That's correct. When he first had the thought, he wrote it down and then kept it with him where he could find it in order to remind himself."

"Are you telling us that he consciously plotted Victor Kojan's murder before doing so?"

Looking directly at her brother and lowering her head, Rita softly answered, "Yes."

"Thank you, Mrs. Reinhold, that's all I have."

"Mr. Barfield?" Judge Heath then asked.

"Nothing at this time, Your Honor."

"Okay, then, Miss Sparks, call your next witness."

"The prosecution calls Detective Herbert Chalmers."

After Herb took the stand, Marilyn Sparks started her examination. "For the record, detective, please state your name."

"Herbert Lloyd Chalmers."

"Are you presently a detective on the city's police force?"

"In a way."

"Either you are or you're not, detective," the prosecution declared.

"I'm actually retired," Herb explained. "I was brought back as a special detective consultant just to work this case."

"Why? Doesn't the police force have enough competent detectives?" Marilyn next skillfully questioned in order for the jury to realize Herb's special qualifications with this case.

"Because the Slaughter House Murderer Case was my first big case and I devoted my entire career to trying to solve it."

"So you're the police force's expert on the case?"

"Exactly!" Herb proudly boasted.

"What type of weapon did the defendant use to kill all of his victims?"

"A slaughter house pistol."

" Please explain, detective."

"Was a .22 caliber pistol designed to kill cattle in slaughter houses. Actually fires a blank round which then forces a metal rod out the end of the barrel which kills instantly by penetrating the brain."

"So the killer actually had to place the weapon directly on the back of each victim's neck when he pulled the trigger?"

"That's correct."

"And on what particular night did Mr. Powers commit all the murders using this slaughter house pistol?"

"He only killed when there was a new moon."

"Do you know why, detective?"

"No, not exactly."

"Care to venture a guess?"

"Objection!" Wyatt Barfield immediately shouted. "Question calls for speculation, not facts."

Judge Heath quickly responded with, "Overruled. I'd like to hear what the witness has to say."

Herb then informed the court, "Mrs. Reinhold told my partner and me during our investigation that Mr. Powers was attending a community college at the time he came down with encephalitis with hopes of getting accepted into a major university's astronomy program. My guess is he was somehow fascinated with new moons."

"Like mesmerized by them?" Marilyn suggested.

"Something like that. There are numerous documented cases of various cults using full moons for their rituals. For some strange reason, then, new moon nights thrilled Mr. Powers."

"Where were all four murder victim's bodies found, Detective Chalmers?"

Murder by Memory

"In a park."

"The same park?"

"No, the first two and then Mr. Kojan's were in the same park, but Steven Watts was found in a different one."

"Were they murdered where they were found?"

"Mrs. Reinhold confessed to luring all the victims to other locations."

"And then she and her brother staged the bodies at the parks. Is that correct, detective?"

"Yes."

"Why, detective?"

"So no physical evidence of the actual murder scene could be found."

"Are you saying, then, that Mr. Powers and his sister methodically plotted each murder as to the exact night each would be committed and then also staged the bodies to throw off the police?"

"Yes," Herb again answered.

"Doesn't sound like self-defense to me," Marilyn declared. "Withdrawn," she next stated. "I have no further questions for this witness. Thank you Detective Chalmers."

"Mr. Barfield, you may cross examine the witness," Judge Heath allowed.

Walking up before Herb, Wyatt then asked, "Did Victor Kojan kill Alvin Reinhold?"

"Yes," Herb replied.

"And how do you know that, detective?"

"Because we found a slaughter house pistol in a storage shed at Mr. Kojan's hunting cabin."

"And how do you know Mr. Kojan used that particular weapon to kill Mr. Reinhold?"

"Because his prints were the only ones on the pistol and then DNA tests positively matched DNA found on the pistol's protruding metal rod to Mr. Reinhold."

"So then, detective, couldn't the defendant have killed Victor Kojan out of fear that he might also kill his sister?"

"It's possible, I guess."

"And wouldn't that be self-defense? You don't have to answer that, detective. By the way, did you ever find the murder weapon which Mr. Powers used for all the murders?"

"No, we only have his and his sister's confessions."

"Thank you, detective. I have no further questions at this time," Wyatt declared as he smiled at the jury and returned to the defense table.

"Miss Sparks, does the prosecution have any additional witnesses?" Judge Heath then requested.

"No, Your Honor."

Banging her gavel, Sandra then declared the court adjourned until nine o'clock tomorrow morning and informed Wyatt Barfield to be prepared to present the defense's case. She then retired to the sanctuary of her office.

As Herb and Lizabeth departed the courthouse building, they were bombarded with questions from the waiting press. Not wanting to say the wrong thing, they repeatedly stated 'no comment' as they fought their way through the clamoring crowd and proceeded to their car. With no other duties to perform other than to partake in this trial, they quickly adjourned to Herb's apartment where they made love several times during the night and also discussed their future plans. One good thing for them was Lizabeth's time in the exchange program had recently been extended so she wouldn't be forced to leave before the trial was over.

At nine sharp in the morning, the court clerk called the courtroom to order and Sandra Heath emerged from another isolated night alone in her secluded office to preside over the case. She started with, "Mr. Barfield, you may call the defense's first witness."

"Thank you, Your Honor. I call the defendant, Mr. Raymond Powers."

Murder by Memory

Marilyn Sparks was somewhat surprised by this move since Wyatt had cross examined the defendant yesterday.

After Raymond was sworn in again, Wyatt asked only one question. "In 1975 did you kill Daryl Woods, Tony Austin and Steven Watts and also plan to kill Victor Kojan because they threatened to hurt Alvin Reinhold?"

"Yes," Ray responded after just a few seconds of pondering the question and recalling the past.

"Thank you. No further questions. Unless the prosecution cares to cross examine, the defense calls Rita Reinhold."

When Marilyn Sparks stated she didn't, Rita promptly returned to the witness stand after first escorting Raymond back to his seat at the defense table.

"Mrs. Reinhold, why did your brother commit all the murders?"

"To protect Alvin."

"Why couldn't Alvin protect himself?"

"You didn't know Alvin, did you Mr. Barfield?"

"No, can't say as I did."

"Well, if you would've, then you'd have understood how he couldn't defend himself from Bruno and his gang. You see, my husband was one of the most sensitive and caring individuals you'd ever want to meet. Wasn't a violent bone in his body, but he truly feared for his safety after Bruno and the others beat him up in the park one night."

From his sight angle slightly behind and off to the side, Herbert Chalmers viewed a puzzled expression on Raymond Powers' face as his sister described Bruno's and his gang's beating of Alvin. He couldn't understand why Raymond suddenly appeared so confused.

"Was this the first encounter Alvin had ever had with Bruno?" Wyatt next inquired.

"Heavens no," Rita declared. "Been going on for years."

"Why?"

"Who knows. Maybe because Alvin was an easy target being how he was slightly different than other boys his age."

"How so?"

"He had a slight build, wore thick glasses, wasn't very athletic and was very smart. Loved to read and write poetry instead of playing sports."

"I see," Wyatt replied. "In other words, Alvin was a nerd."

"You could say that," Rita agreed while shooting him a disapproving stare for using the nerd word.

Sensing her uncomfort, Wyatt clarified his remark. "Please don't be offended, Mrs. Reinhold. That's just how our society seems to be. Bullies are always looking for an easy target. And isn't that what Victor Kojan was - a bully?"

"Definitely!" Rita proclaimed.

"Please tell this court how Mr. Kojan bullied and harassed your husband before the night he actually beat him up and threatened further bodily harm."

"Certainly. Bruno actually started bullying Alvin way back in second or third grade."

"Remember any particular incidents?"

"Yes. One day while Alvin was playing tetherball during recess, Bruno wrapped the rope around him pinning him to the pole and then punched him in the stomach. Also called him 'four eyes' since he wore thick glasses even in those days."

"What else, Mrs. Reinhold?"

"After that incident, Bruno constantly called Alvin names and this continued until our senior year when after getting beaten up, Alvin decided he'd simply had enough."

"So that's when you asked your brother to help?"

"Exactly. Alvin had the right to live a peaceful life and not one in constant fear for his safety."

"Why didn't he tell his parents or go to the police?"

"We were both afraid neither could help and then if Bruno found out we'd told on him, well, he'd just get more violent. And we couldn't take that chance."

"So you took matters into your own hands to protect Alvin?"

"Yes."

"Thank you, Mrs. Reinhold. I don't have any further questions."

"Miss Sparks," Judge Heath next inquired.

"One question, Your Honor," Marilyn responded as she approached the witness.

Wyatt then gave Marilyn a quizzical look as they passed each other on their ways to and from the witness stand.

"Mrs. Reinhold, how was your father killed?" Marilyn asked.

Pausing for a second before answering, she finally stated, "He was killed in a case of road rage."

"Isn't it true that he was shot point-blank by a bully during that incident?"

"Yes, that's correct," Rita acknowledged.

"So your brother had it in for bullies? You don't have to answer that," Marilyn stated as she turned towards the jury and restated her statement. "So your brother had it in for bullies!" She then turned towards Judge Heath and said, "No further questions, Your Honor."

Herb and Lizabeth each turned and simultaneously looked at each other before Herb softly whispered, "Damn, but she's good." Lizabeth simply nodded in agreement realizing how even though Marilyn Sparks was young and relatively untested, she definitely knew how to make her point and influence the jury.

"Mr. Barfield, call your next witness," Judge Heath then ordered after the buzz in the courtroom settled down from Marilyn's pointed statement.

"The defense calls Doctor Stanley Bratt."

William M. Jones

After Doctor Bratt was sworn in, Wyatt began his questioning. "Doctor Bratt, the jurors already understand that the defendant suffers from a memory loss due to a case of encephalitis, but I think it's important for them to learn exactly how he got the disease."

"Certainly," the doctor agreed while at the same time being slightly curious of how his testimony could change any thing. "Was one of the most bizarre cases I ever treated."

"Is that why you remember it after all these years?"

"Yes. When Mr. Powers was first brought into the emergency room, he was already deep in a coma."

"What did you do then?" Wyatt asked.

"Due to swelling with his brain, we first administered penicillin to try to comfort him while we tested all the various possibilities."

"And what was the final diagnosis, doctor?"

"Mr. Powers contracted encephalitis from his girlfriend. You see, she had cold sores which are technically caused by Herpes Simplex Type 1. So you see, by kissing his girlfriend with her cold sores, the herpes virus entered his system and lodged in his brain causing the encephalitis."

"And the encephalitis caused Mr. Powers' memory loss?"

"That's correct."

"What other problems did Mr. Powers have when he finally came out of his coma?"

"He had a severe speech problem and basically had to learn to talk all over again."

"Pretty sad case, wasn't it, Doctor Bratt?"

"Without a doubt, one of the saddest I've ever seen. I mean, what teenager ever believes the rest of his life will be drastically changed just from a little kissing. Really shows how vulnerable we all are."

"Thank you, Doctor Bratt. No further questions," Wyatt stated as he turned to the jury and shook his head. Then

Murder by Memory

hoping to gain some sympathy from the jurors, he placed his hands on the rail in front of the jury box and again stated, "Pretty sad case. Kissing his girlfriend ruined his life." Wyatt then released his grip on the rail and returned to his seat.

"Your witness, Miss Sparks," Judge Heath then allowed.

Approaching Doctor Bratt, Marilyn then asked, "Doctor Bratt, did Mr. Powers' encephalitis have any affect on him before he fell into the coma?"

"No, probably not."

"Explain, please."

"Well, he had various symptoms such as a fever, headaches and was really tired all the time. Stuff like that, and I remember how he'd seen his family doctor and been tested for mono and when those results came back negative it was then thought he probably had an iron deficiency."

"But no symptoms which would alter his personality or make him suddenly violent?"

"No," Doctor Bratt expertly acknowledged.

"And he'd already killed three times before he fell into the coma?" Marilyn then adeptly pointed out.

"I believe that's correct."

"Thank you, doctor. No further questions," Marilyn stated while feeling rather confident knowing she'd made another important point with the jury.

"The defense now calls Doctor Lester Reynolds," Wyatt Barfield called as he recovered from the shock of Marilyn's latest damaging point. He'd heard she was good, and she was definitely showing it.

After Doctor Reynolds was sworn in, Wyatt first asked, "Please state your relationship to the defendant, doctor."

"I worked at the private mental facility Mr. Powers lived at."

"Were you his personal doctor?"

"Psychologist, actually. Mr. Powers wasn't physically sick, or mentally either. His condition has simply left him mentally challenged which requires constant supervision and that's what we provided him mostly with at the facility until it closed last year due to state funded budget cuts."

"Why didn't he live at home like he does now?"

"After he initially came out of his coma, he also had severe speech problems and we had one of the best speech therapy programs in the state back then so he initially came to us mainly for that treatment. Then after the memory issues were fully discovered, his mother basically found it easier for him to remain with us than to provide the constant attention he needed at home."

"Did she abandon him, then?" Wyatt wanted to know.

"Well, I can see where you might think so, but in cases like these you also have to take into account the quality of life of the care provider and taking care of Raymond would have severely limited her ability to work or to carry out any semblance of a normal social life. No, I don't think she abandoned him. She had choices to make in her life and she chose to leave him where he could receive the most attention. Until the later years when her health was failing, she actually visited him on a regular basis and took him home for extended stays with the family at holidays. I think he was well loved and cared for by his family and he appeared quite content with the arrangement."

"So he never caused any problems during his years at your facility?"

"Heavens no. Quite the opposite. Raymond is a gentle and mild tempered individual. As far as I knew, his only problem was his memory loss."

"Please describe that loss so the jury can better understand the defendant's current mental capacity," Wyatt requested.

"Certainly. Ray has what's called Korsakoff's Syndrome. Like you've already heard, it was caused by the

Murder by Memory

herpes virus invading his brain and causing encephalitis. Raymond is typical of other persons with this condition in that he is unable to remember recent events for more than a minute or so. He also has no retention of anything since falling sick back in 1975. He, along with other Korsakoff patients, can, though, recall events from their life dating to before the time they fell sick. The interesting thing about people with this affliction is that when you meet them for the first time, they can appear normal and carry on a regular conversation with you, but in many cases they make things up to fool you just to hold the conversation."

"Is Raymond capable of carrying out his daily personal needs by himself like cooking, eating, hygiene, etc.?"

"Yes, because he learned those traits early in his life. You see, many times he may not be able to recall how he first learned something, but what he learned will stay with him forever. Let me give you another example. I know another case where the person was a pilot before losing her past memory due to a head trauma. That individual didn't have any problem passing aviation knowledge tests, but didn't have a clue about how she initially gained the knowledge. The brain is really a difficult thing for medical science to understand."

"What's your professional assessment of the defendant's ability to commit murder now?"

"Well, to be honest, I don't think he possesses the mental capacity to carry it out by himself."

"But you heard about the notes he wrote to himself?"

"Yes, but in my opinion it would have taken a lot more than a few notes for him to commit murder."

"So are you saying killing Victor Bruno wasn't his idea?"

"Objection!" Marilyn Sparks loudly stated. "Defense is leading the witness."

"Sustained," Judge Heath agreed.

"Sorry, Your Honor. Doctor Reynolds, one last question. Will Raymond Powers' condition ever get any better?"

"No, I'm afraid not," the doctor sadly answered.

"Thank you. I don't have any further questions for this witness."

"Miss Sparks?" the judge then asked.

"Nothing, Your Honor."

"Very well, then, the witness is excused and you can call your next witness, Mr. Barfield."

Wyatt then turned and nodded slightly to the sheriff's deputy standing by the courtroom's rear door and watched as he opened the guarded door and led five middle aged persons in. Wyatt then addressed the court, "Your Honor, all of the witnesses who just came in have basically the same story to tell so to save time I only plan to call one to the stand."

"You may proceed, Mr. Barfield."

"The defense calls Elliot Rumsfield."

After Mr. Rumsfield was sworn in, Wyatt began. "Please describe your association with Victor Kojan."

"Like Alvin Reinhold," Elliot began, "we all went to school together."

"Did Mr. Kojan ever bother you?"

"All the time. He was the local bully and everyone knew it."

"Why do you think he singled you out?"

"He didn't single me out. He bullied anyone he thought was a little different."

"What do you mean by that?"

"You know, smallish and not very good at sports. Someone who wouldn't fight back."

"Why do you think he did it?"

"I don't know. Maybe it made him feel big or something."

Murder by Memory

"So, Mr. Rumsfield, the story you and all the others have to tell is that Victor Kojan constantly harassed all of you."

"That's right."

"And how did it make you feel?"

"Horrible. We were all scared all of the time and cringed whenever Bruno was around."

"Why didn't you tell someone?"

"For fear that he would get madder at us and make things even worse."

"Thank you, Mr. Rumsfield. No further questions, Your Honor. The defense rests its case."

"Miss Sparks," Judge Heath asked one last time.

"One question, Your Honor," Marilyn stated as she approached the witness. "But did any of you ever plot to kill Victor Kojan for being a bully?"

"No," Elliot responded.

"Thank you, that's all," she said as she abruptly turned, looked at the jury and returned to her seat.

Noticing the time, Sandra Heath then announced, "Court is in recess until closing statements at 3 o'clock." With that, she got up and left the courtroom.

As they also adjourned for lunch, Herbert Chalmers looked over and told Lizabeth, "I think my old friend Wyatt has finally met his match!"

Lizabeth quickly agreed, "I think you're right. She sure made some great points for the jury to consider." Saying that, they expeditiously departed back to Herb's apartment for lunch and a quick nooner before returning for the closing arguments.

As they reentered the courtroom shortly before three, Lizabeth noticed another person sitting with Marilyn Sparks at the prosecution table. "Who's that?" she asked Herb.

"The DA. Guess for appearance sakes he decided to show support for the closing."

"She sure didn't need his help during the trial," Lizbeth accurately pointed out.

"No she didn't. She's one tough lawyer," Herb said as he and Lizbeth took their seats and he recalled the snide comment he'd made to her when they'd first met at the Reinhold home. Looking then to his side, Herb caught sight of Benny Mitchell being let in. He was glad his old friend was finally joining them.

Within a few minutes, the court was called to order and Judge Heath began by asking Wyatt Barfield, "Is the defense ready for closing?"

"Yes, Your Honor," Wyatt confidently stated as he stood, hitched up his trousers and then slowly walked towards the jury box. Rubbing his chin a few times, he finally began. "Ladies and gentlemen of the jury, if Alvin Reinhold was on trial here today instead of his protector, Raymond Powers, I'm sure you'd all agree that he'd acted out of self-defense from his shear terror of probable further physical harm at the hands of the bully Victor Kojan and his gang of thugs. I'm also positive that you would have had no other option than to find Alvin Reinhold innocent of murder and only possibly guilty of committing justifiable homicides in the case by acting in self-defense by protecting himself against the unlawful use of force against him by other persons - in this case Victor Kojan and his band of hoodlums. By law, the maximum sentence Alvin Reinhold could have received would have been two to twenty years in prison and most likely he would have been exonerated and have been released or at the most been placed on probation. Isn't that exactly what you would have done?" Wyatt questioned while looking from juror to juror and nodding his head in the affirmative. Hoping he had the jury's sympathy, he then continued. "So if Alvin Reinhold wouldn't have been found guilty of the murders, then how can the defendant, Raymond Powers, be guilty? He can't! Mr. Powers simply went to the aid of a friend who honestly

Murder by Memory

feared for his own life but was too weak or fragile to stand up to Bruno and his gang by himself. In short, Raymond Powers acted out of concern for his dear friend's safety and committed nothing more than a third party self-defense act. Should he be punished for this? I think not. Plus, you've all seen him. He's not a threat to society. Never was and never will be. His life will never get any better than it is right now due to his mental condition. How would you like to live like that?" Wyatt now asked to play on the jury's emotions again. "None of us would. Putting Raymond Powers in prison won't prove anything. The real villain in all the murders was actually Victor Kojan. If he hadn't of been such a bully, none of the murders would have ever happened. In other words, he caused his own death as well as the deaths of his three tag along cronies. Should Mr. Powers be guilty of murdering Victor Kojan? Again, I don't believe so. You've all witnessed the testimony about his current mental state. When he finally killed Victor Kojan, his mind was operating twenty-four years in the past. A reasonable person could only find him innocent by grounds of mental deficiency. Like I stated in my opening remarks, Raymond Powers doesn't belong in jail, he belongs in a special care facility until his sister finishes her plea bargain sentence after which time he should be returned to her care. Ladies and gentlemen of the jury, there's no question that this is an extremely sad and emotional case, but you must remember how the real victim was actually Alvin Reinhold, not Victor Kojan, Darly Woods, Tony Austin or Steven Watts. They were the guilty ones and caused their own demise by being cowardly bullies!" And Wyatt loudly emphasized the phrase 'cowardly bullies'. Then leaving the jury with that thought, he slowly returned to his seat.

Judge Heath then called upon the prosecution to deliver her closing statement. After listening to what she believed was the defense's weak argument, Marilyn Sparks leaped at the opportunity to present her remarks. "Thank you, Your

William M. Jones

Honor," she politely stated as she confidently approached the anxious jurors. "Ladies and gentlemen," she slowly began as she first looked each of the jurors squarely in the eyes, "the defense wants you to believe that the defendant shouldn't be held accountable for the four murders he committed due to being a good samaritan and coming to the aid of a helpless friend. I'm afraid the prosecution views this case in a completely different light. Even though I recognize the admirable act Mr. Powers performed in trying to help his friend, in our society you can't just go around killing others. It's simply not allowed under any circumstances. And yes, the prosecution agrees that Victor Kojan was a bully, but none of the others he harassed tried to kill him. Why? Because it's against the law! There are other ways to handle situations like these and neither the defendant, his sister, nor Alvin Reinhold attempted any other methods to stop Mr. Kojan's harassment. They wrongly assumed that no one would help and then took the law into their own hands. We can't do that in our society. Individuals cannot be allowed to form their own unlawful vigilance committees which simply stated means for good order and discipline in our society it's illegal to act outside the legal authority of the law to keep order and punish crime just because you believe the established law-enforcement agencies are inefficient. And then when you consider the fact that Mr. Powers always committed the murders on new moon nights and enlisted the aid of his sister to draw each unsuspecting victim to him, it's clear to see how each murder was carefully thought out and orchestrated. Thus, each was a premeditated murder. Also, regardless of Mr. Powers' current mental competency, the fact that he wrote himself notes in order to remember to kill Victor Kojan clearly proves how that murder was also premeditated. And ladies and gentlemen of the jury, in our society, premeditated murder, regardless of the circumstances, is a capital murder offense punishable by life in prison or death. And since

Murder by Memory

there isn't a statue of limitations for murder cases and we've also shown how the defendant wasn't suffering from his current mental deficiency when he committed the first three murders, there's no other reasonable option than to find him totally accountable for his actions. You must also remember when you decide the defendant's fate that he didn't surrender himself. His sister's conscience got the best of her and she turned him in. So if you were to consider any leniency towards the defendant, I challenge you against that argument because it's not plausible since he didn't willingly surrender himself - it was entirely an act by his sister. Ladies and gentlemen, I have faith that when you review all of the facts in this case that you'll do the right thing and find the defendant, Mr. Raymond Powers, guilty and fully accountable for murder in the first degree!" Finishing, Marilyn quickly turned and returned to her seat.

After giving the jury a few moments to absorb both closing statements, Judge Sandra Heath then proceeded with the jury's charge. "Ladies and gentlemen of the jury, you've definitely heard two entirely opposing views on this case. It's now your civic responsibility to make a judgment. I know you'll carefully and completely weigh all sides and arguments in this case before delivering your final verdict. Since this case will set a new legal precedence due to the complexities involved with the defendant's involvement and with his current mental capability, this court charges you to accomplish your sworn task with the utmost diligence. At this time, Mrs. Moody and Mr. Chang are removed from the voting jury as alternates. Madam forewoman, this court stands adjourned until your jury returns its verdict." Judge Heath then struck her gavel and retired from the courtroom greatly relieved that the case had proceeded so smoothly so far. Her only hope now was that the jury would act in an expeditious manner and not return as a hung jury. This case decidedly needed closure, not only to finally put the

Slaughter House Murderer to rest, but for her future political aspirations.

After everyone else had vacated the courtroom, Herb and Lizabeth still remained seated along side Benny Mitchell. "Hard to believe it's finally about over," Benny broke their silence with.

"I know," Herb replied. "Kind of like the anticipation of going to the high school prom and then all of a sudden it's over and you wonder where it all went."

"So, what do you think, Herb?" Benny next asked.

"Well, holding strictly to the letter of the law, I think Raymond Powers should get the death penalty and I think Marilyn Sparks did a really good job of presenting that fact to the court."

"But deep down inside after giving years to this case, how do you really feel?" Benny pressed.

Holding Lizabeth's hand tighter and sighing, Herb reflected for a moment before answering. "Benny, I wouldn't want to be on that jury."

"Why?"

"Because it's hard not to feel sorry for Raymond Powers."

"And you think the jury will have a hard time looking past his mental condition and really just judging the case by the facts?"

"Exactly. And especially since his condition really didn't have anything to do with the first three murders, I'm afraid his present condition will cloud their objectivity with those."

"Well, old friend, not much we can do now except wait. Come on, I'll buy you two dinner if that doesn't cramp your plans for the evening," he smiled and then winked at Herb.

"No problem, we'd love that," Lizabeth answered while giving Herb's hand a loving squeeze.

The jury deliberated for two days before reaching their unanimous decision. Throughout the process the forewoman

Murder by Memory

served as the devil's advocate and guided the jury through numerous heated debates. Her purpose for doing so was to ensure they painstakingly considered every possible aspect of the case since she fully understood the magnitude of their decision. And then knowing their decision, regardless of what it was, would be scrutinized by others and possibly by other courts, she wanted to make sure they performed their job to the absolute best of their abilities.

Sandra Heath had remained in the sanctuary of her office while she awaited the jury's decision. Twice during their deliberation, she'd received requests from the forewoman to clarify points of law which she did as rapidly as possible. When word finally arrived of how a unanimous decision had been reached, Sandra felt as if a tremendous weight had been lifted from her chest. She had been so afraid there would be a hung jury due to the emotional aspects of the case, and now that there hadn't been, well, she was ecstatic. She didn't even initially care what the verdict was; she was simply relieved there was a verdict. Her future hinged on it, and now, as she relaxed for the first time since the trial began, her thoughts raced ahead to the future - to the governor's mansion and possibly beyond.

After the court was called to order, Sandra Heath requested of the jury forewoman, "Has the jury reached its decision?"

"Yes, Your Honor, we have," the forewoman clearly replied.

Then ordering the defendant to rise while the verdict was being read, Judge Heath ordered the forewoman to read the verdict.

Looking only at her written verdict and not looking at anyone else inside the courtroom, the forewoman read," For the murders of Daryl Woods, Tony Austin and Steven Watts, we the jury find the defendant fully accountable for their first degree murders and reject the third party self-defense argument." Without pausing, she continued, "For the murder of Victor Kojan, we the jury feel the defendant should be given consideration for his current diminished mental capacity."

Herbert Chalmers sat straight in his seat as the verdict was being read and was greatly relieved that the jury had looked through all the sympathy issues of this case and returned what he believed was also the only correct conclusion. Looking over at Raymond Powers he also knew how he presently didn't fully understand what was happening to him and hoped Judge Heath would take his present condition into account with her sentencing. What really shocked Herb was the quick smile he observed on Rita's face as the verdict was read. Why would she do that? She should have been devastated by the verdict since her brother could possibly be facing the death penalty, so why was she actually smiling? Didn't make any sense.

After the jury forewoman sat down and the buzz in the courtroom settled, Judge Heath first thanked the jury for performing their civic duty and then released them. After they departed the courtroom, she then addressed the defendant. "I'm prepared at this time to award sentencing. I've thought long and hard about this during the trial and see no reason to delay it any longer. Will the defendant please rise," she next requested. After Raymond and Wyatt Barfield stood, Sandra continued. "This court has the ability to award the death penalty in this case, but due to the defendant's current mental state I don't believe any further justice would be served by doing so. I also don't think the defendant is capable of serving time in the regular penitentiary. Mr. Powers, this court therefore sentences you to life, without chance for parole, in the state's mental hospital. This court is adjourned."

CHAPTER TWENTY-ONE

"Hey, sleepyhead, you going to get up or stay in bed all day?" Lizabeth nudged as Herb slowly came to.

"What time is it?" he asked while rubbing his sleepy eyes.

"Almost nine."

"Nine! I'd better get going!" Herb exclaimed with a tone of panic to his voice.

"To where?" Lizabeth questioned.

"To work, of course," he replied while giving her a puzzled look.

"Why? You forget you're retired?"

"That's right, and since the case is over, I don't have to go to work any more," he now realized.

"Correct," Lizabeth said with a devious smile as she pulled the covers back over them and lured him into another playful hour of love making.

Finally rising around 10:30, they first showered together before heading to the kitchen for a leisurely brunch. Lizabeth started by fixing herself a hot cup of coffee and getting Herb a tall glass of water. He surprised her this morning when he also asked for a cup of coffee. While they sat sipping their morning brew, Lizabeth noticed Herb's mood suddenly shift to one of deep thought as he got a far away look and didn't respond to her next question. "Something bothering you?" she then asked.

"Rita," he stated.

"What about her?"

"I don't think she was telling the truth."

"What do you mean, Herb?"

"You remember when we went to her house and I commented about how I didn't know she'd been Alvin's girlfriend?"

"If I remember, you were surprised because Alvin hadn't had any pictures of her in his bedroom."

"Yep. Remember what she said then?"

"Something about you hadn't asked Alvin's mom the right question."

"Exactly. I'd asked to search his bedroom and not the room he was actually living in. Remember what else she said?"

"No," Lizabeth replied with a frown as she tried hard to recall.

"She said I'd assumed a lot and asked if I knew what assume meant."

"That's right. I remember now," Lizabeth acknowledged. "And you think she's been lying about the whole case?"

"To be honest, the more I think about things, the more I think she was. She's been playing us all for suckers, Lizabeth!"

"How so?"

"Because, since she confessed, we, and everyone else, have believed everything she's said. No questions, just blindly accepted her story."

"And you think she's lying? Why?"

"Two things from the trial just don't sit right with me."

"What?"

"Well, first, when Rita was on the witness stand telling about Bruno and his gang beating up Alvin, I happened to catch Raymond's expression and he looked quite confused."

"Like what she was saying didn't register with him?"

"Yep, that's right. I don't think she was providing the whole story."

"What was the other thing, Herb?"

"Did you happen to see her when the verdict was read?"

"No, can't say as I did."

"Well, I did, and she smiled as Raymond's guilt was announced."

Murder by Memory

"Smiled?" Lizabeth questioned in a tone displaying her total disbelief.

"My feelings exactly. Her brother is found accountable of murder to which he could be facing the death penalty and she smiles. Any normal person would have broken down into tears."

"You think she's made Raymond the scapegoat for the murders?"

"Very possibly."

"But he admitted committing the first three murders."

"Yes, but did we ask the right questions? Since Rita told us he'd killed those three boys, all we, and the prosecutor during the trial, asked was if he'd committed the murders. And since he had, he answered yes because his mind was able to flash back in time and remember committing them. Remember, Raymond isn't capable of thinking in the past like you or me, just flashes back and remembers mainly direct facts from before getting sick. He also answered yes to the fact of committing the murders because Bruno had threatened to hurt Alvin."

"And you think there's more to it than that?"

"Definitely! Rita's not telling the whole truth."

"What are we going to do, then, Herb?" Lizabeth pondered.

"Ask the right questions!" he declared.

"Where do you want to start?"

"First, I think we need to find Raymond's old girlfriend."

"But Rita said she didn't know anything about the murders," Lizabeth remembered.

"Didn't know anything or that's what Rita wants us to believe."

"Yeah, I see your point."

"Then I think we need to search the Reinhold house."

"Looking for the pistol?"

"Sure would be nice to finally find it, wouldn't it?"

"Might just tell us an awful lot," Lizabeth informed.

"Exactly, and while we're at it, I think we need to look into the pistol we found at Bruno's cabin a little more."

"You think Rita's lying about Bruno's murder also?"

"Possibly. But one thing's for sure, we're not going to assume anything any more and we're going to make sure the right questions get asked until we're satisfied justice was served, or if it wasn't, until the right person is behind bars! So much for staying home and not going to work," Herb then laughed.

"Can we at least get something to eat first?" Lizabeth joked.

"Of course," Herb agreed while giving her a hug and kiss. "Just let me call Benny and tell him we'll be in to see him in an hour or so."

"Okay," Lizabeth agreed as she turned towards the refrigerator to get some eggs to go with their coffee.

It took Herb and Lizabeth a few days to track down Raymond Powers old girlfriend, Carla Travis. She was now Carla Fields, mother of three, and living in another town a hundred miles down state with her husband of eighteen years. Since her present home wasn't in their jurisdiction, Herb and Lizabeth enlisted the aid of the local detective force to accompany them to the Fields' home. As the three detectives approached the home at mid-morning, Carla was just closing her garage door with her electronic garage door closer when they pulled into the driveway blocking her departure. As they blocked her in, the local detective put on his car's blue police light sans the siren so as to not totally freak Carla out. Herb and Lizabeth then immediately vacated their car and flashed their detective shields as they approached the stunned Carla.

"Carla Fields?" Herb questioned in a loud voice since Carla remained inside her locked vehicle with the windows rolled up for protection.

Scrutinizing Herb's badge, she slowly answered, "Yes."

Murder by Memory

"Please roll down the window," Herb then politely asked in a non-threatening, authoritative voice.

Still not feeling totally secure with the situation, she next only cracked her window just enough to be able to converse better. "What's this all about? I haven't done anything," she proclaimed while beginning to tremble.

"Was your maiden name Travis?" Herb inquired.

"Yes, that's right."

"Ma'am, will you please step out of your car so we can ask you a few questions?" Herb politely asked without trying to sound too threatening or demanding.

"Questions? What about?"

"We need to talk to you about Raymond Powers," Herb flatly stated.

Now beginning to sweat as well as feeling slightly panic-stricken, Carla responded with, "Ray? I haven't seen him in over twenty years!"

"Yes, ma'am, we realize that, but we'd still like to ask you some questions," Herb again politely requested as Carla slowly exited her car.

"Okay," she then reluctantly agreed.

"Are you aware that Mr. Powers has been convicted of three murders he committed while you two were dating?" Lizabeth now joined the questioning with.

Looking directly at the pretty detective, Carla answered, "The Slaughter House Murderer. I read the papers, detective. So what's this got to do with me? You think I had something to do with them?" she next asked suddenly feeling quite frightened.

"No," Herb assured, "Rita informed us you didn't have anything to do with them."

"She was right. I didn't."

"But did you know anything about them, Mrs. Fields? Anything at all?" Herb now asked with a much greater seriousness to his demeanor.

William M. Jones

Beginning to cry, Carla lowered her head and wiped the tears while volunteering, "I didn't know Ray committed those murders! I swear! I didn't know he was the killer. I loved Ray, detective. He was my best friend as well as my boyfriend. We would have gotten married if he hadn't of gotten sick."

"We know all about that too, Carla," Lizabeth added with a touch of sympathy to her voice. Then as Carla really began to break down, Lizabeth placed a reassuring arm around her shoulder. "It wasn't your fault. You know that, don't you?"

"I know," she sobbed, "but that doesn't change the fact that I caused it. I ruined Ray's life. You know that and so do I. He'll never get any better and there's nothing any of us can do about it." Wiping back the tears, she then confessed, "I've tried to block it out of my mind over the years in order to get on with my life, but the trial just brought back all the old feelings."

"Does your husband know about your previous relationship with Raymond Powers?" Herb wanted to know.

"No! And he doesn't need to know!" Carla almost begged.

"Okay, I understand," Herb consoled, "and he won't find out as long as you're not connected."

"I'm not. I told you that and apparently Rita did too. So why are you here, detective? The trial's over. Can't we just leave the past in the past?" she pleaded.

"Wish we could, but I'm afraid some things still just don't make much sense," Herb led on.

"Like what?" Carla wanted to know.

"Well, first," Herb began, "Raymond got a very puzzled look on his face when Rita testified about how Bruno and the others had beaten Alvin up. Said that's the reason she got him to defend Alvin and help her commit the murders. Raymond's expression made me think how Rita possibly wasn't telling the whole story."

Murder by Memory

"And what else, detective?" Carla inquired.

"And then Rita smiled when Raymond was found guilty."

"That devious bitch!" Carla blurted.

Taken somewhat back by her sudden outburst, Lizabeth added, "Some bad blood between the two of you?"

"You could say that," Carla answered. "I never liked her much. She always seemed to be plotting things. She came across as so sweet and innocent, but I just never trusted her," Carla volunteered.

"So can you help us with our suspicions?" Herb asked.

Wiping her reddened eyes while slowly gaining her composure, Carla invited, "Let's go inside the house. There's one thing I'd completely forgotten over the years which the trial caused me to remember which I think you might need to hear."

"Okay," Herb replied as Carla then led the three detectives inside her modest home.

"Did Rita ever mention anything about Bruno threatening her?" Carla asked once they were all comfortably seated in her living room.

"No," Herb quickly returned. "She never said a word. Did he?"

"Yes, and I heard her tell Ray about it one night."

"Did Rita know you heard her tell him?" Lizabeth asked.

"No, she thought I'd gone home."

"What happened?" Herb then curiously inquired.

"Well, Ray and I were all alone in his room one night when Rita suddenly just burst on in. She was crying and all. Seemed really upset."

"So what happened next?" Lizabeth quizzed.

"Well, Ray was always really protective of her."

"Because of his dad's murder?" Herb interjected.

"Exactly. He always felt it was his responsibility to protect her and she knew it."

215

"And did he?"

"Yes, he'd do anything for her. Made me mad a lot. Sometimes I felt he cared more about her than me."

"So, what happened?" Lizabeth continued.

"Ray asked me to leave them alone, so I did, but I didn't leave the house like they thought. I just shut the bedroom door and listened before quietly leaving later."

"And what exactly did Rita tell Raymond?" Herb demanded.

"She told him how Bruno and the others had just assaulted Alvin and her in the park . Said she'd been tied to a small tree and Bruno had unbuttoned her blouse, lifted her bra, and fondled her breasts. Said when Bruno tried to lift her skirt, Alvin had kicked one of the others in the groin. That's when they got really mad and started beating Alvin up. When they left, she told Ray how Bruno had threatened to hurt them both a lot worse if they ever told anyone so that's why they needed Ray's help."

"Did you actually hear Rita ask Raymond to help murder the boys?" Herb needed to know.

"No," Carla confessed as she again began to cry. "I got really scared and left the house."

"But didn't you suspect anything when the murders began?" Lizabeth asked.

"Raymond was my boyfriend. He was so good to me. We were planning on getting married. I didn't want to believe he could be involved and then he got sick. I guess my guilt over that blocked everything else from my mind until the trial began and then all the old memories resurfaced."

"Why didn't you come forward?" Herb next questioned.

"Because I didn't think it would help Ray since you had his and Rita's confessions."

"May not have helped Raymond, but definitely might have placed more blame on Rita!" Herb emphatically pointed out.

Murder by Memory

"Is it too late now?" Carla desperately wanted to know.

"I hope not. That's why we're here, ma'am. Just want to know the truth and put this case behind us all. Thanks for your help because we realize how hard all this is on you. We'll be in touch if we need anything else. Probably won't, and we'll do everything possible to respect your wish of not letting your current family know about this."

"Thank you, detective. I'd really appreciate it," Carla acknowledged as she led the three detectives to the door.

Once inside their car, Herb told Lizabeth, "Rita's behind all the murders and she's played us all for suckers, but she's not going to get away with it any longer! She played on her brother's sympathy to get her way and then used him, her own blood, as her fall guy. What a devious bitch!"

"That's exactly what Carla also called her, and I believe you're both right," Lizabeth agreed. "Where do we go from here?" she next asked.

"I think we need to visit Raymond. It's time we ask him the correct questions."

"Good idea. Isn't his hospital on our way back to the city?"

"Not far out of our way," Herb replied. "We ought to have time to swing by there and still get back to the precinct in time to check in with Benny."

Where Herb and Lizabeth usually talked constantly when they were alone, during the drive from Carla's home to Raymond's hospital, they remained unusually quiet as each reflected on the story Carla Travis Fields had just dropped on them. More and more it seemed like Rita was the real mastermind behind all the murders and unless they uncovered more positive evidence, she'd basically get away with them. Her current plea bargain sentence of eighteen months in the state's minimum security facility was by no means adequate justice if in fact she'd been the driving force behind them all. Herb could visualize her smiling to herself in prison and laughing about how she was getting away with them. Unless he and Lizabeth pursued the matter, she'd not only be free when her time was up, but she'd also be rid of the burden of caring for her mentally challenged brother since he'd remain incarcerated in the state mental hospital for the remainder of his natural life. Oh sure, she'd be the caring sister and periodically visit, but she'd made sure she wouldn't have to provide care for him day in and day out for who could tell how many years. No, she'd definitely seen to it not to be burdened with that responsibility so eighteen months in minimum security was a cake walk compared to the rest of her life behind bars for the murders she probably was responsible for plus the freedom of not having to care for Raymond. Herb was quickly painting a mental picture of the true Rita Powers Reinhold and it wasn't one of a very nice person!

Finally arriving at the hospital, Herb parked in the official visitor's spot as it suddenly started to rain. Fortunately, Lizabeth had thrown an umbrella in the back seat when they left home earlier this morning. Grabbing the umbrella, Herb first got out of his door before opening it and then proceeded around to Lizabeth's door and held it open while she got out. Then walking arm in arm underneath the dripping canopy of the umbrella, they continued towards the hospital. After officially checking in, they were escorted by a correctional officer to a small, empty visitor's room. Within five minutes Raymond Powers was escorted in.

"Nice to see you again, Raymond," Herb greeted as he extended his hand.

"Do I know you?" Ray returned while searching his limited memory for any hint of a previous connection to the individual standing before him right now.

"Yes, Ray, we've met numerous times. Do you know why you're here?"

"Because Rita can't care for me any longer."

"Why?" Herb inquired.

Murder by Memory

"I'm not sure."

"Ray, do you remember Carla?"

"Carla," Raymond repeated as his interest level heightened. "Of course, she was my girlfriend before I got sick. Is she here?"

"No, Ray, she's not, but we talked to her this morning. Ray, can we ask you a few questions?"

"Okay," he agreed.

"Raymond, we want you to think really hard," Herb began. "Did Rita ever tell you that Bruno tried to sexually assault her?"

Thinking only for a few seconds, he nodded in agreement and also softly said, "Yes."

"Was that also the same night Bruno and the other boys beat Alvin up?"

"Yes," Raymond also answered.

"Raymond, did you agree to commit the murders mainly because of what those boys did to Rita?"

"Yes," he again answered.

"Thanks, Raymond. That's all we needed to know," Herb stated.

"Tell Carla to come see me. Will you, please?" Raymond requested as he was escorted from the room.

"We'll tell her, I promise," Herb answered while feeling a deep sympathy for Raymond. Then looking at Lizabeth, he said, "Now we're getting somewhere. As far as I'm concerned, this explains Raymond's puzzled expression and then Rita's smiling at the verdict. Her words of telling us we didn't ask the right questions are going to come back to haunt her! Mark my word, Lizabeth. We're going to get that...."

"Devious bitch," Lizabeth finished his pointed statement.

"Exactly," Herb returned as they headed for the parking lot. Exiting the hospital's front entrance, they witnessed the sun starting to come out with a brilliant rainbow suddenly appearing arched high across the clearing sky. Pointing it out to Lizabeth, Herb informed her, "I don't usually put much faith in signs, but that rainbow's gotta mean we're beginning to see the light with this case and proving Rita Reinhold accountable is the prize at the end of the rainbow!"

Getting hung up in heavy work traffic, Herb and Lizabeth arrived back at the precinct later than they'd expected, but being curious to talk with them, Benny had stayed late and was waiting for them when they finally arrived. After thoroughly briefing him on their day's events, Benny looked directly at both of them and asked, "Okay. What do you want to do? Do you think you've got enough to go back to the judge with?"

"Probably," Herb hesitantly began, "but we really don't want to yet."

"Why?"

"Because we want to make sure we have all the facts this time. We're not going to assume anything, any longer," Herb emphatically stated. "Plus, we've got plenty of time to check everything out since Rita isn't going anywhere for awhile."

"Good," Benny said, "so what's next?"

"Remember what Rita told us about the pistol when Lizabeth and I first asked her where it was?"

"Yeah, didn't she say she didn't know where it was?"

"Exactly! She claimed Raymond disposed of it after he killed Bruno and now couldn't remember what he did with it."

"And you don't believe her?" Benny questioned.

"Nope, not after everything we've heard today. I think it's just another story she's fed us which we've all so gullibly accepted. To be honest, I think she still has the pistol. Benny, can you get us a search warrant for the Reinhold house?"

Murder by Memory

"Sure, no problem. Should have it first thing in the morning."

"Thanks."

"Now, you two go get some rest. I'll make all the arrangements and have a team standing by in the morning to assist you," Benny promised.

After thanking Benny again, Herb and Lizabeth retreated to Herb's place for a quiet evening. Exhausted from their long day, they simply fixed a quiet dinner, took a relaxing shower together and then both fell fast asleep. By eight sharp in the morning they were back at the precinct, rested, and ready to go again. As promised, Benny had procured the necessary search warrant and had four uniformed officers standing by to assist with the search. He also informed them how a real estate friend of Rita's was looking after the house while she was serving her time and would be waiting at the house when they arrived.

Then arriving at the Reinhold house by nine, Herb and Lizabeth exchanged pleasantries with the curious real estate lady before the search team got busy. They spent six grueling hours at the house and meticulously searched every crook and cranny. They even went so far as to sweep the yard with a metal detector and even looked for any evidence of freshly dug dirt spots in the yard, but all of their efforts proved futile.

"Damn!" Herb declared to Lizabeth out of frustration. "I was positive we'd find it here. Maybe she was telling the truth with this one."

Standing off to the side, but hearing Herb's statement to his partner, the real estate lady inquired, "Detective, you do know Rita still owns her mom's old house, don't you?"

"No, I didn't," Herb replied as he turned to face the cooperative real estate lady. "In fact, didn't even give it a thought. Didn't she pass away a few years ago?"

"Yeah, but Rita never did anything with the house. Wouldn't even let me list it. Said there were too many memories inside to let go of, at least for awhile."

"She did, did she?" Herb replied as his interest level peaked and the wheels inside his brain began churning. "You wouldn't happen to have a key for that house also, would you?"

"Actually, detective, I do."

"You do?" Herb said with much surprise.

"Yeah, it's back home. Rita gave me a spare key years ago just in case she was gone and her mom needed something."

"Then you and Rita are good friends?"

"No, not really," she replied. "Her mom and my mom worked together for years and were pretty close. I guess you could say they were best friends. Rita, though, was always kind of aloof, you know?"

"I think I know the type," Herb responded.

"So, I was actually closer to her mom than to her, but after my mom passed away, Rita asked me to look in on her mom every once in a while since I'd gone over there a lot over the years with my mom and knew her pretty well."

"You got time to let us in over there?" Herb next requested.

"Sure, no problem. I can run by my house for the key and be over there in fifteen minutes or so."

"Make it an hour," Herb requested. "We've got to have time to get another search warrant."

"An hour it is then. You know where the house is?"

"I think we can find it," he assured as the helpful lady got into her car and left and Herb reached for the cell phone in his jacket pocket to call Benny for the new search warrant.

An hour later Benny arrived at the Powers' house armed with the fresh search warrant. Waving it as he got out of his

Murder by Memory

car, the real estate lady, who was standing at the front door with Herb and Lizabeth, unlocked the door for them.

"Herb?" Lizabeth questioned as they set foot inside the front hallway.

"What?"

"Do you remember what Rita originally told us about the pistol?"

Thinking really hard, he couldn't. "No, I don't."

"Don't you remember? She said it had been her father's."

"Your right. And he kept it locked in a trunk in the attic!"

"Exactly!" she stated as the real estate lady then led the entire search team to the musty, cobweb filled attic.

Aided by the one 60 watt light which still worked up there, they quickly found a couple of old trunks tucked away behind lots of other dusty old family keepsakes. Within a matter of seconds, the search team had the trunks separated and opened.

"Looky here!" Herb suddenly proclaimed as he carefully held up the missing slaughter house pistol. "Son of a bitch!" he next exclaimed. "Rita had really played us all for fools, hadn't she? But not any more!" he said with determined conviction while projecting a wide grin.

About three hours later, Herb and Lizabeth were hanging around the precinct when Benny got the call they were anxiously waiting for from the crime lab. Raymond's prints were on the pistol, but they appeared quite old. Rita's prints, on the other hand, were clearly much fresher ones. And the preliminary DNA tests also found matches to the three 1975 murder victims, plus Bruno's.

"Jackpot!" Herb yelled when Benny gave him the news.

"So, what do you think, Herb?" Benny then asked.

"I don't think Raymond had anything to do with Bruno's murder."

"You think Rita pulled it off by herself?"

"Yep, and then framed her own brother to get away with it. Sure, why not? Makes perfect sense. Raymond remembers committing the first three murders, so what's one more?"

"So after Bruno killed Alvin, Rita kills him for revenge and then frames her brother," Benny recapped.

"All correct except for one thing."

"What?" Benny inquired.

"Are we certain Bruno killed Alvin?"

"Well, you were, weren't you?" Benny stated.

"I was, but things just aren't always what they seem to be, especially with this case," Herb responded.

"So what are you thinking?"

"I think we need to look a little closer into that pistol we found out at Bruno's old hunting cabin."

"Okay, what do you need?" Benny requested.

"To start with, the names of Bruno's old hunting buddies."

"All right. Shouldn't be too hard. Might take a day or two, though."

"No problem. I've got something else I need to check while you're getting the names."

"Care to enlighten me?" Benny requested.

"Not yet," Herb stated with a smile, "just get me those names."

After they left Benny's office, Lizabeth curiously asked Herb, "What are we going to check out?"

"The notes!" he answered.

"The notes?" she questioned.

"Yeah, I think Rita made up the whole story about Raymond writing himself the notes to remember to kill Bruno."

"Okay, so how are you going to find out? Raymond can't remember and Rita definitely won't tell you."

"You're right, but I've got something she doesn't know about."

Murder by Memory

"What?"

"The letters sent to Bruno back in '75. I've still got them in my old file over in the archives. Remember how she smiled when we told her those letters had really scared Bruno?"

"Yeah, now that you mention it, I do. So you think she wrote them and also wrote the fake notes which, for affect, she planted on Raymond?"

"Exactly. And all we have to do is match the handwriting to find out."

"Again, why didn't we do all of this before?" she asked.

"Because after all the years of looking for the Slaughter House Murderer, we were all so happy to have the confession to finally end this case that we all basically had blinders on when it came to questioning any of it. Why look a gift horse in the mouth? And Rita assumed we'd react exactly like we did. Was just another element of her devious plan to get away with murder!"

"But it appears as if she assumed one time too many," Lizabeth boasted.

"Only because I caught a glimpse of her smile. It was her only downfall. Without the smile, she'd have been home free!"

"But she did, and she's not!" Lizabeth added.

Within thirty minutes Herb and Lizabeth had retrieved his old file and matched the letters to the notes Raymond had supposedly written. Not surprisingly, to their untrained eyes, they matched perfectly. "One more piece of the puzzle coming together," Herb stated as they decided to call it a day and head back to his apartment.

Lizabeth didn't feel very good when she got up the next morning. Feeling slightly nauseous and achy all over, she decided to stay in bed a while longer while Herb took Bruno's old letters and Raymond's notes to the crime lab for analysis. They were positive of the results, but needed to make it official in order to hold up in a court of law. Since

William M. Jones

the lab handwriting expert promised results in a relatively short amount of time, Herb decided to wait at the lab for the results. Twiddling his thumbs and daydreaming about Lizabeth, he was startled back to reality when his cell phone suddenly rang.

"Chalmers," he answered.

"Got the names, Herb," Benny announced from his end of the conversation.

"That was fast," Herb proclaimed.

"Not as hard as I thought," Benny acknowledged. "Think we got everything you needed from the tax records. Appears the cabin had three other owners besides Bruno."

"Know anything about them?"

"No, not yet. None of their addresses were local. When can you get here?" Benny next asked.

"Probably within the hour."

"Why so long?" Benny wanted to know.

"Because I'm at the crime lab waiting for something right now. Tell you about it when I see you. Then I need to swing by the apartment and check on Lizabeth."

"What's the matter with her?"

"Not much, just didn't feel very good this morning."

"Okay, we'll see what else we can find out about Bruno's associates before you get here," Benny promised as he terminated the conversation.

Hanging up his phone also, Herb now wished the handwriting expert would hurry up. What was taking him so long? Just then he appeared from inside his lab. "Perfect match, detective. No doubt about it. Same person positively wrote the letters and the notes!"

"Thanks, I'll pick up your official report later," Herb promised as he hurriedly left the crime lab. Driving straight home first, he was relieved to find Lizabeth now feeling much like her old cheerful self. Then giving her a few more minutes to freshen up, they headed off together to the precinct. Going then straight to Benny's office, they found

Murder by Memory

him engaged in a telephone conversation so after being waved inside, they quietly sat on the couch in his office and waited for him to get off the phone.

"Herb, you're not going to believe this," Benny announced after hanging up his phone.

"What?" he excitedly asked.

"That was one of Bruno's buddies I was talking to. Care to guess what he's the plant manager of?"

"No, couldn't be. A slaughter house?"

"Good guess. His name is Amos Everett. Runs the largest meat packing plant in the state. He's expecting the both of you by the end of the day. Think you can make it?"

"Make it? Of course we can. What is it, about a hundred and fifty mile drive?"

"Yeah, plus or minus a few miles," Benny responded.

"Well, it's 12:30 now. Ought to be there by four at the latest," Herb calculated.

"Might as well spend the night out there instead of driving back late. Any problem with that?" Benny said with a grin as he surveyed Herb and Lizabeth's faces.

"You picking up the tab?" Herb joked.

"Certainly, you're on official police business, you know."

"Okay, since you insist, we'll stay the night and come back tomorrow," Herb agreed as he returned Benny's grin. "One more thing, Benny. Rita wrote those threatening letters to Bruno back in '75, plus, she also wrote the memory aid notes she claimed Raymond wrote. Benny, there's no doubt now that she killed Bruno, not Raymond. No doubt at all about it in my mind. If we have anything to do with it, she'll never get out of jail!"

"No argument here, Herb. Now go talk to Mr. Everett and see what else you can find out."

"See you tomorrow," Herb stated as he and Lizabeth left Benny to his other detective duties and headed back to their car for the afternoon drive to the other side of the state.

William M. Jones

Arriving there around 3:45 after a pleasant trip interrupted only by a quick lunch at a fast food joint and one pit stop at a rest area, they proceeded directly inside the massive slaughter house. Initially taken back by the aroma of the facility, they quickly accepted it and headed straight for the main office. Initially greeted by a friendly receptionist, they were courteously ushered into Mr. Everett's impressive office.

"Amos Everett," he warmly greeted with a firm handshake from his large right hand. "Now, what can I do for you, detectives? Your boss said it had something to do with Victor Kojan. So sad about him, wasn't it? I'd known him for probably fifteen years or so. Weren't you two at his funeral?" he then surprised them with.

"Yes we were," Herb acknowledged while being duly impressed with Mr. Everett's recollection. "How'd you come to know Victor?" Herb next asked.

"Bought a car from him years ago. Was visiting relatives when my old clunker just died. While haggling over the car price, we got to talking about my job here. Been here now over twenty-five years, you know. Came in as floor foreman and became plant manager about ten years ago. He seemed really interested in the slaughter house business. We must have talked for an hour or so about it. I bought the car and one thing led to another and pretty soon he asked me to join his hunting group. We had some great times out there in the early years."

"Why'd you all stop going?" Herb asked.

"Family priorities, I guess. Just kind of drifted away from it. Victor owned about seventy-five percent of it, but we still paid our share of the taxes and were free to go there whenever we felt like it, but I don't think I've been out there in three or four years."

"Did Victor ever tell you why he was so interested in the slaughter house business?"

Murder by Memory

"No, never did. Of course I understand now from all I've read in the papers about the trial. How's Bruno's wife doing?" he next sincerely inquired.

"She moved out of state right after the funeral."

"Oh, didn't realize that. Really nice lady, you know. What she ever saw in Bruno, though, was always a mystery to me. Don't take me wrong, detective, he was a good old boy and we had some great times hunting together, but just couldn't picture those two together. She was so pretty and proper and all."

"Well, sometimes opposites do attract," Herb stated. "Did you ever take a slaughter pistol out to the cabin?" he next directly questioned.

"So that's what this is all about," Everett returned.

"Yeah, we found one out there with Victor's prints all over it. Was used to kill Alvin Reinhold," Herb bluntly said.

"My god, I'd long forgotten about it!" Everett now remembered. "Victor asked me to bring one out years ago. He took it hunting with us."

"What for?" Herb asked while trying to picture what possibly Victor would use it for while hunting.

"In case he maimed an animal."

"Aren't there better ways to put an animal out of its suffering? I never heard of using a slaughter pistol like that before?" Herb honestly proclaimed while wrinkling his brow.

"Neither had I, but he insisted."

"Did he ever use it?"

"Yeah, couple of times. Never gave it much thought back then, but guess it was kind of weird."

"Anybody else know about the pistol?" Lizebeth joined the questioning with.

"No, we were kind of a private little group. Never let outsiders join us."

"So you're sure nobody else knew about the pistol?"

"Wait, Victor's son knew about it. He came out there with his dad once in awhile."

"He ever shoot it?" Lizabeth asked.

"No, not that I can remember. He wasn't really into hunting much. Liked to fish, but that's about it. You two like a tour of the place? Day crew is probably about done," Everett now asked.

"No thank you," Lizabeth quickly replied, "but Herb can if he likes. I'll just wait here."

"Detective?" Everett addressed Herb.

"Sure, why not," he agreed.

When the tour arrived at the killing floor, Herb stood in amazement as he watched the process. Dressed in a blood spotted work coat and wearing a battered plastic hard hat, the killer stood emotionless by the killing area. One by one the cattle were electrically prodded through a small chute into the confined killing area. The killer, armed with his .22 caliber pistol loaded with blanks, then mechanically placed the pistol on the back of each animal's head and slowly squeezed the trigger. Instantly falling dead as the blank charge forced the metal rod out the barrel's end and into the animal's brain, the animal was next moved by a large swinging door out into the main killing floor blood pit where within seconds another worker wrapped a chain around the dead carcass's hind legs and hoisted the animal high into the air before slitting its throat to void the blood. Watching this process made Herb suddenly feel ill as he vividly visualized each of the Slaughter House Murderer killings being committed with the same type of pistol being discharged into the back of each of the victim's heads. Herb was definitely glad Lizabeth hadn't witnessed this. Rejoining her when the tour was concluded, they thanked Amos Everett for his cooperation and then headed for the motel they'd picked on their way into town. Herb told Lizabeth they'd eat later, right now he just didn't feel like it. Both agreed, then, how they needed to look more into

Victor Kojan Jr. when they got back to work tomorrow. Both figured there was possibly much more to him than anyone had previously considered.

"Can I help you?" the attractive lady standing behind the counter at the registrar's office asked as Herb and Lizabeth entered the office.

"We hope so," Herb politely replied. He and Lizabeth had each spent a restless night back in the hotel last night. After talking with Amos Everett and learning about Victor Jr.'s possible connection to the slaughter pistol found earlier at the cabin, both had mentally run various deadly scenarios through their minds instead of being able to sleep much. And then Herb, every time he closed his eyes, graphically visualized the sight he'd witnessed during his tour of the slaughter house of the pistol being placed on the back of the animal's heads and then watching as they suddenly dropped crashing to the bloody floor immediately after the pistol was fired. The sight of each victim from the case being killed kept playing over and over in his mind. The case had been gruesome enough, but suddenly it took on a completely new horrific dimension as he now more clearly visualized each murder being committed and to make matters even worse, his visualizations seemed to occur in animated slow motion which caused him to open his eyes and sit up every time he started to see the pistol's metal rod penetrating each victim's brain. Until he'd seen the cattle being killed earlier today, he'd never actually thought about the true brutality of the murders, but now he feared they'd haunt him forever. So between his nightmares, and Lizabeth's constant tossing and turning apparently from her own mental demons, Herb was sweaty and exhausted by morning. He figured it had probably been one of the longest nights he'd ever experienced in his life. After leaving the hotel around 8:30, he and Lizabeth first went to the IHOP located next to the hotel and had a hearty breakfast along with a heavy dose of hot black coffee. On their drive home, Herb called Benny

William M. Jones

on his cell phone and provided him with a preliminary brief about their trip and informed him how they were proceeding directly to the college when they got back to the city in hopes of learning more about Bruno's wayward son.

"Do I know you?" the registrar lady asked while searching her memory of why the man and woman standing before her looked so familiar.

"Detectives Chalmers and Barcay," Herb introduced while producing his detective shield for her inspection.

"Sure. I recognize you now from the news," she remembered. "You were involved in that big murder trial, right?"

"Yes, ma'am," Herb acknowledged.

"How sad," the lady then said. "We all loved Professor Reinhold. He was so friendly and kind. Students really liked him a lot too. So, what are you doing here?"

"We'd like to get some information on Victor Kojan Jr.," Herb informed the lady.

"Well, I don't really know much about him. He wasn't flamboyant like his dad, you know," she stated obviously well informed about Bruno's former local celebrity status from his used car commercials.

"Can we at least see his academic record while he was here?"

"I'm not sure I can do that," the lady hesitated.

"We can get a search warrant if we need to," Herb quickly informed her.

"Okay. No need for that. Give me a second. Okay?"

"Sure, we'll wait."

"Here it is," the lady said as she returned in a minute or two.

Looking at the grades, Herb commented, "Wasn't a very good student, was he? What's this F in English? Who was his professor?"

"Professor Reinhold," the lady replied after checking another document.

Murder by Memory

"Alvin!" Herb exclaimed. "Do you know any more about this?"

"No. Like I said, I didn't know young Mr. Kojan very well."

"You know anyone who did?" Herb then requested.

"Hey, Mary," the lady turned and hollered at the younger lady in the registrar's back office. "You know anyone who knew the Kojan kid when he was a student here?"

Walking up to the front from her rear office space, Mary greeted Herb and Lizabeth before announcing, "Yeah, I think I know someone he hung around with. Remember that student helper we had in here some months ago?" she asked the other lady.

"Sonya?"

"Yeah, that's her. Sonya Spaulding. I think she hung around with Kojan a lot. May have even been his girlfriend for awhile if I remember right."

"Either of you know where we can find this Sonya Spaulding?" Herb immediately requested.

"Let me check our records, detectives. Maybe we've got an address," Mary offered as she turned and opened a filing cabinet. Finding what she was looking for she then returned and gave Herb and Lizabeth the address to a local off-campus apartment complex. "Good chance she still lives out there. Rent's pretty cheap, you know," she said while handing the address across the counter to Lizabeth.

"Thank you very much ladies. This really helps," Herb stated as he and Lizabeth turned and left the registrar's office. Within five minutes they arrived at the address they'd been provided with. As they parked at the apartment complex and searched the numbers for the unit they were looking for, upon finding it they observed a pretty young female, dressed in jogging clothes, coming out of the door. Getting out of their car, they approached the young woman and halted her before she could start her run. "Sonya

William M. Jones

Spaulding?" Herb asked as he and Lizabeth flashed their detective shields.

Startled, the young woman answered, "Yes, I'm Sonya Spaulding."

"Do you know Victor Kojan Jr."? Lizabeth asked realizing it was best if she took the lead in questioning this girl.

"Why?" Sonya wanted to know.

"Because we asked!" Herb fired back while shooting her a penetrating stern glare.

Suddenly feeling quite afraid, Sonya answered, "Yes, I know him."

"When'd you see him last?" Lizabeth continued.

"Night before he left town."

"Why'd he quit college?" Lizabeth then directly asked.

"Said he needed to get away from here for awhile. Needed to make a fresh start. He was pretty bummed out about his dad's murder, you know?"

"But that's no reason to quit school and run off and join the Army. He have any other troubles here at school?"

"Like what?" Sonya asked.

"That's what we're hoping you'll tell us," Herb added.

"We know he got an F in English, Sonya. Didn't he and Professor Reinhold get along?" Lizabeth then requested. When Sonya didn't answer in a reasonable period of time, Lizabeth probed, "Sonya, something you want to tell us? Was he having trouble with Professor Reinhold?"

"Yes," Sonya finally admitted after formulating her best option for answering this touchy question.

"Why?" Lizabeth asked.

"I really don't know for sure," she lied after deciding to provide the detectives with just enough information to seem cooperative, but not with the entire truth which could possibly get her into a lot of trouble. "Those two never really got along. Junior, that's what we all called him, always said Professor Reinhold ragged on him. Said no

Murder by Memory

matter how hard he tried, he couldn't get a fair break from him."

"So why didn't he drop Reinhold's class or take it with another professor?" Herb asked.

"Because Reinhold was the only prof who taught the class and Junior needed it to complete his requirements."

"Did he ever talk to Professor Reinhold about his grade?"

"Said he tried once, but didn't do any good. Said Reinhold had it in for him."

"Do you know why?"

"Didn't at the time," she again lied, "but after all that's been in the papers from the trial, I can see where Junior's dad and Professor Reinhold had been enemies for a long time."

"Why did getting an F in Reinhold's class bother Junior so much?" Lizbeth next inquired.

"Because his dad would've killed him if he flunked out of here. That's why!"

"So he had a lot of pressure from home?" Herb interjected.

"That's putting it mildly, detective," Sonya answered. "Junior was pretty scared of his old man."

"Really," Herb said. "Looks like he bullied his own kid," he then faced Lizbeth and stated.

"How sad," she returned.

"Sonya," Herb then continued, "did you ever go places other than school with Junior?"

"Sure, like where?" she asked.

"You ever go out to his dad's old hunting cabin with him?" Herb took a wild ass guess with.

"Yeah, twice to be exact. Why?" Sonya admitted and then asked.

"When?"

"Not long ago," she recalled.

"Before Professor Reinhold was murdered?"

"Yeah, I'm pretty sure it was."

"What did you do out there?" Lizabeth then jumped back in with.

"Not much. I just mainly rode out there with him for the company."

"So you didn't stay there very long either time?"

"No, just a few minutes. Was a pretty drive, though."

"What did Junior do out there?" Herb needed to know.

"I'm not exactly sure. He went into an old storage shed and got something and then took something back on the second trip."

"So you never actually saw what he got?"

"No. He just said he needed to pick something up and I never pressed the issue."

"Think hard, Sonya. Can you think of anything he did while you were out there which seemed strange?" Lizabeth prompted her with.

"Yeah, now that you mention it."

"What?"

"As he walked towards the shed I think he took some latex gloves out of his pocket and put them on."

"Latex gloves. Are you sure?"

"I'm pretty sure. Didn't have them on when he came out of the shed either time, though."

"And he never mentioned what he got out of the shed?"

"No, but it was wrapped in an old towel. Told me it wasn't any of my concern so I just left it at that."

"One more thing, Sonya. Do you know where Junior is right now. His mother told us he'd gone to stay with some friends in Texas until his reporting date with the Army."

"Yeah, got a letter from him the other day. Can I call you later with the address?" she requested as she was anxious to get going plus talking with the detectives made her quite nervous.

Murder by Memory

"Sure, here's my card. Be expecting your call by tonight," Herb firmly stated in his best police authoritative voice.

"Okay, can I go now?" Sonya then requested.

"Sure, you've been a big help. We'll be expecting your call, though," Herb reiterated as Sonya turned and jogged off while he and Lizabeth returned to their car.

"So now we know why Bruno passed the lie detector test when questioned if he'd killed Alvin," Lizabeth positively stated.

"Yep, because he didn't do it. His son did!"

"But then Rita killed Bruno thinking he'd killed Alvin," Lizabeth added.

"Well, she assumed wrong, didn't she?" Herb correctly responded. "Guess we'd better have a little chat with Mr. Victor Kojan Jr.," he then declared.

Two days later Herb and Lizabeth were in Van Horn, Texas, staking out the address Sonya Spaulding had provided them with. The house Victor Jr. was apparently staying in was in a run-down section of the dusty western Texas town down along Interstate 10. The surrounding neighborhood consisted of equally run-down one story mainly adobe dwellings littered with countless old junkers randomly parked about. For the stakeout, Herb and Lizabeth were teamed with Texas Rangers and deputies from the local county sheriff's office. With Junior now being wanted for murder in connection with one of the most famous murder cases in the country, the stakeout team had the local neighborhood completely surrounded with Herb and Lizabeth teamed with a Texas Ranger captain and positioned closest to the suspected residence. After about five hours of boring observation, Victor Jr. suddenly appeared sauntering toward the house from another house about two hundred yards further down the street.

"Here he comes," Herb was the first to announce as the Texas Ranger captain then alerted the rest of the surveillance team over his handheld radio.

"Look at him," Lizabeth pointed out, "he looks like he's either drunk or high on something."

"Okay, let's get him," the captain ordered as the three of them got out of their patrol car and approached Junior. "Victor Kojan Jr.?" the captain called to draw Junior's attention. "Texas Rangers," he only had time to anounce before Junior unsuspectedly drew a loaded revolver from underneath his opened shirt, aimed, and shot the captain in the left shoulder.

"Son of a bitch!" Herb screamed as he and Lizabeth hit the ground. By the time they could get their pistols out, Junior had escaped and was running full out for the rear of the one story house.

Momentarily releasing the grasp on his wounded shoulder, the Texas Ranger captain made a radio call to alert the other units. In what seemed like only a matter of seconds, Junior came roaring out from the rear of the house in an old, battered up pickup truck. Almost hitting Herb and Lizabeth as he raced out of the dirt driveway, he spun the truck's tires as he wildly departed the scene. By the time he reached the corner just a couple hundred yards from the house, three other Texas Ranger and deputy sheriff units converged upon him from different directions and joined up in hot pursuit. Herb and Lizabeth remained with the wounded captain and comforted him until medical aid arrived. Having recently completed a first aid refresher course, Lizabeth ripped off part of the captain's shirt and tied a tourniquet around his arm to try to control the immediate bleeding. It looked like the bullet was still in his shoulder and he was initially bleeding profusely. Within five minutes of the shooting, the sound of the approaching ambulance's siren could be heard as it raced towards the wounded officer. As it came into sight, Herb heard over the

Murder by Memory

police radio how Junior had just lost control of his pickup truck and had crashed head-on into a telephone pole. No other details were immediately known. As soon as the medical team stabilized the captain, Herb and Lizabeth raced off toward Junior's crash site. Arriving about seven minutes later, they quickly discovered he'd been killed instantly after being propelled through the front windshield since he wasn't wearing a seat belt after his truck impacted the unmovable pole. Luckily, no one else had been hurt during what was later described as a reckless and highly erratic escape attempt during which Junior had sideswiped six parked vehicles along the way and forced numerous others off the road as he weaved all over the place.

Watching the paramedics place the sheet over Junior's body before removing it from the scene, Lizabeth told Herb, "We need an autopsy."

"I agree," he concurred. "Nothing more we can do here. Let's head over to the hospital and check on the captain," he then said.

After making their visit to the hospital, Herb and Lizabeth didn't have much else they could do right now except wait for the autopsy report. They did, though, call Benny to make sure Junior's mother would be appropriately notified. They also told him they'd personally escort Junior's body to wherever Stella Kojan decided the burial would be. It was the least they could do after everything she'd recently been through. Herb then reflected on what Amos Everett had said just a few short days earlier. He couldn't understand what Stella ever saw in Bruno; they were such complete opposites. In reality, she'd become the victim from this entire tragic ordeal which had originally been caused oh so many years ago by her husband's youthful bullying which escalated out of control into all the murders through the deviously plotting mind of then Rita Powers. What a deadly chain of events which never should have occurred.

William M. Jones

So many lives unnecessarily destroyed. None of it should have ever happened.

Junior's autopsy report wasn't completed until late the next day. As suspected when they first viewed him approaching the house yesterday, the autopsy confirmed he was high on crack cocaine. After reviewing the report, Herb said to Lizabeth, "Know who we need to talk to again?"

"Sonya Spaulding."

"Exactly. I've got a hunch she knows even more than she's already told us."

"Good idea," Lizabeth agreed.

It was a week before Herb and Lizabeth returned home from taking Junior's body to Stella's new home and staying with her throughout the funeral process. He'd been buried in an old family plot from her side of the family. Returning to work, they contacted Benny beforehand and made arrangements to have Sonya Spaulding picked up and brought to the precinct for questioning. She was nervously waiting there when they finally arrived and checked in with Benny after being away now for over a week.

Entering the briefing room where she was being detained, Lizabeth started with, "Nice to see you again, Sonya."

"Detective," she simply replied.

"You know why you're here?" Lizabeth next asked.

"No, not really. I told you everything the last time we talked," she lied trying to again make them believe her previous story.

"Did you, Sonya? Are you sure?" Herb drilled her with as he moved within inches of her face.

Immediately trying to push farther away from him, she frantically cried, "Of course I did. Why wouldn't I?"

"Junior's dead, Sonya. Did you know that?" Lizabeth bluntly informed her.

"Can't be. You're lying to me."

Murder by Memory

"Afraid not. Helped bury him yesterday," Herb emphasized. "And you know what, Sonya? We know he was a drug addict and we think you did too."

Lowering her head and covering her eyes, Sonya suddenly burst into tears. "How did he die?" she wanted to know.

After telling her the whole story, Lizabeth then asked, "So, you going to tell us the truth now, Sonya? Looks to me that if you don't cooperate you could possibly be going to jail as an accessory to murder."

"Murder!" Sonya screamed. "I didn't have anything to do with killing Professor Reinhold."

"But you admit you know something more about it?" Herb pointedly inferred.

"If I tell you what I know, will you let me go?" Sonya almost begged.

"Depends," Lizabeth returned.

"On what?"

"On what you have to say. Was Junior involved in drugs at school?" Lizabeth then questioned.

"Yes," Sonya finally admitted.

"So how was Alvin Reinhold connected?" Herb demanded.

Almost to the point of completely breaking down now, Sonya conceded, "Professor Reinhold found out about Junior pushing drugs at school."

"And?" Lizabeth encouraged Sonya to continue.

"And he threatened to turn him in."

"So he didn't kill him over the F?" Herb added. "You lied to us about that, didn't you Sonya?"

"Yes. I'm so sorry. So very sorry," she confessed as she started to hyperventilate in addition to the constant crying. Finally controlling herself, she continued, "Junior was making a lot of money and Professor Reinhold was going to ruin it all. Can't you see that?" she pleaded.

"So you helped him get the pistol and then helped him kill Professor Reinhold?" Lizabeth demanded.

"No. I'm telling the truth. What I told you about the pistol was the truth. Honest. I didn't really think he would kill Professor Reinhold."

"But you knew about it?" Herb loudly questioned while again moving his face within inches of hers.

"I didn't think he was serious. You've got to believe me! I honestly didn't think he'd do it," Sonya again alleged. "I knew he was really mad and all, but never expected him to actually kill Professor Reinhold. My god, only insane people do something like that and Junior just wasn't like that."

"So what you're telling us, Sonya," Herb said while softening his tone slightly and stepping back a step or two from her, "is that you're like a lot of the recent school shootings where friends didn't take the shooter seriously so they didn't inform the authorities until after the fact."

"Yes," she confirmed while suddenly feeling a tremendous amount of shame.

"Well, Sonya, then I'm afraid you're partially responsible for Professor Reinhold's death," Lizabeth informed her quite matter-of-fact.

"Am I going to jail?" she then desperately wanted to know.

"That's up to the district attorney," Lizabeth informed her. "You did lie to us and conceal vital information in a murder investigation, remember?"

"One more thing, Sonya. How did Junior ever expect to get away with it?" Herb interrupted with.

"Simple," she stated while trying to recover from the reality of what Lizabeth had just told her, "just like what really happened. He knew all about the trouble between his dad and Professor Reinhold so figured his dad would get blamed for it."

"But why?" Lizabeth asked with a curious expression.

Murder by Memory

"Because he hated his dad. That's why. You see, his dad was always bullying him. Said he couldn't ever do anything right to please him."

"But he didn't think someone would kill his dad, though, did he?" Lizabeth added.

"No, that part really surprised him," Sonya agreed. "Thought he'd just go to jail or something like that where he wouldn't be able to bother him any more."

"And he would've gotten away with killing Alvin if Rita wouldn't have smiled at the trial!" Herb said to Lizabeth for probably the millionth time.

With all the pieces of the highly complex puzzle finally correctly arranged, all concerned parties were properly briefed before Rita was unsuspectedly escorted to the precinct interrogation room for hopefully what would be the case's final chapter. The precinct's room was utilized instead of everyone traveling to Rita's minimum security facility since it didn't possess a proper room fitted with one way mirrors. As Rita was escorted into the precinct under armed guard with her wrists also handcuffed together, none of the interrogation team made themselves visible to her. It was only after she was securely inside the interrogation room that Benny Mitchell ushered Wyatt Barfield, Marilyn Sparks and Judge Sandra Heath into their proper viewing positions outside the one way mirror while Herb and Lizabeth proceeded inside to confront the manipulative mastermind behind the entire tragic case.

"Detectives," Rita first said as Herb and Lizabeth entered the room. "Figured I might be seeing you here today. You ready to let me go now?" she said with a smile similar to the one she had foolhardily made back in the courtroom.

"Hardly!" Herb started.

"Then what's this all about?"

"Well, Rita, to be honest," Herb began, "we finally quit assuming and asked the right questions!"

William M. Jones

"What are you talking about?" Rita questioned with a perplexed expression.

"Don't you remember? You're the one who first told me I assumed too much and didn't ask the right question when I first searched Alvin's room all those many years ago. Remember now?"

"Yeah, so what of it?"

"Well, I simply took your own advice and that's what we're here to discuss."

"Okay. Whatever you say, detective."

"Isn't it true that you duped your own brother into committing the first three murders?"

"Are you serious?" she fired back.

"You bet we are!" Herb returned. "You made up some cock-and-bull story about Bruno sexually harassing you to play on your brother's fragile sympathies, didn't you?"

"No way!" she emphasized.

"We've got a witness, Rita."

"You're bluffing."

"Afraid not. You forgot about Carla! You thought she'd left the house the night you dreamed up your deadly scheme, but she hadn't. She'd simply left Raymond's room and listened from the other side of the door."

"You can't prove it!" Rita yelled.

"Yes we can. We asked Raymond, and guess what Rita? When the question was properly asked, well, he acknowledged the truth. You see, Rita, when you were testifying about how Bruno and his little gang beat Alvin up, well, Raymond remembered your version somewhat differently and quietly sat there with a very puzzled look while you provided the actual version from the witness stand. That was your first mistake, Rita, because I remembered Raymond's expression after you made mistake number two."

"Mistake number two?" she demanded.

Murder by Memory

"You shouldn't have smiled when the verdict was read. You would've gotten away with everything if it hadn't of been for that one quick smile. Couldn't control yourself, could you, Rita?"

"You're crazy, detective."

"You think so, Rita. Well, let me tell you about another lie we've uncovered. You must of thought we were all stupid or something. You told us Raymond disposed of the pistol after killing Bruno and couldn't remember what he'd done with it. Not so, Rita. We have the pistol. Care to guess where we found it? I really don't have to tell you, do I?" Herb confidently stated.

Starting to squirm slightly in her seat, Rita replied, "So, what of it?"

"So what! I'll tell you what, Rita. We can also prove how you killed Bruno all by yourself. Raymond didn't have anything to do with it! Did you hear me, Rita? We know how you, and you alone, killed Bruno. We also know how you made up the whole story about Raymond writing himself notes. Pretty good one, Rita. Almost had us believing you, but there was one problem."

"Care to venture a guess?" Lizabeth added.

"No, I bet she doesn't," Herb answered," so I'll just tell her. I still have the letters you wrote Bruno back in '75 and you know what Rita, the handwriting is a dead match for Raymond's little notes. We've got you, Rita. Oh, by the way, you also killed an innocent man!"

Immediately peaking her interest, Rita quickly questioned, "What are you talking about?"

"Bruno didn't kill Alvin!" Herb slowly and clearly enunciated while projecting a penetrating stare which sent chills through the now trembling Rita.

"Then who did?" she really wanted to know as she began to visibly sweat.

"His son, Rita, his son. You killed the wrong person!" Herb loudly proclaimed as he really got into her face. "You hear me? You killed the wrong person! And if you wouldn't have smiled you would've gotten away with everything. Just think, eighteen months in minimum security and you would have been home free. Nothing to it, you figured. But your exuberance got the best of you, Rita. That one smile. That one little smile was all it took for us to quit assuming and finally ask the right questions! Let's get out of here, Lizabeth. She makes me sick!"

"You can't touch me!" Rita screamed as Herb and Lizabeth turned their backs to her. "You can't touch me! What about my plea bargain? That's right, what about my plea bargain? We had a deal. Remember?"

As Herb slowly opened the door to exit the interrogation room, Lizabeth stopped and then turned one hundred and eighty degrees to face the visibly shaken Rita. "You ever hear of perjury?" she first remarked. "You committed perjury, Rita. And you know what? Committing perjury voids all plea bargain deals!" Trembling inside, but appearing cool, calm and collected on the outside, Lizabeth next turned and also departed the room to the now high pitched screaming of the devious Rita Powers Reinhold. Quickly rejoining Herb, they both glanced at the onlooking attorneys and judge and they all just nodded their heads as additional uniformed officers arrived to restrain the super hysterical Rita and haul her off now to a maximum security facility where she wouldn't be able to wreck any more innocent lives, ever again.

CHAPTER TWENTY-TWO

"Herb, where you been? Come on in," Benny requested upon looking up from his mounds of paperwork and suddenly finding his old friend standing at his door. "You okay?"

"Couldn't be better, thanks," Herb returned with a big smile.

"Okay, you wanna tell me what this is all about then?"

"Got any plans for Saturday?"

"Saturday. This Saturday? No. Why?"

"How about being my best man?"

"You and Lizabeth actually going to get married?"

"Yeah, hard to believe, isn't it? Especially after the impression I gave her that first night when you brought her to my apartment."

"I'd say. You were pretty depressing back then, good buddy," Benny reminded him, "but I couldn't be happier for the two of you now. Funny how things just work out sometimes."

"That's for sure. Just when you least expect it, something good comes into your life and turns it all around. Hard to even think where I'd be today if you hadn't of come to get me that night. Sad in a way, though."

"How so?" Benny asked.

"Well, you never would have needed me if Bruno Jr. hadn't of been a drug dealer and killed Alvin."

"But he did," Benny reminded him. "Kind of like fate, Herb. You and Lizabeth getting together was just meant to be."

"I like to think so too. That mean you'll be my best man then?"

"Wouldn't miss it for anything!" Benny gladly stated while approaching his old buddy and giving him a

William M. Jones

congratulatory embrace. "Where you been, though, for the last two weeks?"

"Well, we had some things to work out."

"You staying here after you get married?"

"No!" Herb adamantly stated.

"No," Benny returned," then where you going?"

"Upstate New York, Benny. You remember Lizabeth's dad had been in the Marines?"

"Yeah, I think I heard that once."

"Well, he's gone, you know, but one of his best Marine buddies who Lizabeth is still really close to has a summer place in the country outside a place called Hornell. This friend, Matt Taft, just helped us find a nice place close to his with about fifty acres and a fixer up old farm house so we've decided to move there."

"What are you going to do out there, Herb? You've always lived in the city."

"I know. Pretty exciting, isn't it?" he responded while projecting another big smile. "Lizabeth just got on with the local police department as head of detectives and me, well, I'm going to spend my time writing a book," he completely caught Benny off guard with.

"You're gonna do what?"

"You heard me. Just got a half million dollar advance to write the Slaughter House Murderer story."

"You're kidding?" Benny replied in a stunned state.

"No, it's really true," Herb assured him while really smiling.

"Guess you can finally pay off Irene's debts then," Benny laughed.

"With plenty to spare, Benny. With plenty to spare. Still can't believe how the case changed my life," he then declared.

"For the better, Herb," Benny honestly remarked. "Can't say the same for some others, though."

"What happened while we were gone?" Herb now wanted to know.

"Let's just say it's official now that Rita's not going to cause any more trouble. Got life without parole. And then Raymond is being released to a private facility where he'll most likely spend the remainder of his days."

"What about Sonya Spaulding?"

"Two years probation."

"Okay, that's fair enough," Herb agreed. "Still hard to believe the whole mess started from Bruno being a schoolyard bully and then escalated into all the murders and ruined lives."

"Yeah, really sad. Enough of that, Herb. Let's get you and Lizabeth married!"

"I'm all for that," Herb happily acknowledged.

"You know what, Herb?"

"What?"

"You better keep a spot open for me on that new property of yours."

"What are you talking about, Benny?"

"Going to retire in two months," he then surprised Herb with.

"Good for you. It's about time."

"Yeah, and I just ordered that big RV I've always dreamed about so you'll be seeing us soon."

"Always room for you, Benny. You certainly saved my life."

"No, Herb. Lizabeth did."

Herb just smiled and realized how right Benny was.

THE END

William M. Jones

ABOUT THE BOOK

When a serial killer strikes again after a hiatus of twenty-four years, Detective Herbert Chalmers is returned to the police force. Along with his beautiful new partner, Detective Lizabeth Barcay, Chalmers sets out to finally bring the elusive murderer to justice. One problem - Alvin Reinhold, who Chalmers believed was the killer, is also murdered. Who is the real serial killer? That's what Chalmers and Barcay are determined to discover in this intriguing murder mystery intertwined with numerous plot twists and surprises along the way in their effort to bring the true culprit to justice.

About the Author

William M. Jones is a retired Marine Corps Lieutenant Colonel who served as a Naval Flight Officer with a specialty as a Bombardier/Navigator in the A6 Intruder. Since his retirement in '93, he has been an Assistant Chief Flight Instructor at The University of Illinois. He holds an Airline Transport Pilot, Commercial Pilot, Certified Flight Instructor - Single engine, Instrument, Multi engine and Glider along with Advanced and Instrument Ground Instructor ratings. He is the author of four other books: Two aviation textbooks - *The Pilot's Outline Guide To Basic Aerodynamics* and *Simplified Instrument Flying/Instructing Techniques* and the Matt Taft adventure series novels consisting of *Silent Rescue* and *A Chameleon In The Plumbing*. William and his wife Elane, reside in Savoy, Illinois, during the academic year and spend their summers on their New York country property.

www.ingramcontent.com/pod-product-compliance
Lightning Source LLC
LaVergne TN
LVHW040523090625
813352LV00001B/68